I0658470

Reckoning
A Reverse Harem Tale

Mountain Magic
Book Three

by

Dakota Brown

Reckoning
A Reverse Harem Tale

Mountain Magic, book 3
First Inkwolf Press Printing 2024

All Rights Reserved
Copyright © 2020 by Dakota Brown
Cover Design © 2020 by Camila Marques

All rights Reserved. This book or any portion thereof may not be reproduced or used in any manner whatsoever without the express written permission of the publisher except for the use of brief quotations in a book review.

Names, characters, places, and incidents are the products of the author's imagination and or used fictitiously. Any resemblance to actual events, locales or persons, living or dead, is entirely coincidental.

Inkwolf Press
P.O. Box 473
Ault, Colorado
80610

www.inkwolfpress.com

ISBN : 979-8-9864144-7-8

PRODUCED IN THE UNITED STATES OF AMERICA

Dedication

For Shoshanah

You make all my stories better.

Acknowledgements

I can't even begin to tell you all how excited I am about this series and how well it has been received. Thank you, readers for your kind reviews, for spreading the word, for helping this trilogy do so well.

I want to thank Jen and Sean at Untold for all their hard work helping me get these novels out quickly, their skillful edits, and everything else they do. They really do believe in me and what I'm writing, and I'm humbled and so grateful for everything they do to help make my stories the best they can be.

I also want to give a shout out to my readers group on Facebook. You guys are great! Thank you for your encouragement, support, and all the sexy pictures you post.

There are so many people that help when I need some inspiration, and I appreciate you all. A few stand out time and again for their dedication at helping me through the writing process, the ups and downs, the I can's and the I can't's. Lizzy, Justinn, Shoshanah, and again, Jen and Sean. Without all of you, I wouldn't be half the writer I am today. Thank you.

Chapter 1

Sofia

"Perhaps you should drive faster." Nikolai's voice pulled me out of a light doze. The half Russian-half Tatar mage leaned forward as far as the seatbelt would allow and put his hands on the dash of Doc's pickup.

I was cuddled between my two werewolves, Ed and Allan, in the back seat. Nikolai's alarmed voice woke both of them as well.

"Why?" Doc asked. The dim lights from the dash combined with my currently post-demon enhanced senses, lit up Doc's features enough for me to see him frown tiredly when he glanced over at the mage. His long hair was currently pulled back and I wanted to free it from its restraints and run my fingers through it. That was one of my top priorities when we got back to his cabin in Colorado.

We had left my parents' house in Nebraska the evening after Thanksgiving dinner partially because the longer we were around my parents, the more questions they were going to ask, and partially because now that I was free of the demon that had been forced to possess me, we all wanted to get home and simply spend time together.

It was late in the middle of the night. Nikolai had been keeping Doc company in the front while I slept in the back with Ed and Allan. I put my hand on Allan's arm and squeezed. Ed leaned forward and buried his nose in my hair, inhaling. He had done that at almost every opportunity since the demon had been freed. He liked that I smelled like me again. I did, too.

Allan took my hand and pressed it to his lips, also inhaling before giving me a gentle kiss.

Nikolai sighed and after a long pause, he shook his head. "Maybe it doesn't matter. Someone, probably Ash, is tearing down my wards. Violently."

"Which wards?" The weariness in Doc's voice tugged at my heart. He'd shouldered so much of the responsibility recently.

"The cabin wards."

Doc swore in both Navajo and Nikolai's dialect of Russian.

I understood the Russian, courtesy of Nikolai sharing languages with me when we had first met. Apparently, Doc was picking some of it up, too.

Doc's mother was a Navajo vampire hunter, his father a white preacher. They had traveled together saving souls with word and stake during the turn of the nineteenth century. Doc's mother had been attacked right before she'd given birth. She had not survived, but Doc had, though he wasn't completely human. Sometimes I actually wondered if he wasn't more than half vampire, like he claimed, but maybe no one actually knew for sure how it worked since he was unique.

Ash was sort of a friend of ours, but he was also under the control of our enemy, the Andersons. They were the ones that had forced the greater demon to possess me, hoping to get an even more powerful version of Ash, who was a lesser demon. Fortunately, I was able to avoid being forced out of my body, and Nikolai, who was actually from fourteen fifty or so, had been able to save me.

It looked like the Andersons had figured out we had released the greater demon. Maybe they were retaliating. My mom's words came back to me, about there being ways to hurt people that didn't involve physical violence. She was right.

"What are we going to do?" Ed whispered, but everyone in the car had excellent hearing and even over the diesel engine we could hear the fear in his voice. He and his brother Allan had been turned into werewolves on a family camping trip where they were also orphaned. They ran into Doc a few years later and begged him to get them out of the foster system before their wolfish nature was discovered. They'd already lost everything once. They didn't need to lose it all again.

"Nothing," Doc replied. "There isn't anything we can do. We're still an hour out, even if we drove as fast as I could we wouldn't get there in time to prevent them from doing whatever it is they're doing. All of the important things are here in this truck."

"And, you know, your truck is here, too," Allan added his tone worried but carrying a hint of amusement.

"Yes, everything but you four, is easier to replace than my truck," Doc agreed tightly.

"Why?" Nikolai asked. "Surely it only takes money?"

Doc shook his head. "They don't make diesels the way they used to. I could replace it, but it wouldn't be as good as this one is. Still, all of you are far more important than anything we left there. Whatever they've done, we'll survive it."

"Damn the Andersons," I growled.

Ed pulled me into a tight hug, his light blond hair tickling my cheek. It was getting a little shaggy. He usually kept it reasonably short. Now that I had noticed Ed's longer hair, I noticed that Allan's sandy blond hair was also getting a little shaggy, as if they hadn't gotten a haircut since I'd been possessed. Maybe they hadn't? Another piece of their lives I had disrupted. They swore they wouldn't have it any other way, but I still felt bad about it.

"At least there isn't any traffic?" Allan forced a laugh.

Doc snorted. "It is the middle of the night on a holiday, not to mention most of the roads are actually still closed. And covered in ice. Or snow. Or both."

I leaned forward and massaged his shoulders, trying to ease some of the tension, though I suspected it had been there longer than just the last few hours of what had to be a stressful drive.

Nikolai had provided us with traction spells for the truck and a measure of invisibility so we wouldn't attract the attention of any law enforcement that might be out on the treacherous roads. The whole area had been hit with a couple of massive snowstorms over the last few days and not much was actually open. Nikolai had made it from Colorado to Nebraska with Ed and Allan in a stolen Mustang. Alex Anderson's Mustang, in fact. Fortunately, Nikolai had been able to practice all of his spells on the Mustang, so we and the truck were fairly safe. The Mustang had not fared so well.

I doubted the Andersons were that upset about Alex's car. They were probably upset about losing their demon. One of the mages who had cast the spells to bind the demon to me had probably felt the spell break, much like Nikolai was feeling his wards come crashing down even though we weren't home yet.

Thanking whatever gods and goddesses were listening that I hadn't actually ended up dating Alex, I reflected that I probably wouldn't have survived if I had. The chance meeting with Ed and Allan had saved my life. And while it had turned theirs upside down, they seemed pretty happy about it.

Doc groaned as my fingers dug into his shoulders and neck.

"I'm sorry," I said as I continued to try and ease his tension.

"For what, Sofia?" Doc said.

"This is all my fault."

"No, it's not," Allan insisted. "We didn't have to try and date you. We didn't have to protect you."

"Yes, we did," Ed interrupted, laughing. "I was gone the moment I laid eyes on you. But, what Allan really means is, it was our choice, too. It's not any of our faults. It's the Andersons' fault. They're the ones that tried to enslave you. They're the ones who work for this magic black market. They're completely the bad guys here. And as we've said many times, the truce we worked out with them would only have lasted so long anyway."

"I am grateful that the Andersons were interested in Sofia," Nikolai added. "Otherwise, I might still be trapped in that magical prison."

I had accidently rescued Nikolai from a magical trap his student had locked him in many centuries prior. Though it sucked for Nikolai, I was quietly grateful to Roza. Without her actions, I wouldn't have Nikolai in my life, and I'd be effectively dead. We had saved each other.

Doc took his hand from the steering wheel and put it over mine, gently taking it in his and pulling me forward so he could kiss my wrist, right over my magical pack tattoo. Five pawprints that represented each of us. It was the physical manifestation of the bond we had formed between all five of us. The bond that, along with Nikolai's magic and Doc's vampiric ability to transfer the demon's power to Nikolai, had saved my life.

"I'll stop apologizing, but I still feel bad." All I had wanted was a quiet college experience in a beautiful mountain setting. I hadn't even decided what I was going to major in, or what I was going to do with the rest of my life. Now I really didn't know, though I did hope it would continue to include my four boyfriends. I had only known them for a few months, but already I couldn't imagine my life without them.

"Hmm, maybe we need to distract Sofia," Allan said, pulling me back into his arms and nibbling on my neck.

I moaned. "Not fair. Doc's driving and Nikolai is making sure we don't die."

Ed groaned in mock distress. He and Allan hadn't been sure they would survive the trip from Colorado to Nebraska with Nikolai, who didn't know how to drive at all, behind the wheel. Even being werewolves and virtually indestructible by conventional standards, they had feared for their lives.

"Did not die," Nikolai said hotly.

I laughed, though it ended in a gurgle as Allan bit down on my neck.

"Cheater," I groaned.

"Works every time," Allan replied.

Doc sighed softly, just barely loud enough for me to hear, and Allan muttered an apology before releasing me.

Despite his assurances, Doc had to be worried about whatever was going on back at his cabin. As the Andersons were involved, it couldn't be good. I wondered what we'd find when we got back. I was starting to think of Doc's cabin as home, and I didn't want anything bad to happen to it. None of us did. The guys were right, none of this was our fault. We hadn't done anything wrong. We were just trying to live our lives.

Fucking Andersons.

∞ ∞ ∞

Reckoning

We could tell something was seriously wrong as soon as we crested the pass to drop down into Sunnyglade valley. Emergency lights like the kind you might find on a fire truck or an ambulance flashed on the far mountainside approximately where Doc's cabin was located.

"Fuck," Doc growled.

"What do you think they did?" Allan whispered.

"Probably burned it down," Doc muttered. "It's not like we haven't taken a couple of shots at their mansion."

I couldn't even think of a response. Tears moistened my cheeks and I buried my face in Ed's chest when he pulled me close. Fuck was an understatement.

"What do we tell the cops? Many of the roads we were driving on were closed," Allan asked.

"Check your phone and see if backroads are closed. If not, we took backroads. If we really need alibis, we want to be able to use Sofia's parents."

Allan studied his phone, the light from the screen illuminating his steel gray eyes and making them look blue. "You're in luck. I think there's a way we could have done it. Timing is problematic if we go home now since it would have taken a couple extra hours."

"Sofia, text your parents, tell them something happened at the cabin while we were gone and let them know that if they're asked, we left several hours earlier than we actually did," Doc instructed.

"Okay."

My hands shook while I typed out the text, but before long I hit send.

It didn't take long for my phone to ring. I almost didn't answer, but my mom deserved to know what was going on. Not that I had many answers.

"Honey, what's wrong?"

"Don't know for sure yet, Mom, but the Andersons are being shits again. We're all fine, but the cabin may not be.

Knowing the Andersons, we'll have to prove we were out of state when whatever it is they did happened. We found a route of backroads that are open, but it would have taken longer to get home."

"Okay, we'll let everyone know, but be careful, and text me when you find out what's going on."

"I will. Thank you, Mom."

"It's the least we can do. Without your friends..." She didn't need to finish the statement. My dad may not like my friends, but Mom sure was grateful to them. I even think Nikolai had charmed her completely.

"I know. I love you."

"Love you, too, honey."

I hung up, grateful the phone call hadn't been more stressful. I was running on empty as far as dealing with hard stuff right now.

We fell silent as the truck wound its way down into the valley, through the main roundabout in town, and back up the other side of the mountain. Tension filled all of us, thick in the air, and filtering through our pack bond. Ed and Allan held me while Doc slowed and turned off onto the narrow dirt road that led to the cabin. The truck bounced down the track as Doc drove a little faster than normal. Flashing emergency lights reflected off the deep snow.

The disconnect between my last clear memory of this place being clear of snow and in the midst of fall splendor, and the deep snow that covered everything now, wrenched my heart. I had missed a lot, but it could have been so much worse.

Of course, when we broke out of the trees into the clearing around Doc's cabin, we could see that his prediction was correct. Two fire trucks sprayed water onto what was left of the cabin. One wall stood in the back, and the rest was rubble.

"Fuck," Doc growled as he slowed and pulled off to the side so he wasn't blocking any of emergency vehicles or the police car. We sat there for a minute, letting the truck run, trying to process what had happened, while a deputy sheriff shined a bright flashlight at us and then came over. Doc shut off the truck and rolled his window down.

"Mr. Cassidy?" The deputy asked after shining his light in our faces.

Doc nodded. "That's me. What happened? I mean, besides the obvious?" He managed to sound upset and exhausted at the same time, and buried the anger we all felt deep.

"We're not sure yet. Faulty wiring? Arson? Know anyone who would want to hurt you?"

Doc shrugged before he shook his head, sighing. "Mind if we get out?"

"No, not at all, just stay back."

We all climbed out of the warm truck to stretch our legs. Ed kept his arm around me and I leaned into the werewolf's heat for the warmth and comfort. Allan pushed up against my other side and I cuddled into his heat, as well. Between the two of them I stopped shivering and stared at the wreckage of their home.

Nikolai stood close to Doc while they talked with the deputy. It wouldn't take much effort to overhear the conversation, but I really didn't want to know right now. While I had known that this wouldn't be over once we saved me from the demon, I had hoped we would get a reprieve. Instead, they were escalating. What would we do? What could we do? In Nikolai's time, it would be relatively simple. Nuke them from orbit, as it were. Now? Well...maybe that was still the answer, but it was a lot more complicated.

After Ed, Allan, and I had stretched our legs, we climbed back into the truck and squished together in the back seat for warmth.

I had dozed off again when Doc opened the door, letting in a blast of cold air. "Deputy Morrison wants to talk to you three real quick."

Yawning, I climbed out along with Ed and Allan and looked east. The sky had lightened considerably, and I wondered what time it was.

Deputy Morrison had reached an indeterminate age, where I couldn't really guess how old he was. He smiled at me.

"You just got back from Nebraska?" he asked.

"Yeah, Thanksgiving with my folks."

"You all went?" He sounded surprised.

I shrugged. "My parents like big gatherings. I would have brought my roommate too but she had plans with her family."

"And you just left and drove home even with the weather?"

"We thought there was more snow coming, and wanted to make sure we got back before it hit." That was true enough. I could feel the storm building. Somehow. I wondered if that was left over from the demon. She had left me with quite a bit of knowledge and power. So much so that I wasn't even aware of everything I knew at this point. I had been free from her for maybe 24 hours, and it was already starting to become obvious that she had changed me.

The deputy nodded. "Smart, if a bit of a rough drive."

I nodded.

"Well, be careful. We'll be in touch with Mr. Cassidy. He has my card if you think of anything, or something else suspicious happens."

I frowned. "What do you think happened?"

"It's too soon to tell."

He shook my hand and then Ed and Allan's before heading back to Doc and Nikolai. They spoke for a few minutes and the deputy got in his car and drove off. The firefighters had finished as well, and one spoke with Doc for a minute before they also got in their trucks and drove away.

Once we were alone, I went over to Doc and slid my hand into his. He sighed. I wrapped my arms around him and held him tight. After a moment he returned my hug, but without his usual strength. Nikolai put his arms around both of us.

"We should get some rest," I said. "You're exhausted. We're all exhausted."

He nodded, still holding me. "I guess we should head back into town and see if we can find a hotel." I could tell the idea of driving anywhere didn't thrill him.

"What about crashing in my grove? It's comfortable and safe, and I bet I can adjust the temperature for us."

Doc's shoulders sagged and he nodded. "That sounds fantastic." He glanced around us, and then his gaze landed on his truck.

"I will ward your truck," Nikolai said with a pat on Doc's shoulder and headed over to the silver diesel.

Nikolai gathered his magic and it tugged at me. Mine rose to the surface in response and he glanced over his shoulder at me before gesturing for me to join him.

Doc gave me another squeeze before releasing me, so I went over to the mage.

"It is good practice. Blend your magic with mine, and I will guide you through process."

Warmth filled me as I blended my lavender motes with his dark blue ones. As with other times when I had used magic around Nikolai, my awareness of him increased until I wanted to be pressed up against him, needing to

11

touch him, as much as I needed to feel the magic flowing through me.

This time, Nikolai stepped closer until his chest was pressed against my back. He kissed my hair before turning his attention back to the truck and our magic.

"You are much stronger now," Nikolai said as he guided me. We wove the energy into complicated patterns. A few months ago, this would have exhausted me, but now exhilaration washed through me.

"The demon changed a lot of things."

"She did," he agreed. "Now, lay energy over truck."

We dropped our net of energy over the truck and it snapped into place.

"We will feel it if anyone disturbs truck. Grove is close, and they won't undo this before we can react." Nikolai wrapped his arms around me and held me tightly. I rested my cheek against his shoulder and took a deep breath, reveling in our physical and magical connection.

"Doc's exhausted, let's go." Nikolai released me from his hug, taking my hand and pulling me back toward the others. Allan had his arm around Doc's waist and Ed stood close to them.

"There is some good news," Ed grinned. "They didn't touch the boat."

Nikolai glanced over at the old jon boat and nodded. "Seems unharmed."

Doc laughed. "That would have been easier to deal with."

"Small things," Ed argued.

"True." Doc patted his shoulder and we all headed toward my grove.

My feet were dragging wearily by the time I made it the short distance to the circle of trees I had created the first time Doc helped me access my magic on purpose. I could close it up completely and I thought it might actually take a nuke to damage it. The pine trees welcomed me back and my shoulders unknotted when I stepped inside. Here, I was safe. We were safe.

Once everyone was inside, I sealed up the entrance. As if anticipating my needs, the temperature rose to something I considered comfortable and the moss—certainly not native to Colorado and a variety probably found only in my grove—cushioned my footfalls as I headed toward the center of the small space. There was enough room for all of us to lay down, but not a whole lot more.

I pulled on Doc's hand and he let me guide him to the ground. He wrapped his arms around me and his breathing slowed as he fell asleep almost instantly. Nikolai curled up on the other side of Doc, his arms around the vampire. Ed curled up around me and Allan pressed up against Nikolai. Though it wasn't quite the homecoming I had hoped for, we were safe, warm, and together.

Dakota Brown

Chapter 2

Sofia

Waking up surrounded by my pack, feeling safe and warm, was the best feeling ever. Doc tightened his arms around me and buried his face in my neck.

"You okay?"

"Better now," he mumbled against my neck, sending shivers down my spine.

He clearly wasn't in the mood to start anything, though. Ed remained pressed up against my back and his hands tightened around my stomach. Nikolai reached for me over Doc, pulling us together and Allan's hand found my arm. I sensed contentment from everyone through the pack bond.

Doc hooked a leg over my thigh, as if he could pull me closer, and nuzzled my neck. Maybe he was changing his mind? My pulse sped up from my post sleep languor to something a bit closer to awake and alert.

He rolled me onto my back, hips pressing me into the soft moss-covered ground, resting on his elbows and looking me in the eyes, gaze hungry, not for blood, but for me. I shivered at the intensity in his gaze, forgetting about the others for a moment as I reached up and disintegrated his hair tie. Doc's long, black hair cascaded down, draping on either side of my face, and tickling my cheeks. I grinned.

He smiled back.

My magic stirred as Nikolai did something, then a blast of cool air chilled me.

Doc and I broke our gaze to see Nikolai had used my magic to open the grove and he, Ed, and Allan grabbed coats and shoes from where we discarded them last night and slipped out, leaving us alone.

Sighing, Doc shifted his weight as if he were going to move, but Nikolai sealed up the grove with us still inside.

Doc turned his attention back to me, eyebrows raised.

"I think that's the 'we deserve some alone time' signal." My lips turned up in a sly smile.

"I've had more time alone with you than any of the others recently." He clearly wasn't objecting though, as he stayed where he was, resting on his forearms now, as he brushed some of my short bob out of my face.

"I'd hardly call it alone. Everyone's had a hard time, but you've had to deal with other people more than the rest of us. The only time we were even kind of alone was on the drive to my parents' house." I grinned. I didn't want to remind him about the cabin, but that was also his, and he would have to deal with all of that, too.

"Well, what would you like to do now that the rest of the pack has locked us in here together." His eyes twinkled.

"Mmmm...quiet meditation?"

He cocked one eyebrow.

Laughing, I threaded my fingers through his hair before cupping the back of his neck and pulling him down until his lips met mine. He pressed into me, tongue exploring my mouth. He didn't pull away when I ran my tongue over his fangs, and I smiled while I kissed him. Clearly, he was a lot more comfortable with us seeing his vampire side now. I probably had Nikolai to thank for that.

"You're smiling," he said lips brushing against mine while he spoke.

"Mmmm." He didn't give me time for a proper answer before he kissed me again, driving other thoughts from my mind.

After a few moments, he leaned back, letting me catch my breath.

"Sofia," he whispered.

"Yes?"

"You don't happen to know Nikolai's cleaning spell, do you?"

I raised an eyebrow, confused as to his line of questioning, but I thought for a moment. I had seen him cast it at least once, though my memories of that time were cloudy. However, yes...I did know how. "I do. Why?"

"Because," he grinned mischievously, "we don't have a shower."

My smile matched his. "Oh, were you thinking of getting messy?"

Doc licked his lips, seeming to think for a moment before he nodded. "Yes, I am."

"Hmmm, might be fun," I purred.

"Might be?" He mock growled.

"Well," I teased him, shrugging, though his growl sent my heart racing and I squirmed against him. "I mean, I don't know it will be fun. I suspect it will, but..."

"I guess I'll just have to prove it to you." He nibbled along my jaw before gently nipping at my neck.

Groaning, I dug my nails into his shoulders. "I think I'd like that."

He chuckled. "You're wearing too many clothes."

"Guess you'd better do something about it."

"I intend to," he replied, voice low.

My stomach tightened and my heart raced as my body reacted to the desire in his voice. I freed one of my legs from underneath him and curled it up over his back. He rumbled deep in his throat and kissed his way down my neck to my collarbone, trailing hot fire down my skin and igniting my nerves.

He gripped my shoulders, and gently rolled us over until I was on top. I went to work on the buttons of his flannel shirt, until he hooked his fingers under the hem of my T-shirt and pulled it up, dragging his fingers along my sides as he did and sending shivers up and down my spine.

"If your heart beats any faster, I might have to worry about you," he said as I leaned forward so he could pull my shirt off.

"I'll be fine. You haven't managed to damage me yet."

He held my hips with his hands and sat up. I wrapped my legs around him. He pressed his lips to mine, devouring my lips while he slid his hands up my back until he could unhook my bra. Once that was off, he let me go back to work on his shirt. I slipped each button open slowly, teasing him, leaning forward when I was done and trailing kisses up his neck while I pushed the shirt off his shoulders.

Doc pulled me close and I traced one of the long scars on his back.

"Still wearing too much," he murmured and shifted around until he could lay me down on the mossy ground. He leaned forward, kissing me between my breasts, then going lower, leaving a line of fire down my stomach.

"So are you," I gasped out.

He smiled against my stomach, before finding the button on my jeans and teasing it open.

I panted, trying not to squirm in anticipation as he worked the zipper down and pulled my jeans off my hips. He pulled my underwear off with them, scooting back until they cleared my feet and he tossed them away.

Doc leaned forward, strong hands back on my hips as he kissed my stomach again. Usually the guys checked in with me a lot to make sure I was okay with everything, but he trusted me to tell him if I wanted him to stop, because he worked his way back down without meeting my eyes. I felt an urgency in him, as if he was desperate for this connection. I felt the same. The last few months had been terrible, and all I wanted right now was to be closer to my pack.

I opened my legs for him, and he kissed my folds hesitantly. Moaning encouragement, I titled my hips, giving him better access. That was what he needed. He licked at my nub, teasing it until I was thrusting against him, gasping, hands clenching the mossy ground.

He slid one hand along my body until he could slip a finger inside of me. I arched up, crying out and pushing against him, wanting more, wanting him inside me. Before I could tell him what I wanted, he pushed another finger inside of me, sucking on my clit, and working at me with his fingers until pressure built and I was begging for release.

"Doc," I cried out his name as my hips bucked and my climax overwhelmed me. Doc held my hips for a moment, staying between my legs while I trembled in reaction. Then, once I had calmed a little, he crawled up my body until he was pressed against me as I gasped for breath.

"Having fun yet?" He pressed his lips to my neck and I turned so I could kiss him, not caring that I could taste myself on his lips.

We explored each other's mouths for a while before I nodded. "But I want more."

"More fun?"

"For both of us," I said and hesitated. I didn't think he would object, but it would only be my second time. I wasn't hung up on that so much as I just felt a little awkward asking.

Doc noticed my hesitation and leaned back so he could look at me. "Whatever you want, Sofia, is fine with me," he said, voice soft. "Whatever you don't want is also fine with me."

I took a deep breath and nodded before answering. "I want you, inside me. Please."

It was Doc's turn to hesitate. "Are you sure?"

"Yeah, I am. You don't have to worry about getting me pregnant, either."

He tilted his head, though I wasn't sure that had actually crossed his mind.

"I have an IUD, also there is a spell for that." I winked.

Doc nodded. "I would like that very much, then. You'll have to forgive me, I don't have a great deal of experience." He glanced away as if embarrassed.

"Yeah, me, neither." I blushed and glanced away for a moment. "But that's okay. We can learn together. Or, you know, we can all take lessons from Nikolai."

Doc did blush this time.

"You two are completely adorable."

His blush deepened.

I grinned. "Pants, off. Now," I commanded. "I have no idea what time it is, but I'm sure we don't have all day."

"We have as much time as we need," Doc replied, but he did as I instructed.

I trailed my eyes down Doc's lean body, breath catching at how perfect he was, before holding out my hand and inviting him to come back to me. He complied, pushing me back onto the ground and devouring my lips with his. He slid his hand between my damp legs. I groaned into his mouth as he rubbed until I was gasping and shaking, already sensitive and soaked from before.

"Please?" I begged.

Doc didn't reply, just pressed himself against my opening, then meeting my eyes with his.

I nodded and he carefully pushed into me. Moaning as he filled me, I tilted my legs out further and pressed into him.

"Okay?" His voice shook.

"So good," I replied, hooking one leg over his back.

His hair draped around us as he pulled out slowly, teasing me. He smiled when I groaned in frustration.

"Nice and slow, right?" he whispered.

"Don't you dare," I growled.

He chuckled and pushed back into me, faster this time, but still not fast enough. I pulled him to me but instead of kissing him, I bit down on his neck, knowing that would get him to stop teasing me.

I was right, he shuddered and thrust harder until he was panting and I could feel my next climax building.

"Not sure I can hold out much longer," he groaned. His muscled trembled under my hands.

"Me, either," I managed to get out between gasps.

He pressed his fangs to my neck as he thrust into me. I tilted my chin, hopefully making it clear I wanted him to bite me, reduced to whimpers as I begged for release. He sank his teeth into my neck and my body responded. I cried out as waves of pleasure coursed through me. Doc groaned, trembling against me, holding me close as we both shook.

We lay there, limbs tangled together for a while, before he slowly slid out of me. We both shivered, still sensitive, and he collapsed next to me, arms tight around me, pulling me so I lay cradled with my head on his chest.

It took a while before we were both breathing normally again. I didn't want to move, didn't want to give up the little bit of peace we had created for ourselves.

Finally, I glanced up at Doc. He was studying me, a faint smile on his lips, eyes shining with contentment. He brushed some of my hair out of my face.

"Good?"

"So good, but clearly we both need to practice a lot more. All the time." I winked at him and he laughed in reply.

"Sounds fine to me."

"Hey, Doc?" My thoughts strayed to the other guys.

"Yeah?"

"Ed and Allan, have they ever..."

"I don't think so. Be gentle with them." He smiled. "But, you don't need to be gentle with Nikolai. He likes it a little rough."

I let my eyebrows rise and Doc shrugged. "Thought you might want to know."

It was my turn to blush a little. "Noted."

He kissed the top of my head. "Perhaps we should rejoin the rest of the pack. It probably is late."

I sighed. "I want to join them, I just don't want to leave here. It's safe here."

Doc squeezed me tight before relaxing his grip. "I feel the same way."

"All right." I groaned, and sat up, just a touch sore all over, but so worth it. Gathering my magic, I cast Nikolai's cleaning spell over myself, Doc, and our clothing. My skin tingled and he grunted as the magic washed over us. Then we got dressed and prepared to head back into the world.

Chapter 3

Sofia

The sun was high in the sky, and I was comfortable without pulling on my jacket, when we finally left my grove. If my new senses weren't telling me we were in for a heck of a snowstorm sometime soon, I would have thought we would enjoy some nice weather for a while.

I didn't see Ed or Allan, but Nikolai was sitting cross-legged on the pickup's tailgate.

He turned when he sensed us, eyes shining happily.

"You look much more relaxed." He nodded. "Good. I made us a yurt. Well, mostly." His expression fell for a moment. "Still need canvas and rope."

He hopped off the tailgate and came over to us, putting one arm around Doc's waist and one around mine, before he led us back into the trees. "I would not normally put it in trees, but we can heat it without fire, and unlikely to be fire this time of year in woods. We will need furnishings, but it is comfortable. Spent many winters in yurts."

Nikolai led us to small clearing in the woods right next to where the cabin had stood. He had cleared the space in the middle, probably with magic, and somehow built a circular lattice frame of pine branches.

"Used trees already here. Many were willing to shed a few branches, asked with magic. Made the task much easier when the wood is willing. The land likes you and Ed and Allan."

23

"Wait, are you some sort of druid now?" I asked.

Nikolai shook his head. "No. I am not good with earth magic overall, simply very familiar with this particular task. On the Steppes, we learn this or die. We normally bring our own frames, because not many trees on Steppes, but still, is easier to get wood from willing trees."

"You're amazing, Nikolai." I hugged him.

"Thank you," he replied modestly. "We need to get canvas and ropes, though. Doesn't matter how they're cut, just enough. We can shape with magic. Can we do this?"

Doc nodded. "Yeah. Shouldn't be an issue. We can drop Sofia off at the dorms," his lips twisted at that idea, "and get whatever you want. We need to buy more clothing for everyone and deal with the insurance company, too." He shook his head and I could see his shoulders tensing again.

"Hey, we'll get through this." I wrapped my arms around his waist.

"Thanks. I know. There were a few things I didn't like about the cabin anyway. We can rebuild it a little differently."

"Yes. If we get wood delivered, Sofia and I can work on the cabin. It is a good project."

Doc raised his eyebrows, clearly not having considered that possibility.

"You will probably need to hire someone to do your electricity. Don't understand that enough to use magic, but seems fairly minor compared to the rest."

I clapped my hands together in excitement. "That actually sounds fun."

"What sounds like fun?" Ed asked as he and Allan joined us by the yurt frame.

I let my eyes roam over their muscled torsos. Both were shirtless and their jeans hugged their muscular bodies in a way that made me hope I wasn't drooling on myself. I never got tired of looking at any of my guys.

"Sofia and Nikolai are going to build us a cabin once we can sort through some of the details, like insurance, and getting wood delivered," Doc answered.

"Oh, neat." Ed put his arms around me. "So, how do you like our temporary house?"

I nodded and leaned into his embrace, enjoying his bare skin under my hands. "Once it has canvas it should be cozy."

Allan took me from Ed and buried his nose in my hair. I pressed against him.

"If we're going to accomplish anything with what's left of today, we should get going," Doc said.

Allan swept me up into his arms before I could protest. I laughed. "I can walk, you know."

"Yes, but I can also carry you." His steel gray eyes shone with amusement as he carried me toward Doc's truck.

I let him. When he put me down, I left my arm hooked around his neck and tugged him down into a kiss. He responded enthusiastically, leaving me breathless when we finally broke apart.

Ed claimed me a moment later and I melted into his arms, his lips working against mine, his hands pressed against my ass.

He released me from his strong grip and, winking, put my hands in Nikolai's before climbing into the passenger seat of the truck.

I knew why they always put me in the back when they had a choice, so I could touch whoever was in the back. Doc was the only one who never sat back there with me because he always drove.

Nikolai brushed my hair out of my face before cupping my face with both hands and leaning in. I pressed forward, and remembering Doc's suggestion, bit at his lip and dug my fingers into his back. He rumbled in pleasure and kissed me deeply.

"Maybe I will keep Sofia here, you all go shopping," Nikolai said in jest, as he offered me his hand to help me in the truck.

"If we didn't need you to tell us what canvas to get, I'd tell you to stay," Doc said, starting up the diesel.

Nikolai shut the door behind him and we headed back toward town. I was no longer afraid of being alone, but I wasn't ready to be separated from my guys. Still, the dorms were open and I thought Victoria would be back. I definitely wanted to see her, and they could come get me tomorrow.

∞ ∞ ∞

"Girl! You're back, for real?"

I nodded, and Victoria threw herself into my arms. I hugged her back enthusiastically.

"So, tell me everything." She pulled me into our dorm room and we both sank onto the bed on her side of the room.

"Well, I think you might know more than me. I don't remember a ton from when the demon possessed me. Even when I was more in control than she was. She left me with a lot of knowledge, I just don't know what. Oh, and they burned down the cabin."

Victoria's eyebrows rose, and she put her hands in front of her mouth. "O-M-G."

"Yeah. It sucks." I still hadn't fully processed that change, along with everything else that had happened in the last few months.

"What are you going to do?"

"We're trying to figure that out now. I think Nikolai is in favor of nuking them, but we have to figure out if we can get away with it." I shrugged. "We'll figure it out. At the very least, I'm not in danger like I was before."

Victoria nodded, crossed her arms over her chest, and shivered. She probably remembered the gun against her temple. With Nikolai protecting us from magical attacks and Sam's amulet that Victoria wore, the Andersons had resorted to using a gun and my roommate to get me to go quietly.

Victoria's expression brightened. "Here's some interesting news. The Supreme Court is hearing a case right now that could determine if supernaturals get protected status under the law. It'll be a game changer if it goes through."

"Yeah, for anyone who's willing to expose themselves. Didn't they try and do some sort of registration bill a while back?"

Victoria nodded. "We got that shut down, but you're right, for the protections to work you have to be identified as a supernatural."

"I can think of quite a few races who will not want to be identified, even with protections." My thoughts went to Doc immediately. No vampire, or half vampire in his case, would want anyone to know what they were. Not in the current climate, anyway. He could still pretend to be a mage since he had access to both mine and Nikolai's powers, but I wasn't sure how well that would hold out if it really became an issue.

"Well, the goal obviously is to get to the point where it doesn't matter. This would be a big step."

"Yeah. I'm sorry. You're right, this is a big deal. It would make it easier to fight the magic mafia too."

Victoria nodded. "So, how are things with the guys? They've looked pretty stressed out over the last couple of months."

I stared at the ground, guilt at putting them through so much warring with pleasure as I thought about this afternoon with Doc.

"Good, I think. I mean, they all seem to have worked everything out amongst themselves while I was, um, gone. Now I'm just trying to get caught up with them. I guess."

Victoria's eyes sparkled and her lips turned up. "Enjoy that."

I couldn't help my cheeks reddening. "I will."

"Are you going to spend the rest of the weekend here or back up with the guys? I'm assuming they have some sort of plan for a place to live while they deal with the cabin?"

"I'm not sure. Probably head back up if I can. If not tonight, then tomorrow. Nikolai is introducing everyone to Mongolian camping techniques."

"Okay, cool. My guy will be here before long. He had a little more flexibility with the first part of his week back in classes so we decided to ride out the next snow storm up here. This weather is wild. We don't usually have this much snow this early in the year."

"Great! Do I finally get to meet him?"

"Yeah, want to see if everyone wants to get pizza?"

"Like, my entire pack?"

"That was what I meant by everyone." She winked at me. "It'll be fun."

"Does he know I'm dating all of them?"

Victoria nodded.

I flopped back onto my bed. This was way more difficult than I had anticipated. If I could feel comfortable with anyone knowing I had multiple serious boyfriends, I would think it would be Victoria and her boyfriend. Star, my best friend, knew, but we hadn't had much time to really talk about it. She promised to text me when she got back to Florida and we would talk more then.

"What's wrong?"

"I just...it still feels weird to be dating, I mean, really dating, four guys."

"Weird?"

"Okay, no, with them it feels completely natural. It's only when I'm talking about it with other people that it starts to feel strange."

"David thinks it's cool." Victoria shrugged. "We're good people to practice with. Oh, and I'm pretty sure my parents figured it out, too. Though, they haven't met Nikolai. Uh, I didn't tell David any of your guys were supernatural, except that Doc and you are mages. It was kind of obvious when I freaked out and told him about the asshole who kidnapped you. And so far that's all my parents know about, too."

"Good to know. Thanks. Let me text them."

I pulled out my phone and sent a group text.

Sofia: Anyone up for pizza with Victoria and her boyfriend tonight?

Ed: Yes! Speaking for all of us.

Sofia: Great, see you at 6.

Ed: Get reservations if they take them.

Sofia: Good call.

"They're in. Does the pizza place take reservations? Or call ahead seating?"

Victoria pulled out her phone. "I'll find out."

My phone chimed that I had another text.

Ed: Bring some clothes for the weekend. You're staying with us. Also, Doc wanted me to make sure you knew final exams were coming up for all our classes.

Sofia: Oh. Shit.

Ed: You'll be fine.

"What's wrong? You just got pale?" Victoria asked.

"Ed reminded me we have exams coming."

"Oh, yeah. Shouldn't be a big deal, though. Freshman year and all."

"You've been to your classes. I was trapped in my head." I buried my face in my arm.

"Oh, right. We'll figure it out, Sofia."

I groaned.

"Hey, I got us a reservation and David just got here." She waved her phone at me as if to explain how she knew. "Let's go meet him and then head to town. We've got a hotel for the next couple of nights, so neither of us will be alone here." Her expression fell. "I'm looking forward to having you back."

I hugged her again. "Thanks, Victoria. You really are the best. Let me get packed for the weekend."

Victoria already had a bag packed, and it didn't take long to change the clothes in my overnight bag to fresh ones and make sure I had everything, including my tablet so I could take a look at class material. Maybe I would remember enough of it from the demon going to class, that I could pass my tests.

We shouldered our bags and headed out of our dorm room. I went first, on alert and ready to cast shields thick enough to stop bullets. Fortunately, my caution was unnecessary and we made it out to the student parking lot without trouble.

"David!" Though Victoria had just seen her boyfriend, she still squealed happily and threw herself into his arms.

David was a taller black man with short hair and a blazing smile, at least when he turned it on Victoria. Clearly, he loved her as much as she loved him.

The wattage of his smile diminished from blinding to merely extremely friendly when Victoria led him over to me.

"David, this is my roomie, Sofia."

"It's very nice to meet you." David's deep, soothing voice and his firm but gentle handshake set me at ease. If he was anything like Victoria we would get along great.

"Nice to meet you, too."

"So, I hear we're all getting pizza tonight." His eyes twinkled.

"Yeah, it's our favorite restaurant."

"Meet your guys there?" He said it casually, as if it were the most normal thing in the world.

I still blushed when I nodded.

"Great. Victoria, you want to drive, or want me to?"

"We can leave my car here since it has the parking pass."

"Cool." David drove an Outback and I climbed into the backseat while Victoria took the passenger seat. He had clearly been here before, because she didn't have to give him directions to get to town, though she did give him some advice as to where to park.

I saw Doc's pickup parked on the street not too far from where David stopped and I took my bag so I could throw it in the bed. A quick concealment spell would keep anyone from running off with it, and then I didn't have to remember to grab it later.

Victoria and David watched me while I cast the spells, careful that no one else would see me, then I tossed my bag in the back of Doc's truck. After a quick thought, I also cast a small binding spell so it wouldn't bounce around if I forgot to take it out before we headed back to the cabin. Well, back to the yurt, I guess.

The pizza place was busy, as always, and I scanned the crowd until my eyes were drawn to my guys. They saw me at the same time and Ed waved. The hostess let us head back to our table.

Ed stood and I fell into his arms feeling like it had been forever since I'd last seen him, instead of a few hours. He buried his nose in my hair before giving me a quick kiss and pulling out a chair between him and Nikolai. Doc sat on the other side of Nikolai and Allan was on the other side of Ed. Two other chairs waited for Victoria and David.

Fortunately, though we were at a table instead of a booth, we were in the corner. Doc and Nikolai had their backs to the wall and even Ed and Allan acted extra watchful. Doc was a master of looking outwardly relaxed, but being ready to spring at any moment, and for all of Nikolai's easy smile I caught the hard edge in his gaze as he studied everyone around us, attention never settling in one place for very long. He was a seasoned warrior, and Doc had long years of experience. Ed and Allan were my age and had grown up in the same world I had, though as newly turned werewolves. They were more obvious about their nerves, but no less ready for an attack.

I hoped we could simply enjoy our dinner, but being out in public had me on edge, too.

David and Victoria sat with their backs to the rest of the restaurant, though David angled his chair slightly so he wasn't completely unaware of what went on behind him.

Victoria trusted us to watch her back, though she did glance over her shoulder now and again. She introduced everyone, and they all fell into an easy conversation, interrupted only when the server came to take our order.

Before we could get settled back into a conversation, Doc tensed and glanced over at the door. Ed and Allan's attention was pulled that way moments later. The rest of us looked after that.

Sam, the mage who ran a local curio shop in the touristy downtown section of Sunnyglade, stood just inside the door. She glanced around before her gaze settled on our table.

"Think she's looking for us, or just happens to be here?" I said quietly.

"Hard to say. This is a popular place on a Friday," Allan replied.

"Did something happen with Sam that has you all on edge now? I thought she was a friend? You're way more upset about her than you have been about Ash, and you know he works for the Andersons," Victoria asked.

"We're not completely sure," Allan replied tightly. "Just don't say anything important in front of her. And Ash doesn't have a choice," he added.

Sam came over in our direction after a quick word to the hostess.

"Hello, everyone," she said after a brief awkward silence.

"Hi, Sam," Doc said for all of us.

"What's up?" Ed asked.

"I hadn't seen any of you for a while, so I wanted to see how you were, since I saw you over here." Her eyes fell on me. I wondered how much she knew about the last few months. I had no recollection of interacting with her at all. My last memories of Sam were when she had led us into the trap to rescue the fae from the cold iron traps the Andersons had set near the portal to their realm. We had known it was also a trap for us, but that hadn't stopped us from helping the fae. That fight was when they had figured out Nikolai was a mage, and that had provoked them into taking Victoria hostage so they could get to me before Nikolai could teach me enough to make me useless to them.

If Sam was now working for the Andersons, I wanted nothing to do with her. We had no proof. They could simply have set her up instead. It wouldn't have been hard to do.

"We're fine," Allan said. "You?"

She shrugged. "It's snowing. Ski season brings the tourists. The shop is doing well. Otherwise, nothing remarkable."

Despite the crowds, service was quick, and our food arrived while Sam was talking. She shifted out of the way while the servers put our pizzas on the table. With six of us, two being werewolves with a very high metabolism, we had ordered several. Ed and Allan more than made up for Doc not eating anything, and Nikolai had declared pizza his new favorite food and could nearly put away an entire pizza on his own. Victoria and I weren't shy about stuffing our faces and her boyfriend claimed to be starving, so we had five large pizzas between the six of us.

"Why don't you grab a chair," Doc suggested, voice neutral once the servers left.

"Oh, I don't want to interrupt your dinner."

"Not at all," Nikolai protested. "Sit."

"Okay." Sam got another chair and joined us, sitting between Doc and Victoria.

Doc hadn't touched his water and slid it over to Sam.

Everyone grabbed plates, including Doc and slices of pizza. Since other people were around, I knew Doc and Nikolai would quietly switch plates after a while to make it look like he had eaten something. If it was just us, he didn't bother pretending.

Being a half vampire meant Doc could actually drink pretty much anything he wanted, though he couldn't handle solid food, and if he wasn't getting a steady supply of blood he could get by on protein drinks. I wasn't even sure if he was bothering right now, though. He had plenty of options for blood and with Nikolai's healing spells, it wasn't even taxing for the rest of us to keep him supplied. We enjoyed it, and it kept his powers up in case the Andersons did attack us.

With Sam there, it effectively ended any other conversations we were going to have with Victoria and David, at least meaningful ones, so we kept to safe topics like school and things going on in the town.

All of my guys seemed to like David, and we did make plans to get together next time he was able to come back to Sunnyglade.

Sam said goodbye after we were done eating. She did leave some cash on the table despite Doc's protests that she didn't need to. David pitched in a little cash and Doc paid, then we met outside and made sure David and Victoria got to their car before we all climbed into Doc's truck and headed back for the yurt. Predictably there were no leftovers.

Dakota Brown

Chapter 4

Sofia

"Ed, we should run before the storm hits tonight," Allan suggested as Doc drove down the narrow path on his property.

We could all feel the weather building, though the storm front hadn't hit yet. It would, soon. We had enough time to get the yurt completed though, according to Nikolai. I didn't know how much was left to do, but I think he wanted to have me help him.

Without the lights from the cabin, the clearing where the cabin had stood was very dark. They'd shut off the power at the breaker so we didn't have anything up here right now. Nikolai was completely unconcerned, but it would be very interesting for the rest of us. We were used to having electricity, indoor plumbing, and food storage.

"I'm okay. You go run," Ed replied.

"Ed, you haven't gone running in months. You need to change. Even I can tell you're on edge because you haven't," Allan insisted.

Ed shook his head. "No, that was just because of the demon. I'm fine now."

"Ed," I interrupted. "You need to go run." He was sitting next to me. Allan on the other side and we both twisted around so that we looked at him.

He shook his head.

"Is this about what they did to you? Have you changed since then?"

Ed's shoulders sagged and he sighed.

"Damn them. Ed, it'll be okay. I'll be here for you. I want you to go run with Allan."

"When are you going to come running with us?" Ed whispered.

"Not tonight," I said. "I need to be a little more secure in my own skin before I let you all change me into a wolf, but I will. I promise."

"You will?" Ed's gaze lifted from his knees to meet mine.

"Yes. But you need to change now and run with Allan. Someone's got to watch his back while you're out there and he'll watch yours."

Ed frowned, as if the implications of his brother running alone for months finally hit him. I doubted Allan had complained, but it was safer if they went together.

"I..."

I grabbed his hand. "It'll be okay."

He sighed. "Okay."

"We'll go change," Allan said, "and then Ed can pretend to be a lapdog for a few minutes and then we'll go run."

"If I remember correctly," I turned a sly grin on Allan, "you're just as bad of a lapdog as he is."

Allan grinned and winked.

Some other memories surfaced of my time with the demon. Ash, constantly by my side. Had he slept next to me? I wrinkled my brow as I tried to remember. Now that I remembered his constant presence, his absence felt like a gaping hole. I tried to push the feeling away. We would rescue him.

We all got out when Doc stopped the pickup, and I stood next to the truck and blinked, letting my eyes adjust to the darkness, which they did quickly thanks to the lingering effects from the demon.

The crisp air refreshed me after being down in the small town most of the afternoon and evening. Though I could hear the metal ticking in the truck, the only other sounds were nocturnal animals. I waited until my senses compensated for the night time before I stepped out of the driveway and headed toward where I remembered they had put the yurt.

Ed and Allan went off on their own, barely making a whisper of noise.

I jumped when Doc touched my arm. I hadn't heard him at all. Nikolai was nearly as quiet, appearing on my other side.

"You're going to have to teach me to move like that," I said once I had my heart under control again. "Compared to all of you I must sound like an elephant."

"Have met quieter elephants," Nikolai joked.

"Hey." I punched him lightly on the arm.

He pulled me against him, trapping my arms and kissing my cheek. "I am kidding. It's not hard."

I leaned into Nikolai and sighed, content.

"First we must finish yurt. Come on."

Before we reached the small clearing where Nikolai had started their yurt, two blond wolves stepped into our path.

I grinned and dropped to my knees. The lighter blond wolf, Ed, came forward and pushed himself into my arms.

Though I had never thought to ascribe the emotion relief to a wolf before, Ed the werewolf looked relieved.

I hugged him tightly before burying my fingers in his ruff. "See, you'll be just fine. You two keep your eyes open and use our pack bond to yell if you need us."

Allan pushed his way into my space and I included him in the hug, burying my face in their fur. I needed to get some time with them soon. Getting caught up with all of my guys was a huge priority for me at the moment. That and avoiding the Andersons as much as I could until we had a plan to stop them. We also needed to rescue Ash. Which was really going to piss the Andersons off and we needed to be ready for retaliation.

Ed snuffled my hair before touching his nose to my cheek and stepping backward. Allan did the same before brushing against Doc and Nikolai and then disappearing into the woods.

I stood and let Nikolai and Doc lead me to the clearing. "Wow."

Nikolai grinned, pleased with himself. Doc half smiled and I put my arm around his waist and leaned against him. Piles of canvas lay on the ground, and rope. The frame stood just as it had before, but inside they had put together a low bedframe. Rugs covered the floor, and a few bags lay on one side. Probably clothes and stuff.

"Memory foam?" I grinned.

"Yeah," Doc confirmed. "Got used to it and couldn't bring myself to go back to the old-fashioned kind. Especially after a couple of months sleeping in Allan's bed."

"Why were you sleeping in Allan's bed?" I frowned, trying to remember. When I couldn't, I shivered.

"The demon took over my room, so Nikolai and I used Allan's room and Allan and Ed mostly slept in Ed's."

"Oh. Bet you're looking forward to this one then." I grinned, slipped in through what was probably the front door, and jumped up, landing on my back on the bed.

Doc's low growl caught my attention. He and Nikolai stood close enough that I could see the naked desire on his face. My stomach tightened and I sucked in a breath before letting it out in a soft moan. Nikolai's eyebrows rose before his lips curled.

"Doc, you make bed. Sofia and I will finish yurt. Then, maybe we can see how comfortable it is."

I didn't think Nikolai had actually slept in Doc's bed beyond the first day when we had healed him. If he had, I hadn't been there for it.

"That is a fantastic idea," Doc agreed, voice low.

If I didn't get off the bed now, I didn't think Doc was going to let me get up. His eyes were glued to me as he entered the yurt.

Nikolai slipped an arm around Doc's waist and rested his chin on the vampire's shoulder. "It will get very cold and very snowy, if we don't finish the yurt before we get, eh, distracted."

Doc took a deep breath, a smile tugging at his lips, but he nodded. Nikolai put one hand on Doc's cheek and turned his face until they were inches apart. "Still want to share her with me?"

"Of course."

"Good, I would hate to have to roast you." The mage smirked at Doc before pressing his lips to the vampire's.

I groaned as they kissed, completely turned on now. Clearly, they had grown quite comfortable with each other over the last couple of months.

"You're not helping, Nikolai," I managed to say.

He chuckled and let go of Doc. "I know. Come." He held out his hand to me. "Much as I like winter, I do not like sleeping in middle of snowstorm without shelter."

I scooted off the bed and slid my hand into his, our magic mingling as he called his to the surface and mine responded. We all sucked in a breath as the resonance between our magic affected the three of us. Doc had drank enough of mine and Nikolai's blood that he was still carrying some of our powers and it pulled at him, too.

"Must focus. Middle of battle is bad time to be sidetracked wanting sex." Nikolai laughed. "Is most

41

distracting. First time that happened..." His shoulders shook with mirth. "It is not really funny, I almost got killed, but learned my lesson quickly." He pulled me outside the wooden frame.

That story did a good job of getting me to focus, but thinking about our current living situation and the lack of a shower made me think about another lack.

"Nikolai, what are we doing for a bathroom?"

"Tree?"

"I'm a girl."

He laughed. "Go behind tree."

"Burr."

"You are mage. Use your magic. It will be fine."

"Right." He did have a good point. "How about a kitchen?"

"Have some ideas. I will work on that tomorrow. Have to hope the wolves get a deer tonight. Doc got a few things for breakfast, I think. Will work it out."

"Okay."

"Now, it is possible to create canvas and bindings from other materials, but takes a great deal of effort. Much easier to simply shape existing canvas. I will teach you other method some time, for now, join your magic with mine and follow along."

I did enjoy this method of learning magic. His energies melding with mine caressed our bodies, reaching places we couldn't touch with only our hands.

When he stepped behind me, pressing his chest to my back, and putting his arms around me, the awareness between me and him heightened. Electric tingles spread up and down my body, originating where he pressed into me and setting all my nerves alight.

"You know," I whispered, "It is more distracting with you pressed into me. Thought you wanted to concentrate."

"I can concentrate while aroused."

I leaned back into him, knowing his self-control wasn't amazing and rubbed my ass against his firm erection.

Nikolai moaned. "If we weren't about to get snowed on..." He growled.

It was my turn to laugh. "So, the spell?"

Nikolai grumbled but returned to our magic.

Doc had finished making the bed and lounged on it. I avoided looking directly at him, though I could feel the heat of his desire through our pack bond. I might lose my control if I did, and I also didn't want to get snowed on.

Nikolai and I melded our magics together more tightly than we had yet managed before. I caught my breath, a little intimidated. "Is it supposed to be like that?"

"Sometimes, yes. It is rare. Demon left you with some gifts, also our magic already resonated strongly. Is good." He kissed my cheek then turned his attention back to the spell we shaped.

"This spell reshapes the canvas. Is harder if you don't know exactly what shape you need. I am very familiar with yurts. Goes like this."

I memorized everything Nikolai did as my lavender and his deep blue magic sank into the canvas. Shivering as the cloth changed under our direction, I vaguely recalled a kids' movie about a mage accidently bringing inanimate objects to life. It hadn't gone well for the mage, and I suspected anti-supernatural politics had fueled the popular cartoon.

Nikolai rested his cheek against the side of my head. "Doing great."

Once the canvas had reshaped, Nikolai showed me how to craft another spell to lift the canvas onto the frame. Then, he showed me how to bind it with the rope and secure it.

"Now, we cast a few extra spells to make weatherproof. Yurts without mages are weatherproof but use different methods to achieve this. We cheat."

Once we had finished, he kissed me again before pushing a little of his magic into me, arching my back and almost making me orgasm right as I stood there.

"Speaking of cheating," I gasped out as my legs buckled. He grabbed my arm, as if he had been expecting that reaction.

"Complaining?" he asked, voice mischievous.

I shook my head.

"Good. We should not keep Doc waiting then." He scooped me up in his arms, my legs still too weak for me to protest. Suddenly I figured out the obvious. Nikolai wanted me and Doc at the same time. I didn't know how that would work, but I trusted Nikolai. It wasn't like I hadn't already done things with more than one of them at once, but this was more intense. I fully intended to have sex with Nikolai and I was pretty sure he was on the same page as me by his urgent strides as he carried me into the yurt.

"Do you want me to leave?" Doc asked when Nikolai set me gently down on the freshly made bed. I pulled off my shoes when Nikolai stepped back. Doc was already barefoot.

"No, of course not," Nikolai replied. He glanced at me and I shook my head.

Nikolai shed his jacket and boots then frowned and waved his hand. Blue motes filled the air and my breath no longer fogged the air as it warmed to a comfortable temperature. "Forgot that one."

My breath caught as he pulled his shirt off. Though he wasn't as overtly muscular as the werewolves were, Nikolai had hard, lean muscles from a lifetime of wielding a sword, along with his magic. I wanted to trail my hands up those muscles and trace the scar that ran from his collarbone down across his chest, ending on his opposite hip.

Doc's gaze roamed over the mage, too, drinking in his exquisitely hardened body.

Nikolai climbed on the bed and I scooted toward Doc to give him space. He studied us for a moment before his lips turned up and his dark brown eyes sparkled with a hint of blue from his magic.

He reached for me and I moved into his grasp, getting my wish to run my hands up his sculpted muscles as he met my lips with his. His strong hands clutched at my back and I dug my nails into him. Nikolai groaned appreciatively and devoured my lips. After a moment, when it was still just us, Nikolai paused.

"Doc, you do understand how this works, yes?" Nikolai looked over my shoulder at him.

"I have an idea," Doc said dryly.

"Then perhaps you would do us the favor of touching one or both of us?"

"I wasn't sure."

Nikolai smirked. "Surely you've done this before?"

"In a group? No. Well. Yes. But no."

"Which is it?"

I laughed and claimed Nikolai's mouth again before he could get more frustrated or embarrass Doc more.

"Group sex, no? Group lots of other things that eventually lead to sex but haven't yet, yes," I answered Nikolai after pulling back from the kiss.

"What Sofia said," Doc replied quietly. "Though all the group activities have been with Sofia."

"Good. So, it is easy. You can touch me, you can touch Sofia. Have fun, make sure other people are having fun."

When Doc hesitated, Nikolai reached past me, grabbed the other man's shirt, and dragged him over to us. I ended up sandwiched between the two of them. I was in no way complaining.

"This is not much different than anything else you've done with either of us."

Doc sighed. "You're right. Sorry."

I twisted around and put my hands in his hair, disintegrating his hair tie and then pulling his lips to mine.

Hesitation gone, he crushed me to him, kissing me back, while Nikolai's lips trailed hot fire up my neck.

Nikolai's hands slipped under my shirt and I leaned back from Doc and put my hands in the air so Nikolai could pull it off over my head. I twisted back around and pressed into Nikolai while he went to work on Doc's shirt. It didn't take long before I was happily pressed between two hot, shirtless guys.

Nikolai laid me back on the bed and Doc lay next to me, kneading one of my breasts while Nikolai dragged his nails down my ribs, trailing electric magic along my skin as he did so. Mine responded, and both Doc and I groaned with pleasure as the affects pulsed through him, too. Nikolai nibbled his way down my stomach, nipping gently while Doc worked on my neck.

I shut my eyes, lost in the waves of pleasure that coursed through me. Nikolai pulled my pants off, and Doc worked his fingers into my wet folds. I opened my legs and moaned as he worked soft circles on my clit. Moments later, Nikolai joined him with his tongue, and I could barely think as my body tightened and heat coursed through me. I came so hard, I cried out in surprise and pleasure.

For a moment they let me writhe in pleasure, then Nikolai pressed his lips to my mouth. I opened for him, tasting myself on his lips, finding I didn't mind, and we kissed while he pressed himself into me. I tilted my hips and wrapped a leg around his back while he filled me. My focus narrowed to Nikolai and myself as our magic spun through us as we connected. Sensations intensified, and I came again while he thrust into me. He didn't stop, panting with need. My mind spun and I reached out until my hand connected with Doc. I grabbed at his arm and dug my nails in.

Doc's hands found my breasts and his lips went to my neck. I tilted my chin, inviting him, while Nikolai gasped my name softly as he thrust into me.

Heat built again in my core and I clutched Nikolai's shoulder, digging in nails, not able to do much else as my body responded to my men.

Cold ice stung my neck as Doc sank his teeth in. This time he did more than take a quick taste, pulling at my neck. I cried out again as my orgasm rippled through me.

Nikolai gasped my name, thrusting into me one more time, before shuddering and laying on top of me, chest heaving.

I couldn't have moved even if Nikolai wasn't laying on top of me. My head swam and my overly sensitive body twitched, my nerves on fire.

The three of us lay there, tangled together, until we had all regained some semblance of normal breathing. Then Nikolai leaned on his elbows and looked down at me, titling an eyebrow.

I met his eyes, grinning, though my breath hitched at the emotion I saw there.

"Sofia," he said softly. "I do love you."

His words surprised me. I hadn't even been thinking about love. I should have been. These guys were my saviors, my teachers…my support. My heart melted and I wanted them to know what they meant to me, but I wasn't sure if I could find the words to encompass the depth of my feelings. Feelings I'd barely had time to explore.

"I love you, too," I whispered, testing how the emotion felt to say.

His eyes shone with pleasure and he shifted his gaze to Doc, who lay next to me. "Love you, too."

Doc cleared his throat and I glanced over at him. He also looked surprised, but happy. Blue and lavender magic shone in his dark eyes and it pleased me to see both of our energies marking him. "I love both of you."

I turned my head and kissed Doc gently. "Yeah, definitely love you, too."

"Good." Nikolai nodded, as if something had been settled, though I wasn't sure what.

The warm feeling in my chest remained even after Nikolai slowly slid out of me and stood.

Now that I could think about something other than two of the men who had claimed me, the raging storm outside caught my attention. The canvas shifted with the wind that howled around us.

Though plenty warm, I shivered. "Ed and Allan?"

"Not back yet," Doc said. "They'll be okay."

Doc sounded certain and I didn't feel any alarm through our pack bond, so I put my worry for the rest of my pack out of my mind. We saw to necessities and then crawled into bed, still naked, limbs tangled around each other, and I fell fast asleep.

∞ ∞ ∞

I woke after a few hours when the wolves returned and hopped up on the bed. One of them lay on top of me and rested his head between my breasts. I buried my hands in his fur, shivering for a moment as a little snow melted between my skin and the wolf's fur. The other pressed in between Nikolai and me. The mage put his arms around

48

the wolf, though he still kept contact with me, too. Content, I drifted back to sleep until the next morning.

Waking up in a giant puppy pile of my guys was definitely my favorite way to wake up. Usually the wolves, at least, were up making breakfast before I woke up, but there was no real way to accomplish that yet, so everyone was still in bed. Someone had gotten warm and kicked the covers mostly off last night, and to be fair, with two werewolves, even in human form, practically laying on top of me, I wasn't cold. Nikolai was wrapped around Allan though he still had a leg hooked over mine. Ed still lay mostly sprawled across me and Doc was pressed up against Ed and me.

I sighed contently, though my full bladder was sort of becoming an issue. Still, I didn't want to move.

After a while, I noticed Ed staring at me, lips turned up.

"Morning," I said.

He grinned.

"How was your run?"

"Good," Allan answered for both of them. "Nice to have Ed with me for a change."

"How was your evening?" Ed asked slyly.

"Um, good." My cheeks colored and my body tightened as last nights' activities surfaced in my mind.

"Just good? You two need to work harder if her evening was just good," Ed chided.

Nikolai grunted in annoyance. Doc laughed quietly.

I could tell Nikolai wanted to say something biting in reply, but he kept his comment to himself.

"You're expecting me to be eloquent before caffeine?" I poked Ed in the shoulder. "Last night was great. Do you want details?"

Ed studied me for a minute before grinning. "Maybe later. Right now," he slid a hand up my side before cupping one of my breasts, "I want breakfast."

I shivered under his touch, before thinking he was going to abandon me for food again. Raising my eyebrows, I was about to grumble at him, when he took my other breast in his mouth.

"Oh," I gasped.

Clearly, the guys wanted to catch up with me, too. I think Nikolai had healed me last night after Doc had fed from me. At least, I didn't feel tired or sore from our activities, so he must have, and I had zero objections to Ed's attention.

Allan claimed my lips while Ed worked his way lower.

Someone's phone buzzed and Doc cursed. I lost track of him and Nikolai as Allan and Ed worked my body. I wanted to reciprocate, but with both of them touching me, my mind swam. Neither acted bothered.

Ed went to work with his tongue, while Allan focused on my breasts. My hips rocked and I moaned, encouraging Ed to continue. I finally got some semblance of control over my hands and I dug my fingers into Allan's back, my other hand gripping the sheets as I panted.

It didn't take long before I was crying out as my body responded to their ministrations.

"Hmm, good breakfast," Ed purred.

We lay there for a few more minutes before Allan and Ed both got up. I cast Nikolai's cleaning spell and buried myself back under the covers, not ready to get up after that.

"Sleepyhead," Nikolai whispered, pulling me into his arms, though he left the comforter around me. "Hungry?"

"For food?"

"Yes."

I pulled the comforter down and looked him, grinning. "What's for breakfast?"

"Not as good as usual, but managed cereal and milk."

"Works for me." I finally climbed out of bed, ignored all the eyes on me as I dressed, and went outside into the snowstorm to find a tree. Magic kept me warm and dry, but this wasn't going to be a great solution for very long. I hoped the guys thought of something better soon. The yurt itself was fantastic.

"What's the plan for today?" I asked after I had scarfed a bowl of cereal and climbed back onto the bed since I didn't want to sit on the floor.

"Well, it's still snowing. Deputy Morrison wants to talk to us at some point but said to wait until the snow stopped. I have no idea where you stand on homework, but you might want to check on that," Doc answered.

"Ugh. Yeah. Exams. Shit." I tried out a few Russian curses and earned a nod of approval from Nikolai. "At least everything is online. Though, it feels a bit weird thinking about school when Ash is still a prisoner."

The guys nodded.

"We want him back with us, too," Allan said. "We miss having him around. Even if he is grumpy."

"Can you blame him?" Resigned to focusing on school, I glanced around for my bag and found it in the corner. My phone and my tablet were in there.

"No," Doc agreed with me.

Allan, anticipating what I needed, handed it to me. I gave him a grateful smile. First, I answered a few texts, checking in with Victoria and Mom, then I turned on the tablet and hoped that, somehow, I wasn't super behind on homework.

Dakota Brown

Chapter 5

Doc

Spending the entire weekend basically snowed in with the guys and Sofia had been a fantastic way to end the holiday week. Though he dreaded dealing with Deputy Morrison after he was done with classes for the day, at least nothing unfortunate had happened over the weekend. Doc acted almost relaxed for the first time in months.

Nikolai chose to stay up at the yurt and work on some form of kitchen, now that Sofia was more than capable of taking care of herself. The two mages had spent a fair bit of time in her grove making sure she had a good grasp on at least some of the knowledge the demon had left her, and Nikolai claimed to have learned a few things from Sofia in the process.

Though Doc wasn't sure why the demon had been so generous, he suspected it was on purpose, and probably had to do with her desire to see the Andersons nuked because of what they had done to her and Sofia, and probably Ash, too.

What to do about Ash?

Doc didn't expect the Andersons to let their pet demon out of their sight anytime soon now that they'd broken the bonds on the more powerful demon. Beyond having promised to free Ash if possible—which it now was—Doc hated to see anyone being controlled by someone else. He also missed having Ash around. Hopefully, they could do something for him soon.

They had all gotten up early enough that he could get Sofia, Ed, and Allan dropped off with time to hit the dining hall before class, so he headed to his office instead of his first classroom.

The administrative area of the history building was quiet, and he hadn't expected to run into anyone, let alone Stacy Guen, the head of the history department, and Fred Meyers, the dean of the entire college. They were both seated in the small waiting area outside the cluster of professor offices. Alarm bells went off in his mind.

He tended to keep his extra senses locked down while around lots of people, like on campus, because that much information about the world around him usually did one of two things, made it harder to pass as fully human as his body compensated for the information by getting closer to his vampire side, or got really disorientating.

Carefully, he stretched out his senses, hoping the two of them were alone. He didn't detect anyone else, and it was pretty hard to hide from a vampire. Even with Nikolai's impressive invisibility spell, Doc still usually had a vague sense that someone else was present, though that could have been their pack bond interfering with Nikolai's spell.

He was almost on top of them when Stacy glanced his direction. Her heart skipped a beat and her pulse raced in surprise, though she managed to look only slightly startled. Fred didn't react as strongly. Doc reined in his powers a bit, not wanting to freak Stacy out if she were unusually sensitive. Some people were.

"Roy." She and Frank stood. The administration never used his nickname and sometimes it was weird to hear his given name, he had gotten so used to everyone calling him Doc.

"Hello, Stacy. Frank." He tried to keep his voice casual, as if he had no reason to be worried about their visit.

"Do you have a few minutes?" Frank asked, though it wasn't really a question coming from the dean.

"Of course." Doc gestured to his office, which he unlocked. He dropped his bag onto his desk and leaned against the wall. "What can I do for you?"

"Um," Stacy traded a glance with Frank, her breathing elevated. Frank's eyes were dilated, too. They were both nervous. That didn't bode well.

Frank sighed. "Roy, we've had a complaint from the community."

Doc arched an eyebrow. He could guess who, he just hoped it hadn't been anything close to the truth. Of course, if the Andersons had accused him of being a vampire, the sunbeam he currently stood in from the office window might cast some doubt on that. He suspected if the Andersons had gone that far, Stacy and Frank wouldn't be here confronting him alone. He hoped.

"A complaint?" He prompted when they didn't continue.

"They said you're not human. That you're a mage," Stacy answered words coming out in a rush.

He couldn't help the relieved breath that escaped his lips. Mage he could deal with. He'd been half afraid they would have used Sofia against him. That might have been awkward, but probably survivable. This was both easier and harder to deal with. At least the Andersons hadn't tried to out him as a vampire, they probably were still afraid of him.

"A mage?" He arched an eyebrow, putting as much disbelief in his voice as he could manage.

"Yes."

"Okay?" He shrugged. "Do you want me to deny it? Do you want me to protest? What are you looking for?"

"Well, of course you deny it," Frank said, though Doc hadn't actually denied anything. "But we'll have to suspend you while we conduct an investigation."

"An investigation?" Fortunately, Doc's current identity would hold up to a pretty extensive check if an investigation only checked paper trails. If they started talking to people who might know him, things would eventually crack open. He could be long gone by that point, but that was less than ideal.

"Yes. We can't have a mage teaching at our school."

Doc laughed. "I'm pretty sure there isn't anything in the handbook that says it's illegal."

Frank and Stacy traded a glance. Doc was right, he knew it. They didn't actually have much legal ground to stand on, if Doc was willing to put up with whatever process they invented. Perhaps they'd been counting on him cutting and running? Of course, if they decided he was a mage, Doc had no legal ground to stand on at all.

"You've both known me what, five years now?" He thought it had been five years. "Does anything about the last five years make you think I'm a magic user?"

They both shook their heads.

"How are you going to investigate? Attack me with magic and see if I defend myself?" He crossed his arms and tried not to glare too hard at them.

"Well, your background..."

Doc cut Frank off. "I passed a background check when I was hired. Nothing has changed. What makes you think you'd find anything new?"

They traded another uneasy glance. Clearly this wasn't going the way they had expected, or been led to expect.

"Let me explain something to you. I'm betting your information comes from some rather prominently rich members of our community, potentially even donors to the college?"

Frank and Stacy's uneasy glances were getting almost comical, but he could tell he'd struck the right nerve.

"I'm not going to name any names, but we all know who I'm talking about. They don't like me. They're trying to use you to get to me. I'm going to tell you why they don't like me, and you can take that information as you will. I have something they want." He stretched his arms out so his beaded cuffs were visible, hoping they would take the hint that the cuffs were what the Andersons were after. He had no doubt if they could get their hands on the magical artifact that did actually allow him to cast magic when he hadn't recently ingested mage blood, they would be ecstatic. "Family heirloom." He made it more obvious. "I've been unwilling to give in to their demands, so they're coming after me in other ways."

Stacy frowned as she studied the intricate designs on the cuffs. "Why would they want something like that so badly? They are beautiful, and probably culturally significant, but they're not Native so why would it matter?"

Doc hesitated, wondering how far he should go, then shrugged. Maybe this would help, maybe it would be the nail in the coffin. Maybe it wouldn't end up mattering. If they did free Ash the Andersons were going to completely lose their shit anyway.

He held out his hand and formed a small ball of energy over his hand. The lights danced dark blue and lavender as he was using both Sofia's and Nikolai's magic at the moment.

"They were my mother's. They store a small amount of magic, so, no, I'm not a mage, but I can do a little magic."

Both Stacy and Frank's jaws dropped. Maybe the demonstration had been too much?

"These very rich, but nameless complainers, happen to be a family of actual mages. They want my little heirloom for their collection." He pulled the magic back into the cuffs. "Unfortunately for them, I think its power is tied to my bloodlines anyway. No one else has been able to get them to work. And I'm not willing to give them up."

They were completely derailed with his little demonstration and his counter accusation.

"If they're mages..."

"They're too powerful. Don't go after them, don't even think about it. Leave them alone and eventually things will settle out." Doc knew events had moved too far for that tactic to work, but there was no point in dragging the college into their little war.

"They want you gone."

Doc nodded. "Clearly." He thought quickly. What could he offer them that might make it easier on everyone? He liked his job here, but he didn't strictly have to have it. On the other hand, he didn't want to give up anything to the Andersons that he didn't have to. They'd already taken enough. "What about this, the semester is almost over—no sense in disrupting classes—I'll take a leave of absence next semester, and if things haven't worked themselves out by then, we can reopen this conversation." Doc backed his suggestion with the barest hint of vampiric power. They didn't really want to let him go, or they would have simply fired him. A quiet nudge would be completely undetectable, even by magical means. He'd discovered that in the past.

He knew everything would be settled by the spring, probably even before the end of the year. No one was going to let this conflict drag out any longer than they had to. The longer the Andersons were on the loose, the longer they had to mess things up for Ed, Allan, and Sofia, or cause Nikolai to do something everyone would regret. Doc suspected the Russian had the potential to be very destructive if pushed far enough, and right now he probably wasn't to far from the edge of outright and very visible conflict.

"Roy, you must understand we have to do what is best for the college," Frank said.

Doc nodded.

"Frank, I think Roy's suggestion is a good one. It leaves us the most options," Stacy said.

"Very well, Roy. Enjoy your semester off. We'll get you the paperwork to sign for your leave. If you have any questions about how it affects your benefits or anything, please let us know."

Doc waved his hand dismissively. He didn't care. It probably would affect Ed and Allan's tuition, but that really wasn't an issue, either. There were far more immediate things for him to worry about.

Both of them shot another glance at the magical cuffs before taking their leave.

Once his office door was shut, Doc collapsed into his chair and stared at the ceiling.

"Fuck."

The Andersons really had to go.

Dakota Brown

Chapter 6

Sofia

Though I had hoped to see Ash at class, I wasn't completely surprised that he wasn't present. The depth of my disappointment surprised me, despite knowing he probably wouldn't be there. We would have nabbed him right away, and I wanted to see him. The demon was probably the only thing keeping the Andersons safe right now. While he'd come after us before, under their direction, he hadn't had any real ambition behind the attacks.

I suspected that if the Andersons unleashed him on us now, he'd have some pretty clear and lethal instructions. I sort of wondered why they hadn't gone that route yet. Maybe they still weren't sure they could defeat us, even with Ash?

I suspected, with as closely as Nikolai and I were able to meld our powers, and as much knowledge as the demon had left me, we could stand against Ash. It wouldn't be easy, but we could hold him off. That left Doc, Ed and Allan to handle however many mages they had left and whatever else they wanted to throw at us. It probably would be a pretty tough fight. A big confrontation would get a lot of attention from the authorities, too.

Attention. That thought sparked another idea...what if we could get some attention. Maybe that's what we needed. We needed people to notice the Andersons. The right people. I'd talk to Victoria next time we were alone. Maybe her contacts could help. Had things gone far enough that it was worth the risk?

I didn't know. I'd have to bring the guys in on this conversation.

Doc looked preoccupied when I came into class, though his expression lightened when he saw me.

I tilted my head and he shook his. He could tell me later.

He led class without his usual enthusiasm, though the topic was still interesting and once everyone had filed out, I lingered. I didn't suspect people would think much of it, since I doubted I'd done so for the several months when the demon was in control. No one gave me any looks like they thought I was trying to get too much attention from the teacher. Or maybe I was just being extra sensitive.

"So, what's wrong?" I asked.

"Let's talk after school. I still need to talk to Deputy Morrison, too. I can fill you all in then."

"Should I worry?"

Doc shook his head. "No. I think if Deputy Morrison were going to try and blame the fire on us, he would have shown up and tried to arrest me already and the other thing is interesting, but not actually a problem at this point."

"Leaving me in suspense."

He smiled. "Get to class. We can grab takeout, so Nikolai doesn't starve."

"I think we need to talk with Victoria, too. She may have some contacts that can help us. I think events have progressed enough that we need outside intervention."

Doc's brows furrowed for a minute before he nodded. "See if she wants to come up to the yurt for dinner. She can see our new accommodations. I'll bring you both back down here before it's too late so you can sleep at the dorm."

I pouted.

"Unless Victoria wants to cuddle with a bunch of guys she's not dating, she probably won't want to stay up there," Doc said quietly, eyes glinting in amusement.

I laughed. "Okay, point. Let's plan on that, and I'll tell you if anything changes."

Doc sighed and nodded. He clenched his hands into fists and shook his head. "Pretend I'm giving you a big hug right now, and get to class." There was no way anyone could overhear us, but he spoke even more quietly than he had before.

"See you soon," I replied.

"Looking forward to it."

I left the classroom and made it about halfway to my next class before I ran into one of the people at the top of my never want to see again list.

"Sofia," Alex purred my name. "Looking diminished."

To hear him say my name with such familiarity and comment on how being just me lessened me somehow made me want to show him everything the demon had left me with and leave him a smoking crater in the ground.

I growled, clenching my hands, trying hard to resist destroying him where he stood. As confident as Alex looked right then, I knew I would win.

Ironically, Allan saved Alex.

"Sofia," he came up to me and claimed my mouth with his. It might have been the only thing he could have done to keep me from completely losing control and showing everyone on campus once and for all that magic was very lethally real.

After a quick moment, I could sense that seeing Allan kiss me so openly seriously pissed off Alex so I pressed myself to Allan, using him for a minute in a quick revenge. Of course, I got the impression from our pack bond that Allan was doing the same exact thing.

Alex finally made a gagging sound. "Try not to get a hairball," he growled and stalked away.

"Cats!" I called after him, "Cats get hairballs, idiot."

"Sorry about that," Allan said, cheeks coloring a bit. "I, uh, thought it would piss him off. Not that I didn't want to kiss you..."

I cut off his unneeded apology with another kiss, pressing my lips to his, my body molding to his muscular one, hands digging into his back. Forgetting for a moment that we were on campus and not up on Doc's property.

Someone catcalled and I broke away, laughing.

Allan grinned at me.

"Timely rescue," I said when he took my hand and we headed toward my next class.

"Yeah, I could feel you pulling all your magic. It was pretty intense. Fortunately, the visual show hadn't started yet. I don't think anyone but Alex and me noticed."

"Fucker," I growled again.

"Yeah. He probably was trying to provoke you."

"He has no idea what he's getting into." I clenched Allan's hand.

"No, but we gotta be careful."

I sighed and tried to relax my shoulders. "I know. Thanks for the save."

"Anytime, Sofia. We'll get them. We just have to figure out how to do it."

"I know," I grumbled. "Allan, I..." I hesitated as I met his eyes. The intensity and hint of wilderness I saw in them melted me inside. I needed to tell him how I felt now, in case something happened. We were in a literal fight for our lives. Why was I hesitating? Because I was being dumb, that's why. There was no reason not to tell Allan I loved him. None at all.

"Yeah?" He brushed his fingertips across my temple.

"I love you. You know that, right?" There, that wasn't so hard? Was it?

His eyebrows rose. Clearly, he hadn't been expecting that, but his eyes softened, glistening. "I love you, Sofia."

We kissed gently before breaking apart.

"And, we're going to be late for class." I sighed.

He shrugged. "At least we'll make it. A few weeks ago, I never thought I'd get the chance to tell you how I felt in words."

I smiled. I'd been right. That needed to be said. Now I just had to get some alone time with Ed.

∞ ∞ ∞

Ed and Allan met Victoria and I at our dorm later. We waited in the common area for Doc to show up. A few other students used the space to study, so we kept our quiet conversations to safe topics. Exams were starting to wear heavily on my mind, and I studied my tablet, hoping to unlock more immediate access to the knowledge I had to have gained over the last couple of months.

Though none of the information was new to me, it was becoming apparent the demon hadn't truly applied herself toward paying attention in classes. That didn't exactly surprise me, and I couldn't blame her at all, but I wanted to end the semester with decent grades. I knew my parents would understand if they slipped a little, but if I could at all avoid having that conversation, I would.

Finally, the wolves heard Doc's pickup and we headed outside and climbed in. Victoria took the passenger seat and I got in back with Ed and Allan.

"Did you get takeout?" Ed asked Doc.

"Nikolai said he had cooking covered, so I stopped by the store instead."

Ed and Allan were quiet for a minute before Allan whispered, "What did you get?"

"Uh, normal stuff, I guess."

Ed groaned.

"Hey, I do actually pay attention to what you guys eat," Doc mock growled.

I happened to glance at Victoria. She studied Doc closely, before sighing quietly. Shit, the guys just couldn't seem to remember that she didn't know Doc's secret. Well, at least she wasn't going to jump to the vampire conclusion since she had seen him in the sunlight. Oh well.

Doc glanced over at Victoria and tightened his jaw before shrugging.

"I got lots of hamburger."

"Well, that's something, anyway," Ed muttered.

I laughed. "Guys, it could be worse. You can always go hunt down another deer."

"You all didn't want to stay at a hotel?" Victoria asked.

Doc shrugged. "Nikolai was pretty excited about his yurts and it's actually quite comfortable. We're happier up there, anyway."

Doc hit the main roundabout in town and headed out of the valley.

"You're lucky you found him," Victoria said.

"Yes, we are," Doc agreed.

I couldn't help but grin. I was particularly grateful for a lot of reasons, but I was also glad that Nikolai and Doc had hit it off so well. Victoria might not know about that aspect of our pack dynamic. She was about to get an eyeful if she didn't already know.

Shortly we had pulled off the main road and were bouncing down the snowy driveway.

"It's so pretty back here," Victoria said.

"We like it," Doc replied.

The rest of us murmured agreement.

Once the truck was stopped, we all hopped out. Nikolai waited for us, looking extremely pleased with himself.

"Hello, Victoria," he greeted her before wrapping me in a hug and kissing me soundly. "Day was long without you."

I flushed.

He gave Allan a quick hug before the werewolves jumped in the back of Doc's pickup and grabbed the food Doc had bought.

"I guess he didn't do to badly," Ed said as they headed toward the yurt.

Doc shook his head. "No gratitude."

"Experience!" Allan shot back.

Nikolai laughed and put his arms around Doc, pressing his chest against Doc's back and rested his chin on the vampire's shoulder. "Don't like your shopping?"

Doc sighed though his expression softened with Nikolai's embrace. "I needed some training when they were younger. They haven't forgotten."

I happened to glance at Victoria. Her eyes were wide, though she seemed amused more than anything.

Nikolai kissed Doc's neck before releasing him. "Training?" He headed toward the path we'd made in the snow that led back to the yurt.

"How was I supposed to know what a pair of teen werewolves ate?" Doc replied defensively. "They learned to cook as a survival tactic."

Victoria glanced at me, an eyebrow arched. I shrugged.

She shook her head then glanced over where the cabin had stood. Her expression fell. "Wow, that sucks."

"Yes," Nikolai agreed. "We will rebuild. Just need materials and time."

"Did you lose everything?"

Doc shook his head. "Important documents and most of my guns were in the safe. Nothing else was really all that important. Even the firearms weren't that big of a deal. It's more inconvenient than anything."

"I fixed most of the inconvenience." Nikolai waved his hand. "Busy day. Good to have something to do."

Victoria gasped when we came into the smaller clearing. Nikolai had been busy. The yurt remained where it had stood, but along with everything else he'd done today, he'd taken the time to magic the yurt into something rather fantastical looking. It retained its original shape, but the ropes that lashed it together had morphed into leafy vines. The plain canvas had been transformed into its own piece of art. Earth tone colors swirled along the walls, giving it a kind of camouflage, especially in the fading light, though it was lit on the inside which made some of the colors stand out.

Doc glanced over at Nikolai. "Very nice."

"Thank you."

"There is now a shower and outhouse, too. Magic, of course. Don't let just anyone know about it. It is back that way."

I could make out another path in the snow that led further into the woods.

Ed and Allan came out of the yurt, stunned expressions on their faces.

"Damn, Nikolai, we almost don't need to build another cabin."

His pleased grin widened.

Doc put his arm around Nikolai and side-hugged him before going into the yurt.

"Put food here. Also magic. It will keep everything fresh."

A couple of trunk sized boxes sat near the front door. They were more than adequate for the food Doc had purchased.

Victoria hung back for a moment and I waited with her.

"Wow," she said.

"Yeah, having someone who has actually lived like this before in our pack is really useful. I'd be like...s'mores anyone? That's pretty much the extent of my ability to rough it."

"Well, being able to use magic doesn't hurt."

"No."

"Yeah, so those two..." She raised her eyebrows again.

I grinned and winked. "Can hear you. Come on, let's go."

"Right."

She followed me into the yurt. Nikolai had moved things around a little. The bed was pushed to the side a bit more, leaving room for a low table and cushions. Where he had gotten all of that, I didn't know. Probably convinced a tree to grow them or something. If he wasn't good at earth magic, someday I wanted to meet someone who was.

A slightly taller table looked vaguely like a place to cook. One side of the table was bare wood. The other side had some sort of black stone on it. Under the black stone was another box.

"Gets hot." Nikolai gestured to the stone. "Haven't quite worked out how to let the user chose the temperature. Just pay attention. And this is like an oven. Gets about three hundred degrees, seems to be a common cooking temperature. Not perfect, but will work."

"Not perfect? Nikolai, this is amazing." Ed got in on the hugging action, dragging Nikolai into a tight embrace.

The mage looked a little embarrassed as he hugged Ed back. "Is least I could do. You all provide everything else."

"Ed, Allan, cook something," Doc ordered. "We have a lot to discuss before we drop the ladies off back at the dorm."

The other guys pouted.

"Can't we keep her here?" That was Ed again.

"The semester is almost over. She can stay up here through the break."

"Nikolai, what do we do for water?" Allan came back in holding a tea kettle and a few other things.

"Running water in shower. Was best I could do."

Allan headed back out into the night, assuring Nikolai that it was fantastic.

Trying to stay out of the way, I sprawled on the bed. Victoria joined me, lounging near the foot.

Doc lay down on his stomach next to me, leaning on his elbows as he watched Ed and Allan get familiar with the kitchen. He must have noticed me eyeing the hair tie that kept his long hair pulled back because he reached up and pulled it out before I could disintegrate it.

"I'm running out of them." He grinned.

"Oh, sorry."

"Don't be. I just hate shopping."

Nikolai perched on the other side of Doc. "So, tell us about your day." He buried one hand in Doc's long hair, resting it on the other man's back.

I pushed up against his other shoulder with mine.

"Well, it got interesting fast. The Andersons are not quite hitting full force, but they went after my job."

Everyone stared at Doc in horror.

"It's fine. I talked them out of suspending me, although it amounts to the same thing. I'm taking a leave of absence for the spring semester. Things with the Andersons will be worked out long before the question of if I can actually go back comes up."

"What did they do?" Victoria gasped out.

"They tried to out me as a mage. I managed to convince the dean that the Andersons were lying, and they really didn't want to go through the whole process of dealing with that since I wasn't willing to just walk away. The leave of absence was a compromise."

"That's such crap," Victoria grumbled. "They can't fire you for being a mage."

"They could," Doc said. "And I'd rather they think that I'm a mage rather than the truth, and if an investigation really did happen, it would get messy fast. My current background is tight as far as the paper trail is concerned, but enough people know me, that if they asked the right people the right questions it could get, um, awkward. Of course, they'd have to go to the Navajo for real information and I suspect my mother's people would be fairly tight lipped about the whole thing. Or, the Andersons could just tell the truth. I think they're still afraid to do that, though I'm not completely sure what's holding them back at this point."

"Suspect they're afraid you have friends."

Doc snorted. "Other than you guys, no."

Nikolai nodded. "Still, is better they think that."

Doc buried his face in his hands for a minute before brushing his long hair back and resting his chin on his hands. Then he frowned and glanced over at Victoria.

I followed her gaze. She had a deliberately blank look on her face, as if she were trying really hard not to react to anything we were saying.

Doc sighed. "I'm a vampire."

Her blank mask shattered and her eyebrows rose. That she didn't immediately completely freak out pleased me. She'd known Doc for months now.

"Sunlight?" she whispered. "That's not a real thing?"

"It is." Doc answered. "I'm not a full vampire. My mother was attacked right before I was born. It's a long story."

"Oh." Her gaze met mine, eyes wide. "Okay. Well, I guess that explains about everything then. I can, uh, see why you didn't want to tell me, though."

He shrugged. "At least now if someone asked you if I'm a mage, you can say no with complete conviction, or lie knowledgably if the situation warrants."

She nodded.

Ed and Allan turned back to the meal they were working on and Doc sighed quietly. I was probably the only one who heard him, since I was pressed up close.

"Well, so you have a long vacation. Great. How was Deputy Morrison?" I wasn't sure what else to say about his job situation.

Doc groaned. "Okay. He's not completely convinced it wasn't arson, but no one can prove anything and since I don't have any real information for him, they're going to call it shit luck, I guess. He grilled me pretty hard today, but short of telling him that mages burned it down because we took away their pet demon, I couldn't really say anything other than that I had no idea who might want to hurt us. Took a little persuasion, but he finally dropped it. I dealt with the insurance company, too. We should be able to get replacement supplies before long. Though, I don't know if I want to rebuild until the Andersons are actually handled. Two fires would be awfully suspicious."

"Which leads us to dealing with those assholes," I said once Doc had finished.

Everyone nodded.

"I can't believe they burned down your cabin," Victoria said, voice still airy as if she were trying to cope with all the new information.

It was Nikolai's turn to shrug. "Blew up part of their mansion and burned another part not long ago. Suppose is fair."

Victoria's eyes widened. "Really?"

"Yes."

She shook her head. "How did that not make the news?"

"Magic," Nikolai answered with a grin.

Victoria groaned. "I almost wish I didn't know."

"Sorry," Nikolai replied.

"It would be completely convenient if we could just end them," I said. "We need to rescue Ash and then we need to stop them. I was thinking that maybe it was time to reach out to other groups of mages, see if our problem has gotten big enough to deal with yet."

"It's worth checking into," Doc answered.

"So you want me to see if we have any contacts?" Victoria asked. "I'm guessing that's why you wanted me here."

"Yeah. If you don't mind."

"I'll talk to my parents."

"Thanks, Victoria." I smiled at her.

"Of course."

"I am working on a plan for rescuing Ash," Nikolai said. "Need to do that soon."

"Besides staying alive, that is our next priority, right? That will tip the balance completely," I said.

"If we do rescue him, there's a chance he'll take care of our problem for us," Allan replied.

"How's that?" Victoria's voice sounded a little more normal.

"Well, he's powerful, and I imagine he's more than a little pissed off at them," Allan answered.

"Gotcha."

"Dinner's ready," Ed interrupted.

The increasingly delicious scent of hamburgers was making my stomach grumble and I was grateful for the change in topic, too. We all climbed off the bed and dug in.

∞ ∞ ∞

"So, Doc," Victoria asked once we were alone back in our dorm room. "Really?"

"Yeah."

"He drinks blood?"

"Yeah." I tried really hard to say that last casually. I really didn't feel like sharing those details of my personal life. "He usually gets by on a combination of protein drinks, tea, and occasionally blood. Though, I think he just likes tea. I don't think it actually does anything for him."

She was quiet for a minute and I looked at her. She stared at the ground. "I mean, I guess I never suspected that. It really does explain a lot though. Okay, so what's up with him and Nik?"

I smiled. "Nikolai is into him, he's into Nikolai." I didn't need to share Allan's interest unless she asked. He wasn't as obvious in his affection with anyone, though I had caught quite a bit more casual touching than I'd noticed previously. It made me glad.

"And you're okay with that?"

"I mean, I'm dating like, four guys. If they're also into each other, that's completely fine with me."

"How into each other are they?" She waggled her eyebrows.

"I, uh, guess I never asked. They'll tell me if they want me to know."

"It is kind of hot to see guys that comfortable with each other."

"It's really hot," I agreed, cheeks warming.

She laughed and threw a pillow at me.

Chapter 7

Sofia

I followed Ed as he broke a trail through the snow on their property. Allan trailed behind a short distance. I kept alert for anything that might be magic and the guys kept their noses alert for any strange scents. Even in human form, their sense of smell was nearly as good as when they were wolves.

Nikolai had sent me and the guys on a mission to ring the property in more wards. Though snow still covered the ground, the sun shone, and it was comfortable in a light jacket with our level of exertion. The crisp, pine scented air melted away some of my tension.

It was one of our shorter class days so we had a couple of hours until the sun set, though days were very short and I wasn't sure we would finish before it got dark. Still, Ed and Allan wouldn't get cold easily at all and I had magic.

We were about halfway done when I found a rock on the upper edge of the property with a fantastic view of the valley. The snow had melted off the rock, and the sun had warmed it enough that it was dry. I pressed a bit of magic into it, warming it further before I hopped up onto the rock and sat cross legged, staring out over the snow-covered valley. According to the guys, we should have snow on the ground until spring.

It really was beautiful, especially with all of the pine trees lending green to the winter scene.

Ed sat on one side of me and Allan the other. They sat close so our shoulders were touching and I sighed, content.

"Sofia?" Ed took my hand.

"Yeah?" I rested my head on his shoulder.

"You still really want all of us?" He sounded uncertain.

I could guess that his real question was, 'you really still want me?' and I sighed. I hated hearing that uncertainty in his voice.

"Of course." I put as much conviction in my voice as I could, but I knew he really needed more. "I get different things from each of you." I flipped the hand he held over revealing his wrist and the pack tattoo we had magically formed. With my free hand I lightly traced the pawprints, one for each of my guys and one for me. Our pack bond was probably what had saved me from being completely lost and destroyed when the Andersons had forced the demon to possess me.

He sucked in a breath when I ran my fingers along his skin.

"Nikolai and Doc, well, we got lucky we found Nikolai."

Allan chuckled and Ed nodded.

"Doc holds everything together. Allan," I glanced over at him and took his hand with my free one. "Allan makes sure we all stay grounded and on track, and you are like my sunshine on a rainy day. Always cheering me up. We all have our parts to play in this pack. It's why we work. Besides, without you two, I would have slipped away while Doc and Nikolai were trying to release the demon."

Ed looked in my eyes. I met his sky-blue ones and let my love for him shine through.

"You know I love you, right?" I hadn't told him yet and guilt weight on me. I should have found time to talk to him sooner. He was the least secure in our relationship.

His expression lightened. "I love you, too, Sofia." He breathed the words, as if not quite sure he was actually saying them out loud.

Happy butterflies danced through my stomach at his words. I grinned, letting him see how pleased that made me.

"Besides, I think if it was just me with Nikolai and Doc I'd be way too intimidated." I winked. "You two are pretty badass, but your experiences are still closer to my own. That's important to me."

Ed leaned forward and I met his lips with mine. He pulled me onto his lap and I wrapped my legs around his waist so I was facing him, pressed against his firm chest and drinking in his warmth as the air cooled around us.

I buried my hands in his blond hair and held him tight as we kissed. He gripped my back and held me close, making me feel safe, making me feel like we belonged to each other. For a minute the rest of the world disappeared and it was just me and him. Nothing else mattered.

We leaned back to catch our breaths. The pleased twinkle in his sky blue eyes warmed me. How had I gotten so lucky as to find these men?

Not wanting to leave Allan out, and needing his arms around me, too, I scooted off of Ed's lap and twisted around until I faced Allan. He didn't look like he felt at all left out, more that he was happy to see me in Ed's arms.

I gave him a mischievous grin and arched an eyebrow.

He held out his hands and I let him pull me against him. Instead of pulling me into his lap like Ed had, he leaned me back, supporting me with his arm under my shoulders so that I lay over his lap instead as if he were tipping me backward in a dance. I put my arm around his neck and we kissed. He held me tenderly, but firmly, taking my breath away with the love I could feel in his grip, in the way his lips tasted mine, the intense look in his eyes when he eventually leaned back.

I couldn't help the big smile on my face when I sat back up between the two of them. Ed acted reassured, though it tugged at my heart that he had been worried. Allan, he was, as always, harder to read, but even he had relaxed.

"You know," I said slyly, "we have a little time before the sun sets and I do have a spell to see in the dark now."

Ed and Allan traded a glance and Ed arched an eyebrow at his brother before a grin spread across his face.

"What would you like to do with our time?" Allan shifted until he was pressed up against my back, lips against my neck, fingers threaded through my short hair.

"Oh, I don't know." My words came out in breathy gasps as his warm breath tickled my neck. "Contemplate the scenery?"

"I could go for a little scenery appreciation," Ed replied, slipping his fingers under my shirt and running his warm hands up my stomach as he pulled my shirt higher. "Will you be warm enough?"

"With the two of you to keep me warm? Absolutely." I did let a little more of my magic flow into the rock we were sitting on, warming it more.

Ed tugged on my shirt, and I leaned away from Allan so Ed could pull it off. Allan unhooked my bra and I let that slide off my arms. Then I lay back against Allan while Ed worked on my boots. Once those were off, my jeans and my panties came off fast. Before the roughness of the granite rock could hurt me, Allan had lifted me to his lap. I hooked my legs over his. He scooted us toward the edge of the rock and spread my legs and let me lean back against him, soft lips caressing my neck as his fingers trailed down my stomach.

"Good view," Ed growled in appreciation.

I stared at my wolf, as the wilderness filled his eyes while they roved over me. That hungry look banished any embarrassment I might have felt being so exposed in front of him. Allan rumbled against my back, his hands working into my folds, rubbing gently at first, dipping into my wet core and then circling my sensitive nub.

Moaning, I tried to think through the building pleasure. I wanted them both, but I wasn't sure if they would want to share that experience or not.

Allan's other hand cupped my throat, tilting my neck back until I leaned my head on his shoulder while he gently nipped at the curve of my neck. I trembled as the pleasure built in my core, hips jerking a little as he rubbed. I pressed back against his firm erection, wanting him inside me, but not quite sure if now was the time to ask.

Ed slid his hands up my thighs before he knelt in front of me. Allan's hand trailed back up my stomach and Ed's tongue took over.

I cried out, hips bucking as he licked over my clit before thrusting a finger into my opening. Shaking, sweat collecting between my breasts, as Allan gave them some attention while he nibbled my neck, I groaned as Ed teased me toward a climax. I wanted to tell him to go faster, but at the same time I wanted to enjoy every minute of this forever. This had almost been taken from all of us and still could be. I was never going to take any of the time I had with my guys for granted.

Ed added a finger, working with his tongue and his hand until I was almost begging for a release, thrusting against his face, wanting more.

He finally stopped teasing me, working in earnest while Allan applied his teeth to my shoulder.

I cried out, thrusting against him as I climaxed.

Ed rumbled in pleasure as I shuddered against both of them, lightheaded.

"My turn," Allan whispered.

Before I could really comprehend that they meant to trade places, Ed took me from Allan, spreading my legs with his, supporting my back with his chest, sitting me much as Allan had. I could feel him hard and ready, pressed against my back. I ground against him, relishing the deep groan he rewarded me with. It vibrated through me, turning me on even more.

Allan knelt in front of me, tongue going to work on my sensitive nub. I twitched, still feeling the previous orgasm. He went slowly, gently taking his time and I relaxed into his touch. Ed cupped my breasts, pinching a nipple gently and kissing my jaw when I leaned back against him.

Allan's tongue was like magic as he worked it around my clit. I gasped, tilting my head until Ed could capture my lips while Allan brought me closer and closer to another release.

He slid one hand up my thigh, cupping my hip with the other. Allan worked his tongue down until he was licking into my opening.

I moaned into Ed's mouth, thrusting against Allan's tongue. Allan's fingers found my clit and rubbed small circles while his tongue worked, building me further. I cried out, trembling as my body responded to my wolves.

Allan leaned back, eyes shining with pleasure in the twilight.

Not really able to move, I lay in Ed's embrace, panting, trembling with aftershocks.

"Good scenery," Allan murmured.

"Very good," Ed agreed.

I couldn't quite find the words to reply so I just nodded my head while I recovered.

Finally, I thought I could move without collapsing and I sat up.

"I think it's my turn to enjoy the scenery," I managed to say.

Ed and Allan traded another glance before they grinned. "We still have time," Ed answered.

I purred in pleasure. "I want both of you," I said, then blurted out, "when you're ready," as their eyes widened.

"At the same time?" Allan asked softly.

"Well, I mean, whatever you two want. And it doesn't have to be now." I hoped I hadn't pushed them too fast.

Ed and Allan exchanged another one of their looks before Allan pulled off his shirt and laid it down on the rock.

"Neither of us have ever done this before," Allan said. "But we're willing to give it a try. Just, uh, excuse any fumbles."

My lips curled, pleased, though I realized I needed to ask what exactly they had in mind, because I wasn't even sure how this would work.

"Are you thinking, um, both at once? Or like, taking turns?" I hated that I sounded a little nervous, but I was.

"What do you want?" Ed came up behind me and kissed my neck. "We will do whatever you want."

"I'm not much more experienced than you are," I whispered.

Allan ran his hands down my sides, pulling a moan from me. "That's okay. Let's take turns this time." He kissed my forehead. "Next time we'll see about sharing. Maybe we can take lessons from Nikolai. I'm sure he's got some ideas in that area."

I snorted, though I could tell Allan wasn't completely joking, either.

"Though, I think you're so used to having all of us touch you," he grinned, "that we should share that pleasure." He glanced at Ed and I think he got an affirmative from his brother.

I glanced over my shoulder at Ed. He grinned back at me and gestured toward Allan.

Taking his lead, I put my attention on his brother. Allan pulled his boots off then waited for me, probably making sure I was certain. Reaching forward, I ran my hands over his muscled abs.

He sighed in pleasure, breath hitching as I popped the button on his jeans and slowly slid down the zipper. I pulled his pants and boxers down, and he stepped out of them. I ran my hands down his hard length, enjoying the feel of him as he twitched under my touch.

I took him into my mouth, tongue working along his tip before sucking him into my mouth as far as I could manage. Allan groaned, hands on my shoulders, thrusting gently as I worked him in my mouth.

"Sofia, I'm not going to last that long as it is," he gasped.

I released him, laughing gently. "Totally understandable."

He lay back on the rock, his shirt providing a little protection from the rough surface. "Let me take the beating."

I straddled him, hovering over him for a moment before he nodded and I took him into my hand, guiding him to my opening. He groaned as I slowly slid down his length, letting him fill me. This was the first time I'd ever used this position, and I moaned as he filled me, hitting me in all the right spots.

"Good?" I asked.

"Oh, yes." His hands found my thighs, fingers digging in a little as I began to move.

Ed slid in behind me, hands cupping my breasts for a moment, before he whispered in my ear. "I'm going to let him have you to himself for his first time." He kissed my neck and moved away.

I nodded acceptance and turned my attention back to Allan. He thrust into me, and I rocked my hips with his movement until we found a good rhythm.

Leaning forward slightly, I ran my hands over his pecks, playing with his nipples as he held my gaze. I could feel my climax building again as he hit all the right places, wanting to help it along a little, I took one of my hands back, trailing it down my stomach and grinned as his eyes widened as I dropped my hand to my clit, rubbing. He rumbled in pleasure as I clenched around him while he thrust, building to both of our climaxes.

Mine hit me first, making me cry out, which sent Allan over the edge. He dug his fingers in, joining my cry of pleasure with his own.

I collapsed on his chest and he held me for a while, while we breathed together, bodies trembling. He ran his hands lightly over my back, and I lay there, enjoying the extra attention.

After a little while I carefully slid off of him. He twitched, still sensitive. I lay next to him on the magic-warmed rock.

"Sofia, that was amazing," he said.

"Yeah, it was." I curled against him, forgetting about everything else for a few minutes before I sat up.

Ed stood nearby, leaning against an aspen tree. He grinned when he met my gaze.

"That was hot."

I arched an eyebrow and tilted my head, inviting him to join us.

He shook his head. "I'll get my turn later." He did come over and give me a thorough kiss that stole my breath. "I don't want to wear you out too much."

Though I certainly wouldn't have minded continuing on with Ed, I was a little grateful I would get some recovery time. Both of them were on the larger side and I was feeling a little sore.

"Soon," I promised him.

"Very soon," he agreed. "Shall we finish setting the wards so we can get back?"

"Yeah. Sun is going to go down soon," I agreed and glanced over at Allan. He nodded agreement.

I cast the cleaning spell over all of us, getting a surprised yelp from both of my wolves, before Allan and I dressed.

Ed took the lead as we headed out to finish our task. Allan followed, and before long we had made our way back to the yurt where Nikolai was working on dinner. Doc supervised, though I had a feeling he was spending more time staring at Nikolai's ass then actually helping. Especially since he really couldn't cook.

Ed and Allan jumped in to help Nikolai, much to the mage's relief. They were the real chefs of the family.

I sat on the bed next to Doc and leaned against him, turning his attention from Nikolai to me.

"How'd it go?"

"Good."

He arched his eyebrows and I blushed. Could he tell what we had been up to, even with Nikolai's cleaning spell? Maybe it was just obvious. Maybe they had sensed something through the pack bond? Not that it mattered. Regardless, he looked pleased.

Doc's hair was already down so I ran my fingers through it and rested against him.

"Yes, could feel wards. You did very well," Nikolai added.

We settled into an easy silence while the other guys worked on dinner.

My phone chimed, and I pulled it out of my pocket. I had a text waiting from Victoria.

Victoria: Mom is wondering if you all can come down to Denver for the weekend. She's got someone who wants to talk to you. You can all crash at our place.

"Hey, guys, want to go to Denver this weekend?"

They all paused what they were doing and looked at me. I tilted my phone so Doc could read over my shoulder.

"Victoria's mom has some people who want to talk with us," I supplied for the other three.

"Denver sounds interesting," Nikolai said slowly. "Also interesting to meet other mages."

"How much do the Andersons know about you, Nikolai?" I had no idea what they might have figured out about him since I had been locked in my own head most of the last few months.

"Not sure." He shrugged, unconcerned. "Don't know how much Ash figured out, and no idea how much he had to tell the Andersons."

"I think it's a good idea," Doc said after a few minutes.

Ed and Allan shared a glance before shrugging. "You do realize that Victoria's parents will probably learn all sorts of interesting stuff about us if we go," Allan cautioned.

Doc shrugged. "If Victoria is anything to go by, we can trust them. Though, I would still prefer to be quietly ignored if we can manage it."

"So, we're going to Denver?"

Doc glanced around and when no one offered objections he nodded. "Yes. Tell Victoria she's welcome to ride down with us."

I texted Victoria back and she replied with a thumbs up.

"Well, that's settled. Now we just need to avoid any confrontations for another day or so and then we'll be out of town." I smiled warily.

"And hope they don't take out the yurt while we're gone," Allan said.

"We will not tell anyone we're leaving." Nikolai shrugged.

"Let's hope that works." I sighed. This sucked so much.

"Should." The mage sat down on the other side of me and put his arm around me and Doc. "Will be fine."

"I wish I was as confident as you."

He nuzzled my hair. "All of the irreplaceable things will be with us. Yurts are easy. You should not worry about it."

I stopped myself before I could apologize about the situation again. Nikolai was grateful and the other guys didn't blame me. I wished I could stop feeling like it was my fault, but the guilt wouldn't leave.

Doc kissed my neck. "It's not your fault," he whispered, lips brushing against my skin.

I shivered, distracted from my guilt as he nibbled.

"Hungry?"

He hesitated, as if he hadn't considered that question. "Offering?"

"Yes. We all get dinner, you may as well too."

Doc leaned back and arched an eyebrow at me.

I gave him a sly look.

"I feel like I'm getting spoiled," he chuckled. "Getting offered blood every day."

"Spoiling you is not without its rewards," Nikolai answered for us.

"Our dinner will be done in about twenty minutes," Ed interrupted us while Allan put something into the oven that Nikolai had magicked for us. "We have a little time."

"I'm definitely the spoiled one," I protested.

"Are you now?" Doc pulled me into his arms.

"With the four of you looking after me? Absolutely."

Doc nibbled and I moaned in anticipation.

Doc sank his teeth into my neck, and I could tell he was thinking more about food than sex because his hands didn't wander. He didn't spare whatever it was that made a vampire's bite feel good, though and soon I was seeing stars as I climaxed and cried out in pleasure.

Though I lost track of time, it couldn't have been more than a few minutes before I came back to myself. Ed had joined us and was laying on my stomach, while Doc had curled up around me. He stroked my temple gently while I recovered.

Both of them favored me with heavy lidded, satisfied looks when I glanced at them.

Nikolai had his arm around Allan, and the two of them looked content as well.

An alarm chimed on someone's phone and Allan moved away from Nikolai and pulled dinner out of the oven.

Ed leaned forward and kissed me gently on the lips before getting up to help.

"Thank you," Doc whispered when I reluctantly stirred from his embrace.

"Of course." I pressed my lips to his for a moment before finally getting up. My stomach rumbled, and I sat at the table between Allan and Ed, pressing my knees up against both of their legs. For a few minutes, anyway, everything was all right. Now if only we could keep out of trouble long enough to get some help.

∞ ∞ ∞

Victoria carried the leftover pizza as we walked down the sidewalk toward the parking lot where her car waited. It would be too cold to walk back to campus for months, and it certainly wasn't safe with the Andersons after me. A handful of other residents and tourists wandered through the last open shops, came out of restaurants, or headed to the pub. The still air chilled my warm skin and I could see the brightest of the stars over the streetlights that lit the main road.

We were heading down to Denver in the morning. The guys would pick us up early and we were supposed to meet with Victoria's contacts in the afternoon.

It would be Nikolai's first time in a modern city. Hopefully the internet had prepared him.

Victoria's gasp brought me out of my pizza coma and quiet contemplation. I threw up shields around us without thinking and focused on my surroundings—which I should have been doing all along.

Still, my shields held the blast of sickly green magic at bay. Something I had learned from both the demon and Nikolai was to identify what spells were intended for. This one was nasty. The weaves in the magical net were barbed, designed to cause a great deal of debilitating pain in a short period of time. It was strong enough that it could kill the person it hit or might just take them out of the fight for a while.

Victoria shrieked as the magic settled around us, held back by the dome of my shield.

I snarled, rage flooding my veins, followed by a rush of magic that crackled along my arms in lavender waves. Maybe it was left over from the demon. Maybe I was just done with their shit, but I was not putting up with this any longer.

The target of my fury stood in the middle of the road. I didn't recognize her magical signature, or her physical form, but the attack on me and Victoria I wasn't going to forgive.

Though I now knew several spells that would kill her where she stood, I wasn't quite ready to go there yet.

Instead, I wove a magical starburst that would distract her. It carried the signatures of a particularly nasty spell, but would do nothing more than dazzle her eyes.

I dropped my shield and launched the starburst. It flashed bright in the dark night. As I had hoped, the woman threw a shield over her head. Quicker than she could react, I tossed the other spell. This one I had concealed, and it shot along the ground, a barely visible arrow of purple light that twisted around her legs and coiled up her body.

The mage screamed and her shield fell as the leach I had cast pulled all of her magic out of her body and sent it into the ground. There were other things I could do with her magic, but this was currently the safest.

"Run!"

I grabbed Victoria's arm and we sprinted back the way we had come. I dragged her down an alley and cast Nikolai's invisibility spell. I wasn't as good as he was, but I didn't have to fool anything but a handful of humans.

A few of the tourists shouted and sirens blared in the distance, but they didn't cover the agonized wail of the mage I had taken out. The spell was intended to hurt enough to take someone out of a fight, but the real horror that fueled her cry was probably her belief that I had stolen her magic forever. She would recover, though it would take a day or two. She didn't know that.

I leaned against the wall, panting and trying to catch my breath. My phone buzzed and I fished it out of my pocket.

"Shouldn't we keep running?" Victoria's voice shook.

"They can't find us. We'll need to get to the car but we have a minute. Nikolai?" I answered the phone in a whisper.

"What happened? We all felt you draw on your powers."

"Got attacked," I answered. "We're okay. Trying to get to the car now."

"Come up here for the night," Allan said into the phone. "Bring Victoria."

"Yeah, we'll head that way as soon as it's safe."

"Use invisibility on car. Just, remember no one will see you," Nikolai added. "Did anyone see what happened?"

"I don't know. There were a handful of tourists. We're in town. The cops are probably going to get the mage that attacked us. I disabled her."

"Well, it was self-defense. Hopefully no one identifies you."

"You don't sound too worried."

"We can disappear into Russian steppes. No one will find us." He laughed.

"I don't like winter that much," I grumbled.

He laughed harder. "You should hurry. See you soon."

He disconnected the call and I shoved the phone in my jeans pocket. "They want us to come up to the yurt."

"Yeah, sure." Victoria stared at me.

"What?"

"What did you do to her?"

"Uh, not much actually. Leached all her magic out so she couldn't attack us. She probably thinks it's permanent. I doubt she's seen that spell before. Let's go." I grabbed Victoria's arm. She didn't flinch, which I took as a good sign, and we made our way to the other street and jogged for the parking lot. Victoria still clutched the pizza box in her arms. Good.

Sirens blared down the main street and we could still hear people shouting. The mage had stopped screaming, but unless she had backup, I doubted she would get away. I wasn't about to stick around and find out, but this probably would be the last time they only sent one magic user to capture me, and clearly, somehow, they were watching us.

Victoria's hands shook as she tried to unlock her car. I finally took the keys from her and she wordlessly went around to the passenger side.

I extended the invisibility that cloaked Victoria and I to include the car then booked it out of the parking lot, praying I wouldn't run into anyone else on the road as it was difficult for someone to avoid something they couldn't see and I wasn't used to driving an invisible car.

Once we hit the main roundabout, I hit the accelerator a little hard as I headed up out of the valley. If they were going to attack us, now would be the time. While they might not be able to see the car, they would know we were heading up to the yurt and it wouldn't be hard for them to ambush us. I could think of a lot of ways I would do it. That I had all that knowledge both thrilled and terrified me. In some ways I had earned it by hosting the demon. In others, it felt like I was cheating by suddenly being so powerful.

Of course, until we freed Ash, we would need all the power we could muster.

Victoria had calmed down by the time we pulled off the main road and bounced down the narrow dirt road that was Doc's driveway. I breathed a sigh of relief once we passed through my wards and were once again in relatively safe territory.

"Are you okay?" I finally asked.

Victoria nodded. "Yeah. Wow, that was pretty intense. Are you okay?"

"Yeah. I just hope no one can identify us. Hopefully there aren't a lot of street cameras or anything." I shuddered.

Victoria nodded.

I dropped the invisibility spells and weariness tugged at my limbs. I parked next to Doc's truck and leaned back in the car. By the time I had mustered enough energy to get out, the guys had come over.

Ed opened the driver door and I climbed out and fell into his arms. Doc offered a hand to Victoria and pulled her into a quick hug before we all trailed down the path to the yurt, my hand held tightly in Ed's. I avoided looking at the remains of the cabin, knowing it would only piss me off again. Hopefully soon, we could go back to normal. Though I wasn't even sure what normal was any longer.

Chapter 8

Ed

Victoria sat in the passenger seat while Doc, as usual, drove. Ed was squished up against the door with four of them in the back seat, but Sofia was pressed against his other side and that more than made up for any discomfort.

Nikolai had pressed in against her, and Allan sat between the mage and the door. It was tight with six people in the truck, but Sofia, with Nikolai's direction, had cast some sort of seat belt spell that would keep everyone safe if an accident did happen. No one in the back seat minded being squeezed in with the others.

Some of their classes had exams the following week and Victoria was quizzing Sofia with the occasional input from Allan. Ed stared out the window, having a hard time concentrating on school when they were about to go meet with other supernaturals.

For many reasons, they had kept separate from the rest of the supernatural community. He and Allan hadn't wanted to run the risk of being forced to join an established wolf pack. Now that they were both over eighteen it wasn't as much of a concern, though truth be told, neither of them knew enough about werewolf society to know if that was even a valid concern. Doc was naturally a bit of a loner anyway, though Ed and Allan had changed that to some degree. Nikolai and Sofia had completely broken that tendency in Doc, though Ed doubted anyone would ever call Doc outgoing or social.

He and Allan had stayed apart from others for fear of discovery, not because they didn't want others around. Having Sofia and Nikolai join them made their small pack larger and even more comfortable to a wolf's way of thinking.

Sofia sighed. "I'm going to fail everything."

"You won't," Doc replied. "You answered everything Victoria asked you correctly."

She muttered under her breath. "I still don't feel like I know it. Clearly the knowledge is there somewhere, but it's... I don't know how to explain it. It's like it's not mine and it might vanish at any moment."

"I sincerely doubt it is going anywhere," Nikolai said.

Sofia shifted slightly as Nikolai put his arm around her and squeezed her tightly.

"You will be fine."

Sofia sighed again but fell silent.

Though she didn't say anything, Ed could smell her emotions and she still felt guilty. He hadn't been lying when he had told her they would have ended up in this situation without her anyway, but she didn't believe him. She had stopped apologizing, but he hated that she felt guilty about anything. To him, and the others, there was no blame and they would all rather have Sofia in their lives than the fragile truce they had with the Andersons before she came along.

He hadn't been down to Denver in quite some time and went back to looking out the window as they descended out of the mountains into the more heavily populated suburbs of the big city.

Sofia tucked her hand into his and squeezed.

Her touch warmed him. When he had thought they may never be together again, that had been the worst

94

feeling ever. Now she was nearly as badass with magic as Nikolai was, she just needed practice. She could protect herself, and the rest of them, against magical attacks. That made Ed glad.

Nikolai leaned forward, looking between the two front seats and staring out the windshield, eyebrows rising as he took in the sights. As well as he had adapted to modern technology, he had yet to see a big city.

The snow from the storms had mostly melted in true front range Colorado fashion and the interstate was crowded with midday Saturday traffic.

Sofia put her hand on Nikolai's back. After a moment, Allan did the same.

"Is very different than Sunnyglade."

He remembered Nikolai's reaction the first time he had returned from being down in their small mountain town. He had adapted quickly and he didn't seem nervous now, simply curious.

Traffic thickened as they went deeper into the city. Victoria's parents lived in one of the nicer suburbs and Doc changed interstates to head south.

He glanced at Allan. His brother had clenched his hand around a bit of Nikolai's shirt and looked more nervous than the mage did. Ed probably was, too, if he really thought about it. Big cities were not really his element and he had spent more time in small towns than the city. The reason for their trip hadn't exactly set him at ease either. He wasn't looking forward to meeting these mages that Victoria's parents knew. He was sure they were all right since they were involved in the activist circles and her parents trusted them, but it still made him nervous.

Sofia just looked around and he couldn't smell any hint of distress from her. Victoria was at ease and Doc felt fairly normal. He had been on edge for several months and that hadn't really changed.

After a little while, Doc exited off the interstate and headed back into neighborhoods.

Victoria gave him directions and before long he parked in front of a largeish two story tan brick and wood house.

Everyone climbed out and Victoria led them up to the door. She knocked once before opening it and letting them all in.

The door opened into a comfortable looking living area. The two couches were overstuffed and Ed made a mental note to see if they could get something like that for the new cabin. Books lined shelves and a gas fireplace burned near an armchair.

David, Victoria's boyfriend, looked up from the other armchair and grinned. He waved at everyone else, and got up to pull Victoria into an enthusiastic hug. "Hope you don't mind that I came by."

"Of course not, silly." Victoria melted into his arms. "I would have told you if I didn't want you to come by."

Victoria's parents, Jasmine and Xavier, came out of what was probably the kitchen based on the smell of food, big smiles on their faces.

"Hello, everyone," Jasmine said. "Please, come in." She looked at Nikolai. "I don't believe we've met yet. I'm Jasmine, and this is Xavier."

"Nikolai." He took her hand and bowed slightly before shaking Xavier's with the same bowing motion. That charmed her parents.

They all kicked off their shoes and hung coats on the small rack before following Victoria into the kitchen.

"I made lunch for everyone. Donna Schafer and Adriana Sciarra will be here in an hour or so."

Doc twitched at the second name. Ed only noticed because he was watching, but both Sofia and Nikolai glanced at him.

"Someone you know?" Nikolai inquired.

Doc sighed and nodded.

"Is that a problem?"

Doc ran a hand through his hair and cleared his throat. "Pretty sure she thinks I'm dead. It's a long story." He shrugged. "Should be interesting at least."

"Well, who's hungry then?" Jasmine broke the awkward silence. She glanced at him and Allan and smiled. "I don't think I've met a young man who wasn't hungry all the time. Victoria told me none of you really had food restrictions so I hope these are okay?" She gestured to a plate full of roast beef sandwiches.

Allan blushed and nodded. Ed grinned.

Victoria and David grabbed a couple of sandwiches and everyone else but Doc did the same. Nikolai handed Doc his plate as if they were going to share, and they all found places to perch.

"How are you, Sofia? Victoria says you're doing okay, but going through something like that has to be traumatic," Jasmine asked.

Sofia sighed. "Mostly I'm just really pissed off."

Jasmine nodded. "That's understandable. I hope Donna and Adriana can help."

Sofia nodded. "We just want them to leave us alone."

He noted that she left Ash out of it for now, but they all knew that even if the Andersons were willing to back off now that their plan had failed, Sofia and their pack wouldn't until Ash was free.

Sofia wanted him free because she hated to see someone controlled like that. The rest of them had actually started to like the grumpy demon. He tried as hard as he could to help them even though he belonged to the Andersons.

"How is school going, Victoria?" Xavier changed the subject to something easier to talk about.

"It's fine, Dad. I like classes still. Love Sunnyglade. Well, except for the Andersons. They suck. My roommate is pretty cool." She winked at Sofia. "And I like her friends, too. So, I can't really complain."

"David?" Xavier glanced at her boyfriend.

"If my program at UD wasn't one of the best, I'd consider transferring up to Sunnyglade. Classes are going fine, though."

Xavier glanced at Sofia and she shrugged. "Playing catch up, but it's going okay."

"Ed, Allan?" Jasmine encouraged them to join the conversation.

"It's a great school. Still no idea what I'm doing with my life, but I'm definitely learning a lot," He answered.

"Yeah," Allan agreed. "It's been an interesting semester."

Sofia laughed and shook her head at that. "That's one way to put it."

Before they could continue talking about school, the doorbell rang.

Ed jolted, not used to doorbells.

Doc had a hand on Nikolai's arm. He had probably sensed whoever it was approaching the house. The mage had probably never heard a doorbell before.

Jasmine, either pretending she didn't notice, or ignoring the pack's reaction to the doorbell, got up and went into the other room to answer.

David glanced at Victoria. "Take you out to a movie?"

She glanced at Sofia.

"Yeah, go. We'll be fine. Thanks, Victoria."

David held out his hand and pulled Victoria to her feet.

"See you all later," David said. Victoria waved, and they headed out the side door.

He listened to Jasmine talk with Donna and Adriana, though she didn't do much more than greet them before leading them into the kitchen.

He glanced at Doc. The vampire's shoulders were tight and his jaw clenched, though he smelled more resigned than worried. Sofia had retreated to stand between Nikolai and Allan. She glanced at him and Doc, eyes shifting around, clearly upset.

Nikolai looked more curious than anything and Allan had his arm around Sofia but didn't seem too concerned. Ed wasn't quite sure how he felt either. He didn't want people to know he was a werewolf, but at the same time, he didn't think it would be the end of the world, either. He was more worried for Sofia and Doc.

Jasmine entered followed by two women. Ed's eyes were immediately drawn to the taller of the two. She had dark olive skin, and gray hair pulled back into a tight braid. Piercing brown eyes studied all of them intently. They widened slightly when they landed on Doc and Ed was certain that would be Adriana. She smelled powerful, like Nikolai did, but more blatantly. Nikolai was more casual about his power, and also had practice hiding things, where as this woman wanted people to know she was a badass. Or that's how Ed interpreted her demeanor anyway.

Donna struck him as more of your average suburban woman. Tan skin, even in the middle of winter, short brown hair, light brown eyes, average height. He saw steel in her expression though, too and decided that while she could probably pass for average, she wasn't. Not that he had expected average from anyone involved in the supernatural rights movement.

He just hoped they could also be trusted.

Jasmine made quick introductions. Adriana focused in on Nikolai for a moment. "Nikolai, you're from Russia?"

"Obviously," he replied. He kept his tone friendly, but Ed sensed a bit of tension in him that hadn't been there before.

Adriana arched an eyebrow. "I thought I knew all of the powerful mages in the Russian guilds. How did you stay out of their control?"

That comment got both Jasmine and Xavier to study Nikolai in surprise.

Nikolai shrugged. "Must have slipped their notice."

Adriana arched her eyebrows at his evasive answer, but didn't continue to question him. She turned her attention to Doc.

"It's been literal years, Roy. How are you?" She sounded casual but she studied him intensely.

Ed noticed that Doc had positioned himself in a shaft of sunlight from the window, even before the mages had arrived.

"I'm doing well. How are you, Adriana?" He stayed polite, but didn't offer anything.

"Quite all right," she answered before turning to Sofia. "I hear you have a problem with the Andersons."

Sofia nodded. "I'm surprised more people don't have a problem with them. They're unpleasant."

Adriana actually smiled. Donna laughed. "Everyone has a problem with them. Unfortunately, they have a particular asset that keeps them immune to repercussions. No one can stand against their demon."

Ed glanced at Jasmine and Xavier. They traded concerned glances. He didn't know how much Victoria had already told them.

"Ash is powerful, yes, but he's not omnipotent." Nikolai shrugged. "Could be defeated. Also, he is not terribly willing, so unless the person directing him knows what to say, he finds loopholes."

Adriana and Donna's eyes widened at Nikolai's casual dismissal of Ash's abilities.

"When the Andersons first began making waves we discussed controlling them. Not one of the more powerful mages was willing to try because of the demon."

Nikolai shook his head and muttered something disparaging in Russian. Sofia's lips twitched.

"We will handle Ash," Nikolai said. "We would be happy to handle the Andersons, as well, but will get messy."

"How, exactly, do you plan to handle the demon?" Adriana sounded incredulous.

Nikolai stared at her for a moment before shaking his head again. "With magic. Yes? Is there any other way to handle demon?"

"You really think you can simply handle him?"

"Yes, of course, or I would not say it. Sofia and I can manage Ash." He stressed Ash's name. "Doc, Ed, and Allan would need help with the other mages, however."

It was Adriana's turn to shake her head. "I was under the impression that Sofia was relatively untrained, and I do not think that anyone would be willing to join a fight against the Andersons with Ash still in the picture." She also emphasized Ash's name, but her tone held derision and a hint of fear. "I was prepared to offer to help relocate you all someplace safer and out of their reach."

Ed tensed. He did not want to leave Sunnyglade and he knew the others didn't want to leave, either.

"I can see from your expressions that you don't like that idea."

"No," He answered for all of them.

"It may be the only option," Donna said. "Any overt action would gain too much public attention. Especially now as we're starting to really make progress in the courts."

"Tell that to them," Sofia grumbled. "They attacked me in the middle of downtown Sunnyglade yesterday."

Donna and Adriana shared a surprised glance. "That is quite reckless."

"It's getting annoying," Sofia growled.

"Do you happen to know what they want with you?" Donna asked.

"They wanted to turn me into a host for a great demon. Fortunately, they failed and now they're just pissed off about it." Sofia left out a lot of details.

Ed thought that might actually be wise. Adriana kept glancing at Nikolai like she wanted to dissect him.

"You think we should move," Doc interrupted. "We aren't going to. You can't help us until Ash is dealt with. What can you do if Ash is out of the picture?"

"In the unlikely event they no longer have their demon to hide behind, the Andersons have quite a few crimes that we're aware of they need to answer for. The council can step in and arrest them under some quiet rules we've worked out with the various governments of the world."

"Arrest them?" Nikolai sounded dubious. "You think you can contain them?"

"Yes." Adriana didn't elaborate.

"Interesting." Nikolai looked thoughtful.

Ed knew the Russian mage's solution was usually just to kill the enemy, but he had grown up during outright war. They didn't have the luxury of trying to contain the enemy.

"So, once we contain Ash, how do we contact you?" Nikolai asked.

Adriana and Donna shared another surprised look. "He's a demon."

"Yes, yes." Nikolai waved his hand. "We know Ash quite well. I have a plan. Assuming plan works and Ash doesn't simply kill all of the Andersons in a fit of deserved rage, how do we contact you?"

"You're planning on releasing him?"

"Of course."

Ed supposed it was safe enough to admit that. The Andersons already knew that Nikolai could release demons, so the plan wouldn't be a surprise if it got back to them.

"That knowledge is lost. We've already explored that idea. No one knows how."

Nikolai stared at Adriana for a moment before opening his mouth to say something that probably wasn't complementary.

"Just pretend we actually manage it. It's our lives to risk, right?" Sofia interrupted. "Should we contact you, or handle them ourselves."

"You should contact us," Donna answered. "It would be better if we could handle this with as much legality as we can manage. Otherwise, we could simply provide more evidence that those of us in the supernatural community simply can't be trusted."

Nikolai muttered under his breath again.

Doc put his hand on the mage's shoulder and Nikolai fell silent.

Adriana handed Sofia a card and Donna did the same. "Our phone numbers. If you change your mind about relocating, let us know and we'll help you with the details and help you find a safer location."

"Thank you," Sofia said politely. "Is there anything else you can tell us that might be useful?"

Donna shook her head. "Lay low, don't get discovered. If you do and it causes problems, we'll support you of course. That's what we do right now."

Sofia nodded, but that wasn't new information and Ed thought it was fairly useless.

"Roy, I would enjoy a chance to catch up. I must admit, I hadn't thought I'd ever see you again," Adriana said.

Doc shrugged. "I'm pretty hard to kill. Glad you made it out okay."

"You as well."

They had clearly helped as much as they could for the moment, so everyone stood.

"Thank you for coming down to see us. It has been interesting to meet you all. If we can be of assistance in the future, don't hesitate to contact us," Donna said.

They both thanked Jasmine and Xavier as well, then Jasmine walked them to the door.

As soon as they were out of earshot, Nikolai let loose with a bunch of what had to be Russian cursing. Sofia laughed.

"Nikolai, we did warn you," she said.

"Modern mages," he said in disgust. "Useless."

"Hey." Sofia put her hands on her hips and glared at Nikolai.

"Present company excepted, obviously." He pulled her into a hug.

"Well, I hope that was at least somewhat helpful," Jasmine said quietly.

"Yes," Doc answered for all of them. "It was, actually. Despite Nikolai's attitude," Doc smiled fondly at the mage, "we know a lot more and once we rescue Ash, we can get help."

"Do you really think you can?" Jasmine asked.

"Of course," Nikolai replied. "We rescued Sofia, didn't we? Will be similar."

"What exactly do you mean by modern mages being useless?" Xavier asked.

Nikolai glanced at Doc, looking a little embarrassed at his slip in words. Doc shrugged.

"Eh, I am from a different time. We used magic constantly. Makes a difference."

"How did that happen? Am I even allowed to ask about that?" Xavier asked hesitantly.

Nikolai shrugged. "My student stabbed me in the back and locked me in a dimensional prison. Sofia let me out."

"Oh."

Jasmine and Xavier didn't seem to know what to say to that, so they fell into an awkward silence.

"Why don't we take Nikolai out for a drive since he's never been to Denver before. We'll come back this evening," Doc offered.

Jasmine brightened. "That's a fantastic idea. Do you know the city well?"

Doc shook his head. "Well enough, but I'm open to suggestions if you have any. You're both welcome to join us."

To Ed's relief, Jasmine and Xavier declined to join them. They offered a bunch of suggestions and Doc led everyone out to the truck with the promise they would be back in the evening.

Dakota Brown

Chapter 9

Sofia

"Well, that was interesting," I said once we had all piled in the truck. Ed took the passenger seat and Allan and Nikolai had gotten in back with me. I sat between them, hooking a leg over Nikolai's thigh, and leaning back against Allan.

"They certainly don't think we can actually handle Ash," Ed added.

"It will not be easy," Nikolai said. "I have a plan. Should rescue him soon."

"I think that's our next course of action," Doc said. "I want to say we should do it tomorrow, but this week is exam week. He can probably wait until next weekend." Doc's tone of voice made it clear waiting was not his preferred option, but he was right, there were only a couple of weeks left in school and getting the exams taken care of was important. Maybe not as important as rescuing Ash, but it would give me a little more time to practice with Nikolai if nothing else.

"Do you think they'll actually help with the Andersons if we can save Ash?" Allan rubbed my hip as he spoke.

Nikolai traced random patterns on my thigh with his finger as he stared out the window.

"Yes." Doc answered.

"We're not going to be able to disappear off their radar after this, are we?" I asked.

"Radar?" Nikolai said absently.

"Um, actual radar is, well," I hesitated not actually sure how to explain it. "A way ships keep track of things at sea. And, well, airplanes and stuff. Technology. The saying means we won't be able to stay out of their notice now."

"Ah." He glanced at me. "No. Not likely. This Adriana is far more interested in Doc than I like and I suspect I'm interesting to them, as well."

I glanced at Nikolai. Was that jealousy I heard in his voice? His brow was furrowed as he looked at our vampire.

Doc shook his head. "She thinks I'm a mage. She was interested, many years ago. I was never about to get involved with her. Not safe. Not interested."

Nikolai's expression lightened a bit.

"Convenient that everyone thinks you're a mage," I said.

Doc nodded. "Even if something changes in the next few years and it becomes safer to be known as a supernatural, I doubt it will ever be safe to be known as a vampire. We're too dangerous."

"And difficult to contain," Nikolai agreed. "How many do know?"

Doc shrugged. "A handful of my mother's people know what I am. Sofia's dad's friend. The Andersons. Which, basically, once we take Ash, I bet a lot more people are going to know." He sighed.

"We will deal with that if becomes an issue." Nikolai leaned forward and put his hand on Doc's shoulder.

"So, we'll spend the next week taking tests and preparing to steal Ash away. Then we'll deal with the consequences." I turned the conversation away from the more disturbing topic and back to tests.

"Yes," Doc agreed.

"So, where are we going now?"

"Natural history museum. Then we'll wander up the 16th street mall, grab some dinner, and head back to Victoria's house. Tomorrow we'll go home," Doc answered. "I have no idea what their rotating exhibits are, but it's a really good museum."

It didn't take long before Doc had parked the truck and we stared at the banner advertising the current attraction. Mongolia, past and present.

Ed laughed. "Well, this should be interesting."

"Very," Nikolai agreed.

We hurried inside, got tickets, and started working our way through exhibits. The natural history ones really caught Nikolai's attention, and we spent several hours wandering the museum before we got to the Mongolia exhibit. I thought Doc and I spent more time watching Nikolai's reactions than actually paying attention to the things around us, but his intent interest was quite entertaining. The building wasn't super crowded, though there were plenty of adults and children around, so we weren't real free to talk. Even Nikolai remembered not to be too obvious about his gaps in knowledge.

I threaded my hand into his as we went into the exhibit about his part of the world.

"It is very strange to see this in museum," he whispered as he studied some of the modern pictures of life on the Mongolian Steppes. "Would say, not much has changed."

Ed and Allan wandered ahead. We let Nikolai take his time, though he didn't let go of my hand and he stood close, occasionally pointing out a small detail to me.

He studied one picture of a Mongolian family and pointed at the woman. "She is mage. See, her sash signifies her position."

"I wonder if they are more accepting of magic users," I said quietly. The picture was dated more recently.

109

"Steppes are difficult land to live in. Would be silly of them to reject someone who could mean the difference between life and death." Nikolai shrugged. Nikolai was half Tatar and half Russian and had spent time both on the Steppes and in Russian cities.

We worked our way back in time, and details got more speculative, though Nikolai filled in a lot of information. Quietly. As we approached his time, details in the exhibit about magic became more prevalent. His hand clenched on mine as we read details of how the Renaissance had affected that part of the world.

He growled softly, muttering about stupid humans, though I saw him studying the descriptions intently. Maybe looking for mention of people he knew?

"Here." He pointed. "Roza Orlov. Court mage." He curled his lip.

"Orlov?" I questioned.

"Cousin."

"Ah."

Doc stood close, listening, though he watched the people around us while Nikolai read.

"Did not go well for her." He pointed at one of the documents. Not long after she had stabbed Nikolai in the back, the war with the Tatar was won and the magic purge took its toll on the Russian courts. "She did not enjoy her success for long." Nikolai laughed. "It says she gained ascension after the previous court mage mysteriously vanished. Few records of that individual remain." He snorted.

I squeezed his hand and leaned against his arm.

"We should leave," Doc said quietly.

"Why?" I turned to look at him then followed where he was looking.

"Huh, wonder what she wants?"

110

That got Nikolai's attention. "Adriana followed us here?" He frowned.

"Apparently," Doc replied.

"Well, is obvious she knows we're here. I would like to finish reading this. See how much they got wrong." He smirked. "I do not think we're in danger. Currently, anyway."

Nikolai turned back to the documents in front of him and I stayed twisted around, watching the other mage approach.

"Touring the city?" Adriana didn't even pretend she was there by chance.

"Neither Sofia nor Nikolai have been here before," he answered. "Why are you here?"

"How are you alive, Roy? You haven't aged a bit, either." Adriana crossed her arms, not answering his question directly, but it was clear why she had followed us.

He shrugged. "Just lucky, I guess."

Nikolai pulled me on as he finished reading. Doc and Adriana followed.

"You don't look that much older, yourself."

"Yes, but I have aged. It's been thirty years, and no one should have made it out of that alive. Your magic isn't that strong."

Nikolai muttered something I didn't catch but I glanced at him. He was studying something about the war between the Russians and the Tatar. Maybe he was looking for references to his friend Peter?

"I didn't get hit when the building came down and was able to get out before the smoke overwhelmed me. I got lucky." Doc kept his tone mild, but I could sense his annoyance through our pack bond.

"Why didn't you find me?" She actually sounded a little hurt.

It was my turn for my hand to clench. Nikolai pulled his attention away from the exhibit and turned toward Doc.

"Maybe I didn't want to answer your questions." Doc smiled slightly. "We had accomplished our goals and I moved on. I don't usually stay in one place for very long."

"Why?"

"Life of a cowboy," he drawled.

Ed and Allan wandered back over, though I saw both of them stiffen as they recognized Adriana.

Nikolai and I stepped up to either side of Doc, though our hands were still joined behind his back and we made it very clear with our body language that he was quiet spoken for.

Adriana's eyebrows rose and she glanced between me and Nikolai then back to Doc. "Seems you have settled down a little."

He shrugged. "For a while." He slid his arm around mine and Nikolai's backs.

"Something tells me my initial instincts about you were correct. You're not really a mage, are you?" She said it casually, as if it didn't matter to her, but I could sense the intensity behind her question.

"Perhaps this is not best place to be talking about any of this?" Nikolai suggested.

We hadn't exactly drawn an audience, but we were getting curious glances.

"Of course," Adriana agreed. She turned her attention to my mage. "I still want to know more about you, as well."

Pink lights flashed in her eyes as she pulled on her magic. I thought she was using some sort of sensing spell.

I growled softly, but Nikolai blocked her.

"You seem awfully confident discovery won't cause you problems," Nikolai lowered his voice.

"People know who and what I am." She shrugged. "I'm not worried about discovery. I fight for our rights."

Nikolai shook his head and gestured toward the exit. "If you want to talk, we should leave."

"Where are we going?"

Nikolai glanced at Doc, who shrugged. "Dinner, perhaps."

She nodded acceptance.

It would be dark by now or I would have suggested that we go someplace like a park where there were less likely to be people close enough to overhear our conversation. Though, I supposed, there was a spell for that.

Ed and Allan trailed behind us as we headed out of the museum.

∞ ∞ ∞

Doc made good on his promise to take us to the sixteenth street mall. My luck with restaurants and never having to wait for a seat held and we got seated right away at a restaurant claiming to have the best cheesecake. They certainly had a wide variety, and I debated skipping dinner and going straight to the dessert.

I ended up ordering pasta. Doc ordered the same thing though he and Nikolai had a lengthy discussion about various dishes which Adriana watched with interest as it became quite clear the Russian was not familiar with most of the stuff on the menu. We sat on either side of Doc. Ed sat on my other side and Allan sat next to Nikolai. Adriana sat between the two werewolves.

She acted at ease, but I noticed her shoot uneasy glances at the two werewolves now and again. They had put us in a corner of the restaurant and Nikolai discreetly cast a spell that would muffle our words to anyone not at the table or standing right next to us so we could talk freely if we wanted to. Adriana watched him with interest, but didn't otherwise comment.

Once we ordered food, we fell into an uneasy silence. She seemed to be waiting for us, and I knew we were waiting on her.

Finally, once our drinks arrived, she took a drink and leaned back in her chair, head tilted slightly, almost regal in her demeanor as if she viewed supplicants.

"We want to help you, you know. The Andersons have needed handling for a long time now."

"Then why do you not handle them?" Nikolai grumbled.

"The demon, of course. They have not yet done anything worth risking other mage lives over."

Doc's water glass shattered in his hand and his growl vibrated through me. Blood dripped through his clenched fist, mingling with the spilled water on the table. Adriana's eyes went wide as she jumped in her seat. Either she had discounted what they had attempted to do to me, or didn't consider it that important.

Both Ed and Allan glared at her.

Nikolai quickly cast another spell and the spilled water, blood and broken glass vanished. Then he made a show of casting a healing spell over Doc's already closing wounds, before he put his hand over Doc's wrist. I pressed up against the vampire's other side.

Nikolai's magic tugged at me, though we had managed to get some of our reaction to the resonance between us under control, my stomach still tightened and I had to concentrate on my anger to keep from losing my focus.

My mage glanced at me, winking before he turned his attention back to Adriana.

Doc was so pissed off that he didn't even react, though he had to have felt it just as I did.

"Perhaps you are unaware of what they've been up to recently?" Nikolai said voice low.

"We keep some watch on them, but we only have so many resources," Adriana replied defensively.

"They wanted Sofia to host a greater demon," Doc growled through clenched teeth. "Nearly succeeded, too."

Adriana blanched. "How far did they actually get."

We all traded a glance before I shrugged. At this point I didn't think it mattered what she knew.

"Let's just put it this way," I said. "Much of my education came from the greater demon. She was kind enough to leave me alive long enough for Nikolai to figure out how to send her home. Nikolai has taught me the rest of what I know."

Adriana's eyebrows rose. "You were able to release the binding on a greater demon?" She directed that at Nikolai, "and you were able to resist being pushed out of her mind?" The last was said toward me.

"The demon was just as interested in going home as I was in staying alive, so she worked with us. The Andersons didn't think we'd manage it and we tricked them into leaving me with Nikolai while he figured out how to unravel the spell."

"How did you do it?"

Nikolai rolled his eyes. "Unraveled the spell."

"But how?" she repeated.

"You are not skilled enough to do it. No sense in teaching you."

Burn, I thought to myself, fighting a smile.

Her eyebrows really rose at that. "I am one of the more powerful mages in the States."

Nikolai waved his hand dismissively, currently every inch the court mage in posture and attitude. I hadn't seen him act like that in quite some time, so I was certain it was deliberate.

"Where are you from, Nikolai? No one has heard of you."

"Course not." He didn't elaborate.

Adriana clenched her jaw, but her attention strayed to Doc and she tensed.

I ran my hand up his forearm, before folding my hand over his clenched one. He took a deep breath and relaxed marginally.

The food arrived, interrupting our conversation. We ate for a while in silence before Ed finally broke it. "Did you follow us just to tell us again how you couldn't help us?"

Adriana shook her head. "Nikolai seemed certain that he could take their demon away from them. I wanted to know why." Her gaze strayed to Doc and her eyes narrowed. "And I needed more answers about Roy."

"You don't need anything," Allan said a distinct growl to his voice as well. "You just want information."

Ed and Allan had finished their dinners and Ed eyed mine speculatively. It tasted good, but the conversation had stolen a lot of my appetite, so I passed my plate off to him. He grinned. Doc handed his plate to Allan, and the werewolves dug in.

"You are werewolves?" Adriana asked hesitantly.

Ed nodded.

"Where is your pack?"

Ed tilted his head as if he didn't understand the question. "Sitting at the table with us."

"No, your other wolves. Werewolves rarely, if ever, are on their own."

"It's just me, Allan, and the mages. We're a pack. Doc rescued Allan and me from the foster system. Sofia and Nikolai joined us more recently."

"How did you end up in the foster system?" Adriana frowned.

"Our family was attacked on a camping trip. Ed and I survived. Our parents didn't. Relatives couldn't take us. We managed," Allan finished the story.

"I see." Her tone indicated that she was still confused. However, she dropped the questions.

Another uneasy silence followed, broken when the waiter came to see if we wanted dessert.

"You do." Allan grinned at me.

That settled, everyone ordered cheesecake, though I probably wasn't the only one that wished Adriana would leave.

When dessert arrived, I took a bite. "Oh, this is good." I moaned a little, which got all the guys to stare at me. I ignored the heat in their gazes, partially because of our unwanted dinner guest, and partially because the cheesecake was that good.

"Yes. Is truly made from cheese? Delicious." Nikolai stole Doc's piece.

"Hey," Doc protested.

"Get another. I have been missing out on this entire life."

Doc laughed and gestured for Nikolai to keep it.

The werewolves finished quickly, and Adriana grabbed the bill before Doc could. "Least I can do. Now, since you seem to think you can, once you rescue the demon, call us and I will have people move in to arrest the Andersons. If you change your mind about relocating, don't hesitate to reach out. Try to keep the damage to a minimum." She directed the last comment at Nikolai.

Adriana put cash down for the bill and left.

We stared after her for a minute before I burst out laughing. "She doesn't know you, but she's already figured out you're destructive."

Nikolai snorted, passing the last of the cheesecake he had taken from Doc to the werewolves. "She is not wrong."

∞ ∞ ∞

We were all exhausted when we made it back to Victoria's house. She and David were home and playing cards with her parents.

"Have fun?" Victoria grinned.

"Yes. The museum and dinner were great." I didn't mention Adriana tracking us down at the museum. They didn't need to know.

We all found places to sit, though I ended up sprawled in Nikolai's lap while Ed and Allan shared the other couch with Doc.

They finished their card game, then Jasmine stood. "Let me show you where you can sleep. I'm sure you're all tired."

I nodded for everyone.

"We have a couple of options, but Victoria said you guys were used to sharing?"

"It's a werewolf thing," Ed offered. "We talked the mages into it. Now they're just used to a puppy pile."

Jasmine's eyes widened slightly though she smiled at Ed's phrasing. She glanced at Allan, who nodded agreement.

I was surprised they had told her, but it was probably just as easy that way.

"We have a guest room with a queen sized bed or we can set up a few air beds. David stays in Victoria's room when he stays over, but we can kick him out, if you want to sleep in there, Sofia."

"I, uh, I'll just share with the guys." I tried not to stammer too much.

"Sounds good." She didn't act like it surprised her, so I just rolled with it.

118

"We'll take the guest room," Doc said. "No need to go to any extra trouble. We do appreciate you putting up with us for an evening."

Jasmine's smile warmed me. "It's no trouble at all."

I reluctantly climbed off of Nikolai's lap and we followed her up the stairs. "In here. The guest bathroom is attached. If you need anything, don't hesitate to let us know."

"Thank you," I said.

"You're quite welcome, Sofia. It's been a pleasure meeting all of you. Get some rest. Pancakes in the morning."

"We love pancakes," Ed replied, eyes glinting with excitement.

"I'll make a lot." Jasmine sounded pleased.

Once we were alone, Nikolai cast his sound barrier again. I groaned as his magic washed through me.

"Do not think will need it, but still, can talk if necessary." Nikolai studied the bed, glanced at all of us and shrugged. "Cozy."

"I can..."

I cut Doc off. "Squeeze in with the rest of us. We'll fit." There was no way I was letting him sleep on the floor.

He didn't argue, and before long we were all curled up in bed. Doc spooned around my back and Nikolai had pressed into him. I spooned around Ed and Allan lay on his other side. We fit. Barely. Still, I wouldn't trade these moments for anything. Especially since I had almost lost them.

∞ ∞ ∞

After waking up surrounded by my guys, followed by a fantastic pancake breakfast, and the general feeling that we were actually safe, I didn't want to head back up to

Sunnyglade. I loved it there. Not being safe weighed heavily on me, however. I hadn't realized how much until I spent even a few hours away from it all. As we climbed into Doc's truck, the weight settled back around me.

Nikolai might have sensed something because he kissed my hair and wrapped his arm tight around me. Allan had pressed against my other side and gave me a curious look. Maybe he caught the same sense of depression that weighed me down because he took my hand and echoed Nikolai's kiss on my hair.

"It'll be okay, Sofia," he murmured.

"Thanks." I snuggled into them.

Ed reached across Allan and put his hand on my thigh.

Victoria finished saying goodbye to her boyfriend and climbed into the front of the truck. We all waved and headed home. Now it was time for exams and busting our demon out of his shackles.

Chapter 10

Sofia

"I feel like that was too easy," Victoria said at the end of a long week of exams.

"Oh?" I for one was grateful for a quiet week.

"Yeah. I think I passed everything. I wasn't stressed about any of my tests, and we weren't attacked all week long."

I laughed. "Well, yeah. I guess I think I did okay, too." I hadn't told her we were going after Ash this weekend. The semester was effectively over now that exams were done, even though we had a final week of class to attend. "You're going home this weekend, right?"

"Yes. Why?"

"Just, um, probably a good idea."

She cocked an eyebrow then shrugged. "Be careful, whatever it is."

"As careful as I can be."

We headed into the dorm and she grabbed her overnight bag and keys. I got my bag as well and looked around the room wondering if I would actually see it again. Our plan was dangerous. Leaving Ash in the Andersons' hands was even more dangerous.

Hopefully this would work.

"Hey, what's wrong?" Victoria asked as we headed back down to the parking lot.

"Nothing. Sorry, Victoria, lots on my mind."

"Yeah. I get it. Hey, like I said, be careful. You need anything, call, and don't hesitate to just show up. My parents like you and your guys."

I blushed.

"They really do. They think your guys are adorable."

"Uh, thanks." I was glad that they, at least, had accepted us. My parents were starting to make noise about a Christmas visit. They wanted me to come and visit for the holiday. I hadn't yet asked if I could bring anyone along, nor had I asked any of the guys if they wanted to come. I really hoped I could talk my parents into coming here to visit instead, if we had managed to handle the Andersons by then. It seemed so far away compared to what we needed to deal with now. Not to mention, I hadn't even begun to go Christmas shopping for the guys. That was one disadvantage to dating so many guys. I wanted to get them all gifts.

One thing at a time, Sofia, I thought to myself. Rescue Ash. Get the Andersons arrested. Deal with mundane things like the holiday. Easy. Right? Right...

I fought back a sigh, and forced a smile when I hugged Victoria before she got into her sedan. My smile turned into a real one when I heard the growl of Doc's diesel truck. My enhanced senses hadn't faded much from the demon's presence, though I was getting used to it. I still thought Doc and the wolves had way better hearing, smell, and sight, but mine was far better than it had ever been before.

Victoria waved, and winked, as she pulled away.

I headed for the street where I would meet the guys.

To my surprise, Nikolai was driving Doc's truck. His distressed expression reminded me of when we had first brought him into Sunnyglade. Doc, in the passenger seat, looked relatively serene in comparison.

"Is it safe to get in?" I tried to keep my expression serious, but I had to laugh when Nikolai's slightly panicked expression soured.

"Of course," he grumbled.

I climbed into the backseat and leaned forward to kiss him on the cheek by way of apology.

"Love you," I said.

Nikolai's expression lightened. "And I you."

Doc already had his hair down. I ran my hand through it, hoping that was subtle enough that no one would notice should anyone happen to look our way.

"You, too."

Doc smiled. "I love you, Sofia."

I grinned. "Where are the guys?"

"Running," Doc answered. "They got done earlier and I took them home and picked up Nikolai."

"So, learning to drive?"

Nikolai sighed. "Ed and Allan can drive."

"You don't actually want to learn?"

Nikolai shrugged. "It is good idea. It was not my idea."

I laughed. "It is a good idea, just in case you have to drive the truck. Wouldn't want to wreck it like you did Alex's Mustang."

Nikolai paled. "Do not want to fuck up Doc's truck."

Perhaps that was his real problem. It wasn't that he didn't want to learn to drive, more that he didn't want to make a mistake and damage Doc's precious truck. It was a reasonable concern, though I thought Doc would forgive Nikolai just about anything.

Hesitantly, Nikolai put the truck in gear and pulled away from the curb. His eyes darted between the mirrors and the view in front of him. He drove smoothly enough, though I was surprised at how relaxed Doc was. Of course, with his reflexes, he could probably prevent an accident pretty easily.

Once we hit the roundabout and headed up the mountain I managed to relax enough to think about something other than Nikolai behind the wheel. "What's the plan?"

"We're going after Ash tonight. We want to be well rested, so we're going to relax, spend some time together, and plan a little more. Then we're rescuing our demon."

I thought Doc's choice of words very interesting, but at this point I agreed. Ash was ours, though I didn't know where I had come up with that possessive feeling, and I wanted him free. Something told me the demon wasn't going to go anywhere if we rescued him, though I didn't know what that would mean for our little pack.

Still, I wasn't going to worry about that now. Like Christmas presents, there were a lot of things I needed to accomplish before we got to that point. If we got to that point. I wasn't nearly as worried about the Andersons as maybe I should have been. I was extremely worried about Ash. Nikolai and I would have to overcome him fast, and I was certain his instructions wouldn't leave any loopholes this time.

Nikolai thought we could do it. We had worked out the combination of spells we would use, and we had practiced them. We were as ready as we could be.

We pulled off the main road onto Doc's driveway and bounced down the snowy rutted road. The mage sighed in relief as he put the truck in park. We waited for a minute for the diesel to idle and then he turned it off.

Doc patted Nikolai on the shoulder and slid out of the truck. I jumped out and wrapped my arms around Nikolai. "Good job."

"Would be less stressful to steal another car to practice in," he grumbled into my shoulder as he sagged in my arms. Nikolai claimed it wasn't cold enough yet to need a coat and Doc had mentioned that he only needed one when it got really cold, so I was the only one wearing a jacket. Colorado, I had learned, could be comfortable on a twenty-degree day if the sun was out, without much more than long sleeves and a light jacket. It was one of those days.

"Good motivation to drive carefully," Doc answered, putting his arms around the two of us, sandwiching me between the two of them. Their firm bodies pressed against me got me thinking about other ways I might like them pressed against me.

Doc, likely sensing the way my body reacted to my thoughts, ran one of his hands down my side, curving his fingers around my hips.

I made an appreciative sound.

Nikolai shifted against me, distracted from his original train of thought. He cupped my cheeks with his hands and pressed his lips to mine. I eagerly explored his mouth with my tongue.

Magic crackled between the three of us. Doc pressed into me from behind, hand tightening on my hip. His other arm was still around Nikolai and he pulled the mage closer into me.

"How much time do we have?" I asked.

"Depends on how you define rest," Allan said, startling all of us.

I glanced toward Allan. He and Ed stepped out of the woods, shirtless, sweat glistening on their muscular torsos despite the chill in the air. Their pantlegs were wet from the snow.

"Rest for us is a run through the snow and a nap. I'm not sure how mages define it, and Doc really just needs blood to have energy," Ed added, a mischievous glint in his eyes.

Nikolai grumbled.

I laughed and pressed my lips to Nikolai's. He kissed me, but I could tell he was still distracted by Ed's dig, so I dug my fingers into his back and bit at his lip. That got his attention and he focused on me.

Doc released us and I lost track of the others as Nikolai slipped his hands under my jacket and pressed his hands into my shoulder blades. The attention he paid to me, along with his skilled tongue made me feel as if I were the most important person in the world to him. Doc was right, Nikolai was an excellent kisser.

Groaning, I pressed into him, pushing a bit of my magic into him. He rumbled in pleasure and moved one hand down to cup my ass. I was about to do the same when someone cleared their throat Nikolai released me.

"We've decided we have time," Allan said.

"Sun isn't down yet," Nikolai agreed, grinning at me. "If you're interested?" He arched an eyebrow.

I thought about joking around with them, but I wanted my guys and we were about to face a demon who, while he didn't want to hurt us, probably would and I couldn't even get the joke to form on my lips.

Nikolai must have seen my answer in my eyes because he scooped me up and carried me to the yurt, the other guys right behind us.

He tossed me on the bed. Before I could do anything but giggle as I bounced, he pulled the laces off my boots and started undressing me. He kicked off his shoes and crawled onto the bed with me. The others did the same, though they let Nikolai take the lead on pulling my clothing off.

He was efficient, and soon I was naked, and my guys were wearing too many clothes. I attacked Nikolai's shirt, impatiently undoing the buttons.

Ed's warm hands caressed my sides as I worked on Nikolai's clothing. I glanced over and noticed Allan and Doc working on undressing each other and was grateful I wouldn't have to take the time to remove all their clothing myself. That might be fun some other time, but the urgency I felt didn't leave room for a great deal of patience.

Nikolai's gaze captured mine as I ran my hands over his chest before pushing his shirt off over his shoulders.

He used that move to pull me close again, kissing along my jaw before nipping at my ear and digging his strong fingers into my back.

I murmured in appreciation.

"I don't mind having Sofia to myself," Nikolai said. "But that wasn't the point."

I leaned back and looked at the others.

They were all looking at us as if they weren't sure what to do. We had done group activities before, but not quite like this. Even when I had been with Nikolai and Doc, it had mostly been Nikolai and me together.

"What?" he finally asked when they continued to stare.

Ed glanced down at the comforter and Doc and Allan both shrugged. "We only have a general idea of group sex," Doc said. "Same as before." The corner of his lip curled slightly in the suggestion of a smile.

"Oh. No shame in that," Nikolai replied. "Was not expecting to be giving lessons, but is no problem."

His casual acceptance of their lack of experience eased their tension and they relaxed, though I could tell he was amused. They probably could, too.

"I must know what you're comfortable with." He looked at me.

I shrugged. "I'm willing to try most things at least once."

He glanced at the others, who all traded a look before nodding.

"Hmm, okay, well, is one of her and four of us." He considered, and I wondered what was going through his mind as we all watched him. Finally, he shrugged. "Two more than I've ever dealt with, too." He grinned. "Doc, take off clothes and lie down. Then one of us can, um, take her from behind, while the others participate other ways."

I raised my eyebrows, but I was certainly game to try.

Ed, still close behind me, tensed. "Maybe I'll just watch," he said quietly.

Twisting around, I faced the werewolf. "What's wrong?"

"Nothing. I just..." He clenched his fists. "Later." He hopped off the bed and stalked out of the yurt.

"Fuck." I flopped back on the bed. I was still the only one without clothing, but I couldn't feel self-conscious in front of my guys. Ed, apparently, did. Which was fair. I just wished he felt more comfortable about saying he wasn't.

"I'll talk to him," Allan offered.

"Nope. I'll fix it," I replied and got off the bed. "You three entertain yourselves. I'm all about trying this group sex thing but I'll need a raincheck."

Nikolai nodded agreement and smacked me on the ass when I was in range. "Enjoy your wolf," he said.

I yelped in mock anger before I followed Ed out of the yurt, not bothering with clothing and relying on a spell to keep me warm and prevent my feet from damage on the ground. With the wards in place, either myself or Nikolai would know if someone else was on the property and it was dark anyway. My demon enhanced eyes could see well enough, and I followed my sense of Ed through the pack bond until I found him standing near my grove, looking out over the valley.

"Hey."

"Hey," he replied and glanced at me before he looked back over the valley. Then he did a double take and looked back at me. "Aren't you cold?" His eyes roamed over my body.

"No."

"I'm sorry. I just, well, chickened out." Ed dropped his eyes to the ground.

I walked over to him and pushed against his front, wrapping my arms around him.

His warm hands cupped my bare ass and he held me tightly to him.

"That's okay, Ed. I should have realized you might not be comfortable with that yet. I'm willing to try anything, because I trust you all, but if I'd never actually had sex, I'd be way more nervous, too."

"Yeah, that's part of it. I just feel, I don't know, nervous. None of them would say anything, but..." He shrugged.

"You know," I whispered. "They're perfectly capable of entertaining each other for a little while." I leaned back so I could meet his eyes and grinned. "Let's head to my grove."

He let me take his hand and tug him toward the entrance to the grove.

"I can't believe you're walking around naked."

"No one else is on the property. Who's going to see? You and the other guys have seen me completely naked how many times?" I grinned.

"True." His eyes twinkled.

I sealed up the grove behind me and pulled him to the center. He was still shirtless, and shoeless. His skin shivered as I trailed my hands down his muscled chest. He put his hands on my hips and I leaned forward, tilting my head so he could kiss me. Ed took the hint and met my lips with his.

We explored each other's mouths for a while and his hands roamed up and down my back. Like Doc, the wolves healed so quickly that they never built up callouses, and their hands were smooth. I continued to trace my fingers along his muscular torso for a while before I moved down to his jeans. Running my fingers along the inside of the waistband, I teased him. Ed sucked in a breath and his hands tightened on my back.

"You good?"

"Yes," he answered.

I popped the button on his jeans and slid down the zipper. He wasn't actually wearing boxers at the moment. Kneeling, I slid his jeans down, running my hands along his firm thighs, feeling him shiver under my touch.

On my way back up, I ran my tongue along his firm length. He gasped, clutching my shoulders as I rose.

"What would you like?" I asked when I was standing again, pressing my stomach into his erection.

He groaned and tightened his arms around me. "I want you however you'll have me, Sofia."

"Do you have a position you'd like to try first?"

Ed kissed the curve of my shoulder. "Maybe we can try a few?" He hesitated, blushing. "We have a little time."

"Mmmm, sounds good." I tugged his hand until we were down on the ground.

He gently laid me back until I was cradled on the soft mossy ground. "I love you, Sofia."

"I love you, Ed. So very much." My stomach fluttered at the strength of my emotion. His eyes shone in the low light, wolf-like and I shivered at the naked passion on his face.

He kissed my throat before nibbling down my collarbone and then taking one of my breasts into his mouth and sucking it gently.

I moaned encouragement and he dragged his fingers down my sides. I threaded my hands into his shaggy hair. He still hadn't gotten it cut and I kept my hands in his hair as he worked his way lower, nipping softly as he worked over my belly. I opened my legs as he found his way between them.

"That's good," I managed to say as he licked my folds and rubbed my sensitive nub. Before long I was soaking wet and thrusting against him, small, urgent moans escaping my lips as he pleasured me.

"Ready?"

"For you, always," I replied.

Ed moved, but stopped just short of touching. I wanted to cry out in frustration, but that wouldn't help his confidence. Instead, I met his eyes, slid my hands along his ribs and tugged gently.

"You're sure?"

"Yes. More than sure."

Ed finally moved forward, guiding his hard length to my opening. I tilted my hips and he pushed against me.

Groaning, I pushed back as he slowly entered me.

"So good," I moaned as he filled me completely.

"Yeah?"

"Yeah." I pulled him to me and pressed his lips to mine. I hooked one leg around his back and he slowly thrust into me. Though I wanted him to move faster, Ed needed to find his pace and it did feel good, slowly sliding into me, hitting me in the right places, slowly building my pleasure.

"So good," I said again.

I met his sky-blue eyes and grinned. He smiled back, wonderment in his expression. Gripping his hips, I encouraged him to keep going, to move a little faster.

"I don't want to hurt you," he said.

"You won't, and if you get close, I'll let you know."

"Okay." He thrust harder and I wrapped both legs around his waist. Soon we were both panting, and I was just on the verge of an orgasm.

He slowed, maybe feeling the same thing. "I want you on top, too. That looked like fun."

"It's all fun," I replied with a small laugh before grabbing his shoulders and shifting my legs until I rolled us.

Groaning as I sunk onto him at a whole different angle, I almost lost it, but I wanted Ed to last a while longer so he could experience this position.

"I'm not going to last too long," I warned him as I began to move.

His breaths came fast as he nodded. I took that to mean he was the in the same situation. I tried to get myself to slow, to enjoy this a bit longer, but my need for release built and I rocked my hips, sliding up and down his hard length, crying out each time he filled me, ready, just on the verge.

"Sofia!" he called out my name, thrusting hard into me, holding my hips as he came. I joined him as my orgasm hit me hard.

I collapsed onto Ed's chest and he held me, our hearts pounding.

"I love you, Ed."

He tightened his fingers on my back, holding me close. "I love you, Sofia."

After we cuddled for a while, I carefully slid off him. We both groaned, still sensitive.

It wouldn't be hard to get Ed going again, but we needed to get some actual rest, too, damn it. Still, I needed a few more minutes to cuddle with my wolf and I curled up next to him. He probably needed me to tell him I had enjoyed myself. It should have been obvious, but I knew Ed needed some encouragement.

"Thank you," I whispered. "That was perfect."

"Yeah." He tightened his arms around me and nuzzled my hair. "You're the best, Sofia."

"You're not so bad yourself." I put my hand on his cheek and tilted his head until I could kiss him. "We should do this again very soon."

He nodded enthusiastically, making me smile. "I think I'd even be okay with a group now," he offered.

"Only if that's what you want."

He grinned. "We'll see when we get there but I think I'll be fine. I was just nervous."

"Well, no need to be." I smiled and gave him a quick kiss.

Ed blushed.

"That was great, but it's okay to be nervous. I'm a little nervous about what Nikolai has planned for me. I'm excited to try it though, too. I trust you guys."

Ed answered with another kiss, almost convincing me we should go again just with his tongue against mine.

"We should get back, huh." He sounded a little wistful.

"Yeah. We need to rest so we can go rescue our demon." I reluctantly pulled away from Ed and cast the cleaning spell over us. It was seriously the most useful spell ever. The shower Nikolai had made us was nice, but this was more efficient, and I was ready to curl up with my pack and sleep.

"What do you think Ash will do once we set him free?" Ed asked.

"I don't know. If he can't go home, he may want to stay with us for a while. He's been a prisoner for a long time."

Ed nodded. "We should keep him, if he'll let us."

"Keep him?"

"He's kind of grown on me," Ed explained. "He could join our pack, if everyone wants him." He held me with his gaze for a moment.

I raised my eyebrows. "I, uh, had not really thought of that. I mean, I hope he will stay with us, but fully bringing him into our pack?"

"You don't have to, you know. It's just a thought. He's going to need us, I think. We certainly owe him for helping us keep you safe and I'm not saying he should join us because we owe him, but we should give him the chance at least."

"Yeah, I'm fine with that. We'll help him however we need to." That was more than fair to me.

"Good." Ed held out his hand and I slid mine into his. He blushed again but his grip was firm as we left the grove. He didn't bother with his pants either.

When we pushed back the flap on the yurt, Doc, Allan, and Nikolai were already cuddled into bed, asleep, though Doc woke up enough to glance at us. They had left room on one side and I crawled in, curling up against Doc and Ed slid under the sheets behind me, wrapping his arms around me and to some degree Doc, as well.

"We're getting up in a few hours," Doc whispered. "Allan set an alarm."

I kissed his shoulder and nuzzled into his hair. "Sounds good."

Ed drifted off quickly.

I couldn't help but turn the details of my part of the plan over in my mind again and again. So much hinged on my ability to keep up with Nikolai. If we couldn't take out Ash fast, we were screwed.

Doc took my hand in his and tucked my arm against his chest before he kissed my knuckles. "You'll do great, Sofia. Now get some rest."

He must have used some of his vampire powers on me because I drifted off quickly and didn't dream.

Chapter 11

Sofia

We parked Doc's truck at a trailhead close to the Andersons' and got out. Nikolai muffled the sound of us closing the doors, just in case. There shouldn't be anyone awake at two in the morning, but better safe than answering awkward questions. Cool, crisp air stole the breath from my lungs and fogged it as it escaped my lips.

The hope was that we could sneak in, snag Ash, and get out. None of us believed it would be that easy and we had several contingency plans. Hopefully we were prepared.

It wouldn't take us long to walk there, and Nikolai thought he could hide us from the wards around the Andersons' house. He had managed several times in the past, but they might know that now and be prepared.

Ed and Allan slipped through the pine forest in wolf form, barely visible. Their job was to watch the perimeter and keep us informed through the pack bond. We had all been practicing, and it was much easier for us all to communicate. Though the wolves didn't use words, but the images, scents, and sounds they conveyed were as clear to the rest of us as if they had spoken in our minds. From Nikolai and I they had gained some ability to sense magic and were on the alert. They would split off as soon as we were through the wards.

Doc seemed to have fully embraced his vampire heritage. The only reason I knew where he was at was because I could sense him through our bond. He moved with us, silently, not even a whisper on the still night air.

Nikolai, though he was quite skilled at moving quietly, sounded loud in comparison to the other three. I hadn't even pretended I could keep up with their abilities and cast a muffling spell on myself. There was always the chance it would give us away, but it was either that or my crashing through the forest that would alert anyone even half aware for miles around. Someday I would learn that skill, but until then, I would have to make do with magic.

I split my attention between my awareness of Nikolai and the magic he worked and scanning our surroundings with my demon enhanced senses and magic. Knowing exactly what I needed to do, even before Nikolai showed me his method, was a little freaky. The demon really wanted me to succeed against the mages that had imprisoned her.

We had also informed Adriana of our plans. It was a risk, but one we thought we had to take. Otherwise, the Andersons might bolt before this council of hers could get their hands on the assholes. Well, I should say that I sent her a text message about ten minutes ago, checked to make sure it went through, then put my phone on silent.

We slipped through the trees, the sharp bite of pine strong on the crisp air. The snow was patchier on this side of the valley and we avoided stepping in it as much as we could.

I felt like I should be tired, but adrenalin coursed through me and I was on high alert, the smallest noise making me jump.

Nikolai took my hand and squeezed.

Trying to relax was like trying to bench press a truck. There was no way I could do it.

Well, maybe with magic.

Now I was distracting myself. I focused, or at least tried to. I was so not cut out for this sort of thing. As much as I hated to admit it, if Nikolai didn't need me to help cast magic, I might have sat this fight out. No. I really wouldn't have. The demon gave me everything I needed to succeed. I just had to trust myself.

We crossed the outer wards without any apparent notice, so Nikolai sent the wolves off to circle the mansion. They brushed against my legs, and I let my hands trail across their backs, sinking my fingers into their thick fur. Then they were gone, off in opposite directions to both keep an eye on things while we were inside and hopefully cover our retreat as we escaped. Nikolai called them our scouts and had managed to make them feel good about their roles despite them wanting to be in on the actual fight. He was right though, without knowing what was going on outside the mansion, we could walk right into another trap. Their role was just as vital.

It both seemed to take forever, and no time at all before we were crouched in the tree line staring at the mansion.

A few lights illuminated the grounds, and one light burned in an upstairs window, but otherwise it was quiet.

Ed sent us a quick image of sleepy guards walking the grounds. Two, not terribly alert. Allan echoed with the same information from the far side of the house.

I nearly jumped out of my skin when Doc appeared next to us. "Want me to take them out, or leave them?"

The deadly intent in his voice sent shivers down my spine.

"Leave them. Still trying for surprise," Nikolai answered after a quick hesitation.

Doc vanished again, after a quick brush of his fingers across my cheek.

I had thought my heart was pounding before, but that was nothing compared to the way my pulse raced as we snuck across the open grounds. Nikolai had already chosen our entrance, a second story window in a room he claimed was not used much. Doc could climb to it, slide it open and he and Doc could help me up. Or so he claimed. Doc had reluctantly admitted that he could use his powers to break into places, and we hoped that vampire abilities were so poorly understood in these days that the Andersons wouldn't be able to set alarm magic for it.

We made it to the edge of the house without being discovered and Nikolai directed us to the window he was after.

Doc, still more a shadow than anything, scaled the stone siding like it was a ladder, spent a moment at the window, and then slid it open. He disappeared over the sill and then returned, looking a little less like a shadow as he leaned out to grab me.

Nikolai made a stirrup with his hands and I stepped into it. He boosted me quickly and I reached for Doc's hand. He gripped me and easily hauled me into the window.

Doc held me tight for a moment while I trembled. "You're doing great," he whispered in my ear, barely loud enough for me to hear.

I nodded, not trusting my voice.

He released me and leaned back out of the window. Moments later, Nikolai stood with us. He also hugged me briefly.

Doc shut the window, though he left it unlatched, and then slunk to the door. He listened before cracking it open and slipping out.

Nikolai and I waited until we sensed from him that it was clear, then stepped carefully as we followed.

According to Nikolai, some of the floorboards creaked, because of course they did.

If my pounding heart didn't give us away, a false step would, and I followed behind the other mage as carefully as I could.

The house was dark, though here and there a nightlight lit the halls. It was just enough to see by, and we crept to the staircase. Nikolai claimed that the only reasonable place to keep Ash would be in their dungeon-like basement. Especially if they were planning on a trap for us. Which was possible. There was no way we could expect them not to anticipate this move.

Though every moment stretched into an eternity, it didn't take long before we were down on the main floor.

Doc appeared and grabbed both of us and shoved us into a deep shadow. We crouched there, huddled together, Doc sheltering both of us with a cool touch of his powers deepening the shadows around us. He had never used so many of his abilities around me, and I made a note to ask him about it later. He hadn't really hesitated to use borrowed magic, but this was a side of him I hadn't seen.

Nikolai pressed against my back. I could feel his heart pounding almost as hard as mine was, and I was strangely comforted to know he was also nervous.

Moments later a pair of footsteps announced the passage of two people passing our location. Probably mages.

This time Doc didn't ask, he simply crept away. A few seconds later I heard a quiet thud then the soft click of a door. Nikolai held me until Doc returned.

"They'll be out for a few hours at least," he whispered.

"Should have killed them," Nikolai answered.

"Probably," Doc agreed.

Nikolai patted him on the shoulder. "Perhaps is good only one of us comfortable killing."

We moved out of the deep shadow and crept down the hallway until we reached the stairwell to the basement.

Nikolai paused for a long time before he touched the knob and turned it. We were all alert for magic. So far everything we had sensed was passively detecting anyone moving about in the house, and we had avoided being noticed. At least for now.

The wolves checked in. Nothing much had changed.

Waiting to be discovered was almost worse than actual discovery. Maybe. Probably not, but still it felt that way right now.

Doc moved ahead of Nikolai once the door was open. There were no lights on down there, but that wouldn't stop Doc. Nikolai and I were a touch more hindered and after a minute I reached out through our bond and *borrowed* Doc's lowlight vision, like the wolves had done with our ability to sense magic. My perception changed drastically, and I stumbled.

Nikolai caught my arm and pulled me against him, but we didn't talk. I adapted quickly, probably thanks to some innate memory from the demon. I realized I was seeing heat. That's how he did it. He couldn't see without light, he could see heat. Why had we never talked about this before?

Sensing that I had my feet under me again, Nikolai released me, and we continued down the stairs.

My memories of the stone basement were vague, but I recognized the quarried stone walls, the prickle of magic along my skin, and the musty smell.

Doc located Ash in a cell near the room where they had forced the demon to possess me.

I got the sense from the vampire that Ash was watching the doorway. He knew we were here, but so far he wasn't acting. Surely his orders would be to kill us on sight.

Nikolai and I crouched in the doorway.

"It's much harder to convince myself you're not a vampire when you're acting like one." Ash's voice shattered the silence, though he spoke quietly.

Nikolai and I both flinched.

"They still ordering you to kill the vampire?" Doc asked, his voice barely audible.

"Lucky for you, yes. Kill the vampire, kill the mages on sight. You'll have to kill me quick or I might not be able to resist my compulsions long enough to keep from murdering all of you."

He sounded so tired. Resigned. Like he no longer cared to fight for any sort of independence.

Damn it.

"If they don't already know you're here, they'll know as soon as we start. I'm sure they've prepared. They know you're coming after me."

Nikolai and I shared a glance and shrugged. The only way out of this was to rescue Ash or die trying. The Andersons would never quit while they still had his power to hide behind.

His lips brushed across mine and we prepared ourselves, shaping the spell we needed before drawing on our magic. It wasn't easy to shape the spell before calling our powers and having it work, but Nikolai and I had drilled all week.

The spell was twofold. It would blast through just about any magical barrier, and then, if Ash were still standing, it would stun the crap out of him. The spell was draining, hard to cast, and generally lethal to anything on the other side of it. We were counting on Ash's demonic nature to save him.

It was also easy to block if you knew how and we had a backup plan in case the wards we sensed around Ash deflected it. Doc knew to duck and cover as soon as we cast to avoid any backlash. His abilities laced with our magic should keep him safe. We'd made sure he was well supplied with both of our blood before we had left.

As soon as we had the spell formed, we leapt out from our cover, drew on our magic as deeply as we could, and blasted the spell toward Ash.

The resulting flash of light blinded me. I staggered, shrieking in pain as it overwhelmed my borrowed vision.

Nikolai grabbed my shoulder and dragged me forward, while I clutched at my face.

We slammed into the bars around Ash's cell just as something slammed down around us, attacking my ears with a pressure induced pop.

Nearly totally blind and unable to hear, I clutched at Nikolai's arm.

It took me a moment to sense them both through my bond and them trying to reassure me that it was all right. I hadn't even known I could use Doc's vision like I had, and I certainly hadn't been ready for the heat and light show that overwhelmed me.

Nikolai placed his hand on my forehead, and healing energy cooled the fiery pain.

"Thank you."

"Welcome. Is okay. Look."

I hesitantly opened my eyes. When I wasn't assaulted with blinding pain, I looked around. Soft light illuminated the space, probably from a spell Nikolai cast. Ash was sprawled on the floor. Long platinum blond hair covering his face. His chest rose and fell gently, reassuring me that we hadn't killed the poor guy.

Bars still separated us, but Doc touched them hesitantly, before gripping them in his hands and snapping them back easily.

"Don't be too impressed," he said, a small smile curling his lips when he saw the expression on my face. "The magic weakened them considerably."

Nikolai snorted. "You could have broken them if it hadn't. Don't lie."

Doc shrugged. "Maybe."

"Okay, we're trapped." Nikolai looked at a nearly visible shimmer surrounding us. "We release Ash now. Don't want them to see what we're doing. Sofia, secure our location. They may have us trapped but doesn't mean we can't also keep them out."

I got the idea of what he was after and cast an opaque shield around us. It would keep most everything out long enough for Nikolai and Doc to work on Ash.

The shield sprang into place just as footsteps crashed down the stairs to the dungeon.

There was a much longer pause than I had expected before I heard some muffled what the fuck whispers.

That reminded me... I pulled out my phone. Adriana had gotten my text and replied with a 'be careful.'

I suspected she didn't think she would ever hear from us again. Before they did something to block cell signal, I sent her another text.

Sofia: Ash is down. We're releasing him now. Could use a save though.

I put the phone back in my pocket. They would either come or they wouldn't, and I needed to concentrate on the shield spell I had up.

My skin prickled as someone probed the shield with magic. I glanced at the guys. Doc's long black hair mingled with Ash's as he leaned over the unconscious demon, fangs in his neck.

"Are you okay?" Nikolai said hesitantly.

"Not as bad as last time," Doc said when he leaned back, "but not pleasant. I'm not going to be feeling very good for a while." He wiped a bit of blood off his lips, wincing.

Nikolai clenched his jaw as Doc bit his own wrist so he could transfer the demon's magic to Nikolai. That was the big secret about releasing the demon, you needed some of their magic to do it. Doc had the ability to transfer powers between people with his blood. It was super secret. If the wrong people knew, they might lose their fear of the elusive race and start hunting vampires in earnest.

The mage took Doc's wrist and pressed it to his mouth.

I had tasted Doc's blood before. The first time he had taken Ash's blood in a successful attempt to subdue the demon. He hadn't known how badly demon blood affected him, though he had burned through a lot of the borrowed power rescuing me, it had still almost killed him. I'd taken the magic out of him by drinking his blood. It hadn't exactly done me any favors either, but at least I had been able to handle the demon magic better than Doc. Once I'd gotten beyond the fact that I was drinking blood, I hadn't found it distasteful. Nikolai clearly didn't share my experience in that regard by the twisted expression on his face.

He side-hugged Doc for a moment before falling into the spell to release Ash. It wouldn't take long, though the prickling on my skin intensified as they assaulted my shield in earnest.

"Sofia," Alex's voice washed over me, and I shivered at the slimy feel it coated my skin with. "There's still a way out of this for you. With some training and a few promises, you'd be welcome amongst us."

I shuddered. Though I hadn't seen much of Alex recently, which I appreciated, I couldn't forget what he had done to me and everything he had helped do to our friends. Putting Victoria in danger, using Ash, helping kidnap me so they could use me to host a greater demon.

"Go fuck yourself," I replied.

"Now there's an idea." Alex snarled and proceeded to describe what he was going to do to me when our shield finally fell.

My eyes widened and I hunched in on myself. Doc crawled over, though he clearly felt like shit, and wrapped his arms around me.

"Don't listen," he whispered in my ear. "Just keep the shield up. We'll take care of him as soon as Ash is free."

I wanted to point out that he didn't feel like he could lift a kitten the way he held me, but his eyes glowed with Ash's amber magic and I thought he might have a few reserves once he got over how awful demon blood made him feel.

He helped me tune out Alex, kissing my neck gently while I poured my attention into keeping the opaque shield up while they assaulted it with magic on the other side.

Someone else joined in, and I groaned under the strain. Doc leaned against me and pressed his fangs into my neck. Moments later energy poured into me. It was Doc's energy laced with the demon magic and even some of the magic Nikolai and I had given him.

"Don't wear yourself out," I said.

He couldn't reply but he tightened his hands briefly on my arms.

The boost helped, and though two more mages joined the onslaught against our shield, I held it.

Sweat streamed down my back and matted my hair to my head and my muscles shook. At some point Doc removed his fangs from my neck, but the connection remained.

"Got it," Nikolai groaned, collapsing to the ground next to us.

"Are you okay?" Doc asked the mage.

Nikolai nodded. "But now we need to fight our way out, and we're all exhausted. Releasing Ash was much more difficult. Magic was quite ingrained."

"Is he okay?"

"Will be," Nikolai answered. "Unconscious still." Nikolai took a deep breath and heaved himself off the ground, kneeling next to me. "I've got it." He poured his energy into the spell protecting us, and I gratefully took a rest.

Doc eased the connection between us and I collapsed to the ground, my limbs dragging me down like lead. The cool concrete floor pulled some of the heat from my body and the sweat chilled until I shivered so I forced myself up until I was sitting instead.

Doc had his fangs buried in Nikolai's neck, and I could see them sharing energy, so I crawled over to Ash.

His chest rose and fell. I brushed some of his long hair off his face. His skin was so warm my hands felt icy when I touched him. I took his arm in my hand and looked at the deep scars on his wrists. They looked raw and painful so I spared a bit of my energy and pushed a bit of healing strength into them.

He gasped, eyes fluttering as he woke. He zeroed in on me, and gathered his powers, anguish twisting his handsome features and darkening his husky blue eyes.

"Ash, you're free." I didn't want him to blast me on accident.

His eyes narrowed and he held up his arms and stared at the ugly scars on his wrists. He darted his gaze back to me, disbelief warring with suspicion on his features. He glanced around and saw Doc supporting Nikolai as the mage held up my shield, though both looked at least as tired as I felt.

"Before you pull on your magic any more than you already are," I said as something I had noticed but not

146

really acknowledged, clicked into place. "Feel the magic around us. I think they were prepared in case we did manage to free you. The wards will trigger to your magic."

His jaw clenched and he nodded, expression darkening. Ash rolled to his feet, coiled tension in all of his muscles. He still hadn't said anything, but he hadn't attempted to kill me on sight either, so I took that as a good sign.

Ash stalked over to Nikolai and Doc and knelt behind them. Nikolai glanced at Ash when he put his hand on both of their backs. Magic flowed from him into them and I could feel their flagging energy strengthen. Filtered through Nikolai, the magic shouldn't trigger as demon magic.

Fortunately, Alex had given up on his descriptive tirade, focusing instead on taking down our shield.

Unfortunately, even with Ash, we were all tired, though I suspected I had more energy than Nikolai at the moment now that I'd had a chance to catch my breath.

I tapped him on the back and he let me take over the shield.

"So, what now?" I asked.

"Cavalry is on the way," Nikolai said quietly.

"Did you call in the wolves?" I did not like that idea at all.

"No," Doc said. "But they did tell us that Adriana and some others had just arrived."

"That was quick," I muttered.

"Suspect they were in area," Nikolai agreed.

For whatever reason they happened to be close, at the moment I was grateful. The slight worry that they weren't on our side tried to tickle at my brain, but I pushed that away. We were screwed if that was the case. Or, someone would be anyway. I suspected that if Ash, Nikolai, and I really wanted to, we could level this place, even as wiped out as we felt. We held back now, but if it came down to it, we would fight.

"See if you can wake that demon up," we heard a female voice order over the crackle of magic against our shield.

I shivered. The voice was familiar, but I wasn't sure who it belonged to. Maybe Alex's grandmother? The woman who looked like she could be his older sister. However she had managed to extend her life and youthful appearances, I doubted it was ethical.

"Ash, wake up." The words were simple enough, but the note of command in the tone and the push of magic caused Ash's head to go up and his eyes to narrow. His coiled muscles tensed more and I hoped he wasn't about to lose control. I wouldn't blame him, but I didn't think it would help at the moment. Hell, if it had been me, they'd have to hold me back. I couldn't do anything but watch as I concentrated on the shield.

Doc put his hand on Ash's shoulder. "There will be a time," he said quietly.

The demon's expression eased slightly, and he nodded, platinum blond hair falling into his face.

The magical assault on my shield grew and I dropped to my knees on the hard concrete. Sheer determination kept me from giving under the onslaught. We'd either be saved in a moment or have to unleash everything we had.

Ash's hot hands touched my back and supported me as he poured some of his energy through me into the shield. I groaned as it washed through me, not entirely certain if his magic brought pleasure or pain, but grateful for the assist.

If nothing else, we were keeping them distracted, and wearing them out while the others infiltrated. One of the mages moved from a steady attack on the shield, to lobbing magic at it randomly. The spell was an 'unraveling,' and it was starting to have an effect.

Nikolai joined me, reinforcing our protection.

"Doc, be ready to defend us, should this shield fall," Nikolai ordered.

I wasn't sure exactly how long I held the spell with Ash supporting me directly, and Nikolai helping before we heard shouting over the crackle of the magical assault.

"Just a little bit longer," Ash whispered into my ear as I wilted. At some point I'd fallen into his arms. He was the only thing keeping me from becoming a puddle on the ground.

Doc supported Nikolai, though the mage looked to be in better shape than me. I burned up inside and it took everything I had to keep mine and Ash's energy pouring into our shield under the onslaught.

"Sofia, let go," Nikolai ordered, voice urgent.

"But..."

"Now."

I released the energy and collapsed into Ash's arms. Now that I wasn't channeling so much power, I could feel what had concerned Nikolai. I was at the end of my abilities and everything felt frayed. Anymore and I might have permanently hurt myself. As it was, I wasn't going to feel good for a while.

Moments later the assault on the shield ended. Nikolai dropped it, hands up ready to cast an offensive spell.

Alex and his grandmother were gone and the two remaining mages only had a moment to comprehend that the situation had changed before Nikolai blasted one backward into the stone wall behind him. If the blast hadn't killed him, by the sickening crack as he hit the wall, the force was more than a human skull could deal with and he slumped to the ground, leaving a red streak behind him.

Doc snapped the other mage's neck, his eyes shining in the low light.

I tried to get up from Ash's grip, but my limbs wouldn't cooperate.

"Carry her?" Nikolai asked Ash.

The demon nodded and fell in behind Nikolai and Doc as they headed for the staircase.

Hating feeling so helpless, but unable to lift the lead weights my hands had become, I let the demon carry me as we carefully made our way up the stairs. I rested my head against his warm chest and trusted him not to drop me.

Doc and Nikolai crouched by the door and after a quiet discussion, Doc darted out onto the main floor while we waited.

A few minutes later Nikolai gestured, and we followed. Whatever had held my vampire back from killing before, he'd gotten over it. At least temporarily. Two bodies littered the ground, heads twisted at unnatural angles, and we caught up to Doc in the main hallway, another person dead at his feet, blood leaking from the wound in his back.

Now that I wasn't focused on slinging magic, I could feel my wolves. They were out in the forest, fighting. Fortunately, they were in their element, and doing well with a little mage backup.

The people Adriana had brought were mages, but the Andersons had apparently added a contingent of werewolves since we had last fought them, and the mages had their hands full.

I caught a hint of powerful magic before the house shuddered around us. Dust and plaster rained down from the ceiling, and Ash dove into a doorway as chunks fell around us.

I managed to get my arms to corporate long enough to wrap them around Ash's neck and take some of my weight off his arms.

He glanced down at me and I smiled at him.

The corner of his lips twitched as if he had almost smiled.

Doc and Nikolai joined us as the house shook again.

"Hope we wore them out enough for Adriana to handle," I said.

"She's reasonably powerful," Doc answered. "And experienced in this kind of fight. She'll be okay."

"Should we help?" Nikolai asked.

Doc shook his head. "Give them a minute. We will if we need to."

One last blast of powerful energy pulsed through the air and more of the house crashed down around us.

Nikolai cast a shield over us, and we huddled under it. The doorframe mostly protected us, but his spell kept the debris and dust away.

As things fell silent, Doc gestured and we hesitantly followed him toward the main entry to the manor house. Nikolai and Doc glanced around the corner and gestured for us to follow.

"I think I might be able to walk now," I said quietly.

Ash didn't put me down and I didn't ask again, distracted by the sight in the main hall. Someone had blown half of the front house out and pieces of it littered the ground outside. Cold winter air competed with Ash's warmth, making me grateful he still held me as my sweat chilled me.

Alex was out cold on the floor. At least, I didn't think he was dead.

Ash growled, rumbling in his chest and through me, as he saw the asshat on the ground. Alex's grandmother was nowhere to be seen.

A few other mages I didn't know were also unconscious at Adriana's feet.

"You thought I'd be destructive?" Nikolai laughed as he surveyed the damage.

A couple more mages and Donna joined Adriana. They all looked warily at me after quick glances at Nikolai and Doc.

No, they weren't looking at me, they were looking at Ash. Suddenly, I was glad he still held me. Hopefully, it made him seem less dangerous.

"Well, it seems you have accomplished the impossible," Adriana said after an awkward silence.

"Is not impossible." Nikolai shrugged. "Simply difficult."

"Your name is Ash?" Adriana asked.

Ash nodded.

"You will come with us." It wasn't a question, and Ash stiffened.

"No, he won't." I glared at her.

"Where will you go then?" She apparently realized she couldn't force him, because she backed down.

Ash might not be able to do much inside the manor house without the wards locking down on him, but once he stepped outside, or off the property, he was one of the most powerful magic users in the area, if not the world.

"He can come with us," Doc said. "Until he figures out what he wants to do. I very much doubt he wants anyone telling him what to do right now."

Adriana shifted her attention from Doc back to Ash. The demon nodded, still not speaking to anyone but me.

"Very well. We'll be in touch." She gave Doc another hard look before she gestured to the fallen mages. A few of the others cast simple spells, raising the unconscious mages, including Alex, in the air and leaving the house with them. Adriana followed.

I knew we weren't out of the woods as far as dealing with Adriana and her group, but hopefully we could move on from dealing with the Andersons.

"What do you want to do, Ash?"

"I don't know," he admitted.

"You don't have to come with us," Doc said, "but it might be wise to at least pretend you're doing that until Adriana and her mages are gone."

"If you'll have me, I'll go with you." He sounded nervous.

I tightened my arms around his neck. "We're happy to have you with us, Ash."

He twisted his lips, probably not believing me, though he did follow when Nikolai and Doc left the house.

We'd been here longer than I thought. The sky had brightened considerably in the east.

Doc flinched as he glanced toward the growing light.

"Doc?" I asked.

"I may need a bit of time to recover from this," he muttered. "Fuck."

The wolves found us then. Both of them were matted with blood. Before I could even ask if they were okay, Nikolai wrinkled his nose and cast his cleaning spell on the two.

Doc caught the mage as he collapsed, unconscious. The wolves looked like they had just come out of a drier, their coats standing on end. I'd have laughed if I wasn't so worried about Nikolai.

Allan sniffed Ed and yelped, jumping backward as he got shocked.

"He probably just overdid it," Doc said, voice tight with worry. "We should go before I find out how badly I screwed up." He glanced east again before hefted Nikolai into his arms.

"You still have a heartbeat," Ash said. "You'll be fine in a day or so."

Ed whined and pushed against Doc.

"It's okay, Ed. Just don't want to get a sunburn." Doc headed toward the woods where we could hike back to his truck.

"We can take my car," Ash offered though he glanced at the wolves and frowned. "You may not fit."

"Ed, Allan, meet us at the truck," Doc said.

The wolves both huffed in agreement and took off into the woods.

Ash led us to a black Camaro.

"I don't remember this one," I said, thinking back to when Alex and he had taken Victoria and I dancing.

"Alex didn't like the color when they bought it for him after someone destroyed his favorite car, so they gave it to me."

I snickered.

Ash finally put me down and opened the door. Doc crawled in the back with Nikolai. He handed me the keys to his truck when I climbed in the passenger seat. Before I could object, he fell asleep in a tangle with Nikolai. It didn't even look comfortable, but neither of them were moving.

"Vampires can fight the compulsion to sleep during the day, but it is unlikely that Doc has ever had to even try. He'll be okay," Ash said again.

"He's not a vampire, though."

"May as well be." Ash hit the start button and the sports car rumbled to life.

I contemplated Ash's statement as he pulled away from the Anderson's mansion. "Do you know where his truck is?"

"Down the road?"

"Trailhead, yeah."

He nodded and we fell into a silence I wasn't sure how to break, or even if we needed to. There was a lot that probably needed to be said, but right now maybe it was enough that he was free, and we might be free, as well.

Shortly, he pulled the Camaro into the trailhead parking lot. I gave one more quick glance at Doc and Nikolai passed out in the back seat before looking at Ash, trying not to convey my worry. I trusted him. I really did, but part of me still remembered how he had helped bind the greater demon into me. I didn't blame him, but it was on my mind as I left Doc and Nikolai in Ash's care.

"I'll follow you," he said gruffly.

"Thanks." Though I wasn't a stranger to large trucks, I wasn't terribly comfortable driving Doc's since I knew how much he liked it. I resolved not to screw it up.

"Sofia," Ash said before I could shut the door.

I leaned down and met his eyes.

"Thank you."

"You're welcome."

"I'm sorry."

I tilted my head, tensing, before I realized he meant for everything before. I hated that I immediately expected betrayal, but it had been a rough couple of months.

"You have nothing to be sorry for, Ash. You weren't responsible for any of that."

His eyes softened but he didn't agree with me. It would take time, for all of us. I shut the door and nearly jumped out of my skin when Ed and Allan slunk out of the underbrush.

"Sorry," I muttered as I opened the backdoor of the truck so they could jump in.

Ed pushed his muzzle into my hand before he hopped in. Hopefully, that meant he wasn't offended. I didn't sense anything negative through our bond.

"I love you two. I'm glad you're safe." I tried not to think about how badly this all could have gone. We'd done it, with help, sure, but we really had done it.

155

The wolves whined in acknowledgement.

"Doc is passed out in the back of Ash's car with Nikolai," I said once I climbed in the truck and shut the door. "The mage overdid it, the vampire, well, apparently did too much vampire stuff and the rising sun knocked him out."

One of the wolves huffed in surprise. I didn't see who as I slid the seat forward so I could reach the pedals and fire up the truck.

Ash followed me as we pulled onto the road and headed back to the yurt.

Chapter 12

Sofia

Nikolai had woken by the time we made it back to Doc's land. Both of the wolves were asleep and didn't wake up when I turned off the truck, so I left them and hoped they wouldn't be upset. I didn't think they would be, though.

Nikolai helped Ash with Doc and I followed, weariness dragging at my feet until I just couldn't move forward anymore. I leaned against a tree and drifted off while I was on my feet.

"Sofia, not so comfortable to sleep against a tree," Nikolai murmured.

I groaned.

Strong hands picked me up. I woke up long enough to help struggle out of my clothing and crawl under the sheets next to Doc before I was out.

∞ ∞ ∞

The smell of food woke me up some time later. I was curled up with my thigh thrown over someone's leg and my head resting on their shoulder. Someone else was sprawled next to me, with their arm over my back, holding me tight. It took me a moment to figure out I was laying on Doc, and Nikolai, still snoring lightly, was pressed up against my back.

By Doc's steady, slow breathing, he was actually awake. He probably didn't want to disturb me or Nikolai. I tilted my head up and stared at him.

He glanced at me and smiled. "Feeling better?"

"Exhausted still," I admitted. "You?"

"I feel better than I did."

Nikolai mumbled in his sleep and tightened his arms around me.

"Can we all get a vacation now?" I groaned, not ready to wake Nikolai up so I could move. I wanted a real shower, food, and some extracurricular activities wouldn't hurt my feelings, either.

"Maybe." He sighed. "I feel like we deserve one."

"Me, too."

"Food's ready if you want some," Ed said, coming into my view.

I grinned, admiring the shirtless look with a spatula in hand. He could cook shirtless any day. "You're the best."

He raised his eyebrows and smiled.

"Get some food," Doc ordered. "If Nikolai doesn't wake up, we can feed him later."

I slid across Doc, to get out from under Nikolai, and briefly considered changing my priority order as his lips twitched into a smile. I kissed him before I made it all the way out from under Nikolai and slipped out from under the covers and off the bed.

Ed caught me up in a one-handed hug and kissed me deeply, again making me reconsider my trip to the shower. Maybe I'd just have to go back there later. Wouldn't that be a shame.

Allan wasn't in the yurt, but I ran into him as I was heading out to the shower Nikolai had made for us. His hair was damp and he was also shirtless despite the winter chill. I had grabbed a jacket, not feeling up to casting any magic even to keep warm, but it didn't stop me from feeling the firm planes of his chest as I pressed myself into a hug and then another deep kiss.

"I was worried about you," he said.

"I'll be okay. Still tired, but I think I'm all right."

He kissed me again and I almost dragged him to the shower with me.

Allan tilted his head, as if sensing that I had something on my mind.

What the hell. The shower was big enough for two. If they liked each other. I tugged on his hand and tilted my brow suggestively.

His smile let me know he knew exactly what I was thinking as he followed me back toward the bath house.

"Where's Ash?" I asked before I got completely distracted.

"He's around. He slept for a while but was pretty restless and said he was going to wander the property. He promised not to leave until we all got a chance to talk about what was next, though. I don't think he knows what to do with himself."

I could think of several things off the top of my head, then I blushed, not completely sure where those thoughts had come from.

Allan's smile turned sly. "I wouldn't object."

"Got a thing for a certain demon?" I grinned as I pulled him into the small bathhouse.

"Maybe." It was Allan's turn to blush. "Maybe I just like having a big pack."

"We'll see what Ash wants. Right now, I want you."

Allan slid the jacket off my shoulders and hung it on one of the hooks. Then he cupped my face with his hands and pressed his lips to mine. His pants and the clothes I had slipped on to walk through the snow quickly followed. He turned the handle and the water poured from the faucet.

Being magic, it only took moments to warm up and he pulled me under the water.

For a few moments, we simply pet each other, running our hands over the other's body, feeling them, grateful the other was still alive as the water and Allan's body warmed me.

I finally pressed my stomach against his firm erection. Allan groaned and cupped my ass.

He pressed a soft kiss to by temple. "How do you want to do this?"

"Standing room only." I smiled mischievously.

"Just making sure we were on the same page," he whispered as he lifted me easily. It wasn't that I was particularly light, it was more that my men were all very strong.

I wrapped my legs around his waist and guided myself until he pressed against my opening.

"Ready?"

Allan nodded and he lowered me inch by inch. I moaned in pleasure as he filled me, hitting me just right. He moved until my back was against the smooth wall, the water hitting us perfectly to keep me warm and wet. Allan held me as he slowly withdrew and thrust in again.

I cried out in pleasurable agony as he slowly pulled out, wanting more, but enjoying the sweet torture. I tightened my legs around him, hoping he would take the hint and move faster.

"No patience." He laughed.

"I'm hungry, damn it." I was, but I wanted this more than I wanted food.

He laughed harder. "Yes, ma'am. Never stand between a pack alfa and her food."

Before I could comment on his choice of words, he thrust into me hard. I yelped in surprise.

"Too much?" He hesitated before moving again.

"No," I purred.

"Good." He thrust again, carefully a few times before seeming to take me at my word and driving into me.

The intensity had me gasping his name, pleasure building in my core. He dropped one of his hands to where we were joined and rubbed at my clit. I clawed at his back, no longer coherent as the intensity built, bringing me right to the edge and leaving me there as he slowed his fingers.

I groaned.

"You can have some patience," he teased.

Unfortunately, it wasn't as easy to break through Allan's control as it was with Doc or Nikolai. I couldn't just bite him and make him give me what I wanted. Before I had to try and get creative, Allan went to work again building me right to the edge. This time he didn't stop, and my orgasm crashed into me, bringing him over the edge at the same time.

Allan held me while my body quaked around him. His face buried in my neck as he kissed me gently.

"Mmmm," I mumbled appreciatively once he set me down.

"Good shower," he agreed. "I'm glad you talked me into taking another one."

I laughed and cuddled into his chest while he wrapped his arms around me.

"We should get you fed, though," he said.

I nodded. "Let me actually get clean and we can head back."

Allan stepped out of the shower. There wasn't room for two if we were actually trying to clean up.

"Remind me to educate Nikolai in the need for larger showers when we rebuild the cabin," I said as I rinsed off the lather.

Allan laughed. "Especially if I get to watch?"

"Hmm, didn't realize you liked that sort of thing."

He shrugged when I glanced at him. "Might learn a thing or two."

I laughed. "We still need to get the pack together for some group activities," I said. "We can bring it up then."

Allan's eyes twinkled at that. He held out a towel when I stepped out from under the faucet. I tried to take it from him, but he gestured me forward, winked, and rubbed me with the towel.

I wanted to melt into a puddle at his feet. I felt so loved.

"Maybe I should get wet again," I said, double meaning intended.

Allan laughed and gently tossed the towel at me. "Later. I already ate and the way your stomach is grumbling is making me hungry again."

Pushing my lips out in a pout, I tried to look upset. He just laughed harder and handed me my shirt.

"Thanks." I dressed and we headed back to the yurt. We passed Doc and Nikolai on the way.

I raised an eyebrow, but they both dragged their feet and I guessed they weren't up to anything but getting clean and making sure they both made it there and back without falling down.

"You two okay?"

Nikolai grumbled in annoyance, something about magic not usually knocking him on his ass, but he nodded.

"Yes, and I'm sure I'll feel better once the sun goes down." Doc sighed.

I brushed my hands across his cool skin. Nikolai had thrown on a shirt, though he claimed that the cold didn't bother him until it was really cold. Doc hadn't bothered. I could really get used to all my guys walking around shirtless.

"You could go with them." Allan winked at me.

"Hey, Nikolai, when we build the showers for the cabin, let's make them bigger," I said, instead of following them.

"Why?" he grumbled out.

Even Doc looked amused at Nikolai's confusion. "I'll fill him in."

Allan and I snickered as we headed for the yurt, the smell of food luring me away.

Ash was seated at the low table, drinking some of Doc's tea when we arrived. Allan pulled me over to sit next to him. "I'll get your plate."

My momentary burst of energy flagged, and I leaned my elbows on the table and buried my face in my hands.

"Are you okay?" Ash put his mug down.

"Just exhausted. I used more magic yesterday than I think I have in my entire life." I wasn't even sure if that statement was really an exaggeration.

He touched my shoulder hesitantly. "I'm sorry."

"It's not your fault the Andersons wanted me. It's not your fault they're a bunch of asshats. It's also not your fault any of this happened. The guys have been telling me this for months now. I'm starting to believe them."

He let his hand fall from my shoulder, but he didn't contradict me.

Allan slid a plate in front of me. Bacon, eggs, toast. Simple but fantastic. I groaned as I dug in.

Munching on some bacon, Allan joined us at the table and Ed sat next to his brother.

Nikolai returned just as I had finished my meal. "I have been properly educated on the need for larger shower." He sounded a little less grumpy than before but still not his normally cheerful self. He helped himself to the food Ed had cooked.

Allan and I traded an amused grin, though Nikolai's expression didn't really give any clues as to how Doc had educated him.

Doc joined us about the time Nikolai finished his food. Allan volunteered to clear the table.

We all sat in silence until Allan rejoined us.

"Ash," Doc said. "What do you want to do now?"

The demon hunched his shoulders and stared at the table. I pushed my shoulder against his.

He flinched, but before I could pull away, he leaned back into me. He probably wasn't used to being touched, at least not kindly.

"I had wanted to return to my plane. I don't think I can. I've been here too long. Unlike a greater demon, who needs a host on this plane, this is my body, and it's been held here too long." He sounded so lost, it broke my heart.

"Ash, you can stay with us as long as you like," Doc said.

Everyone nodded agreement when Ash looked up in surprise.

"If you don't want to stay with us, just let us know and we'll help you if we can."

"Why?"

Doc frowned, tilting his head as if he didn't understand the question.

"Why wouldn't we help you?" Ed asked.

"Among other things, I destroyed your house. I've put you all in danger. I've fought against you."

Nikolai waved his hand dismissively. "That was the Andersons."

"You helped us as much as you could," Doc insisted. "You did more to keep Sofia safe while the greater demon was here than any of us could. We want to help you, if you want us to. You don't have to decide now, Ash. We just want you to know you can stay."

The demon's expression twisted. "I'm not used to having a choice."

"We know." I put my hand on his. "Take your time. Get used to it."

He took a deep breath and nodded.

"One day at a time," Allan said.

Doc studied the demon for a minute then shook his head. "Nikolai could wear my clothes, but I don't think you can. We'll have to go shopping."

The demon frowned. "For?"

"Clothes. Unless you want to magic something all the time."

Though Doc didn't say it out loud, I also knew that he didn't have many to spare at the moment, either, since most of his things had burned in the fire. There was no need to bring that up, however.

Ash raised his eyebrows. "I, uh, thank you."

"We'll go tomorrow. I don't know if any of us have the energy to do anything with what's left of today," Doc said.

The sun was almost down. I had slept until nearly three and it was almost four in the evening now. Doc was visibly starting to perk up, though I didn't know if he had noticed.

My left over demon senses tingled with the hint of snow, too. It wouldn't be tomorrow, but we were in for another storm soon.

"So, now that the Andersons are handled, should we start looking at building a new cabin?" I grinned. Excited about the prospect.

"I can see about getting supplies delivered," Doc said.

"Supplies?" Ash glanced at me and Nikolai.

"Is easier to build a house when supplies are already present."

Ash shrugged. "I can help with that, if you want. Some of the trees can be thinned, dirt and stone can be repurposed. It's been a while since I've been able to create anything with magic."

Nikolai raised his eyebrows. "Yes, that would be good."

"So, no supplies needed?" Doc asked.

"Save your money for furniture," Ash said. "The mages and I can build the cabin with what's here." A faint smile crossed his lips. "With larger showers."

"I vote for a large bathtub, too," I put my hand in the air.

"Fireplace," Nikolai said. "If we're taking requests."

"Bigger kitchen," Ed and Allan said together.

Doc laughed. "Whatever you all want."

Ash did smile then. "We should make some plans. We don't need full on architect plans, but some ideas of where we're going before we get started. We'll be able to make minor modifications once we've finished, but it will be easier to get it close the first time."

"You have done this before?" Nikolai asked.

Ash nodded. "Quite a few times. I believe I can even mimic modern electricity, so guests won't notice anything strange."

Doc raised his eyebrows. "We probably still want to use some, just in case anyone ever raises questions about utilities, but I certainly won't complain about a lower electric bill."

Ash nodded and magicked some paper onto the table. "Let's get some ideas then."

We spent the next few hours looking at pictures on the internet and developing plans for building our new cabin. Neither Nikolai nor I were ready to start right away, but plans for the following weekend were underway. That would give us some time to finalize our design, too.

Chapter 13

Sofia

"They want to come out for Christmas." I groaned and flopped back on my bed in my dorm Monday evening.

By this morning I had felt mostly recovered from the fight against the Andersons. I still didn't really want to perform any magic, but I didn't feel like I might collapse if I tried and school had gone okay. Nikolai had recovered quickly. Unfortunately, Doc was still actively avoiding direct sunlight, though it didn't seem like it was as big of a problem for him as it would be for a full vampire. He had looked exhausted in class, but still managed to keep everyone involved. Ed and Allan had also recovered physically, but they were both pretty quiet about the fighting they had engaged in. Ash was settling in well enough, though the yurt was getting a bit crowded with all of us up there.

"Your parents?" Victoria spun around in my office chair.

"Yeah."

"Well, I mean, it makes sense that they want to hang out with you for the holiday."

"It would almost be easier if I went there."

"But you don't want to be gone from your pack?"

"Would you want to be gone from all of that?" I grabbed my phone off my chest so I could reply to my mother.

Sofia: Sure, Mom, that sounds great.

Mom: I'm glad, Honey, we'll let you know when we've made all the arrangements. You'll be staying with your friends while the dorm is closed?

Sofia: Yeah.

I groaned. "And I have no idea what I'm going to do about the guys. She seems cool with me staying with them while the dorms are closed, but... yeah." I trailed off, not even sure what to say.

"Just own it. If they give you grief, you can bust their asses."

"Yeah, they're my parents."

Victoria laughed. "Oh, right."

I needed to text the guys. I brought up the group text.

Sofia: Hey, so my parents are coming out for Christmas.

"So how was your weekend?" Victoria gave the chair another spin.

"Oh, okay." I really didn't know how much to tell her. Finally, I decided she knew everything else. "We rescued Ash. He's free now."

Victoria was silent for a minute. "That's why you wanted me out of town."

"Yeah."

"Everything go okay?"

"Better than I expected. No one on our side died, anyway."

Her eyebrows rose, but she didn't ask me to clarify.

"Where is he now?"

"Up at the yurt."

"What are you going to do with him?"

I shrugged. "He's staying with us for now. It's up to him, but he probably needs some time to get on his feet and figure out what he wants."

My phone signaled that I have a text.

Doc: We'll just have to get the cabin done before they get here. It'll be okay.

Sofia: At least we can tell them it was magic.

Ed: LOL.

"Last week of school. Did you get all your classes arranged for next semester?"

"Yeah, I did, and I'm glad we're roommates again." I grinned at Victoria. "Hopefully, with a little less drama."

"Girl, you've got that right."

"Hey, so, I have another problem." I kept my face neutral.

She focused on me. "Uhoh."

"Christmas shopping for so many guys."

Victoria's eyes lit up. "Oh, we've got this, no problem. I'll help."

I gave her a relieved smile. "Thanks. I knew I could count on you."

"Hey, small problems or big ones, I've got your back."

∞ ∞ ∞

The rest of the week sped by and I was almost sorry for it to end. Friday was the last day of classes before break, and this was just about the most normal week I'd had since the semester started. Trying not to think about the time lost over the semester, I left my last class, bag slung over my shoulder, and headed for the dorm. We had all weekend to clear out. I was already packed. I just needed to grab my things, give Victoria a quick hug, and meet the guys.

The snowstorm I had sensed building all week had the clouds heavy and low in the sky. We were in for it tonight. A few fat flakes drifted through the air and one landed on my nose.

"Sofia!"

I stopped and turned, heart racing for a second before I recognized Ash. A handful of students flowed around me as I waited for the demon to catch up. He wore a pair of jeans that hugged his hips, and a long-sleeved T-shirt, despite the chill in the air. I guess the temperature didn't bother him much, either. His long blond hair was pulled back in a tail and he smiled when I waited. I warmed just looking at him.

"Hi, Ash."

"I hope you don't mind," he said as he jogged over to me. "Doc asked me to give you a ride up to his place. He's getting a few things done to the truck before the storm hits and he got delayed."

Doc had mentioned something about an oil change.

"Why would I mind?" I bumped my shoulder against Ash's when he fell in next to me.

He shoved his hands in his pockets and hunched his shoulders as we headed to my dorm so I could grab my things.

"I don't know," he muttered.

I mentally sighed, but managed to keep myself quiet outwardly. I didn't want him to feel bad. At least Ash couldn't smell my emotions like Doc and the wolves could.

The door was propped open for move-out and Ash followed me up the stairs and to my dorm.

I knocked on our door before opening it. Victoria was sitting in her office chair, staring at her phone when I walked in.

"Hey," I said as Ash followed me.

Victoria's eyes widened. She cleared her throat and obviously forced a smile. "Hi, Ash."

"Hi," he muttered, shoulders hunching more as he leaned against the doorframe.

I touched his arm before heading over and giving Victoria a hug. "Keep in touch."

"Yeah, as soon as this snow breaks we need to go shopping." She winked and gave me a hug. "I'm sure you can talk one of your guys into driving you down to Denver for some girl time."

"One of us will get her there," Ash said, voice a bit softer.

Victoria raised an eyebrow and mouthed "Oh really?"

I shrugged, not having a good reply. The idea had certainly crossed my mind more than once. Allan had already voiced approval. None of the rest of us had talked about it and Ash had not pushed the issue in any way. I wasn't even sure if he wanted anything more than to not be someone's slave at the moment.

It didn't take me long to gather my things and say another quick goodbye to Victoria. We would see each other soon, so we didn't need an extended goodbye.

Ash took my suitcase and wheeled it out after a quick nod toward Victoria. He didn't say anything as we made our way to the parking lot and his black Camaro. A few more flakes of snow sprinkled out of the sky and he grumbled as he put my bag in the trunk. I put my backpack in next to it and he shut the truck before opening the passenger door for me.

I smiled at him. "Thank you."

He nodded sharply and got into the driver's side. The Camaro roared to life and we pulled out of the parking lot.

I let the silence linger until we reached the turn out of town up into the mountains.

"We haven't had much chance to talk," I started. "How are you doing?"

Ash shrugged. "I'm fine."

I twisted to look at him while he drove. "What's up?"

He frowned and glanced at me before darting his eyes back to the road.

"You don't have to tell me. I can pretend everything is okay, but if you want to actually talk about it, I'm here for you."

He took a breath and nodded. "I'm okay. It's an adjustment. I'm still not sure what to do with myself."

"You don't have to decide right away, but once you have an idea please let us know."

Ash nodded.

I put my hand on his arm and he flinched. I pulled away. "Sorry."

"It's not you. Touch me if you want. Just not used to it."

Hesitantly, I put my hand back on his forearm. His muscles quivered with tension, but he didn't flinch, and I left my hand there.

He made the turn off and I let my hand fall back into my lap. Some of the tension had eased out of his shoulders though and that made me happy.

"How are your wrists?" I asked once he parked.

He tucked his hands under his arms, clearly uncomfortable. I pulled up the sleeves of my jacket and showed my scars. They weren't as bad as his would be, but if anyone paid much attention when I wore short sleeves, they would be obvious.

Ash unfolded a little and took my hand in his. Electric shivers trailed up my arm as he gently ran his fingers over the scars. He gently turned my arm revealing the pack tattoo on the underside of my wrist.

That skin was particularly sensitive when he traced the colorful pawprints. My breath hitched and he let go of me as if I burned him.

"Sorry," he muttered and got out of his car before I could try to reassure him that nothing was wrong. I caught up to him at the trunk.

He wordlessly handed me my backpack and took my suitcase to the yurt. I followed. Doc's truck wasn't here so I guessed it was just me and Ash if Nikolai wasn't here.

I hurried to the yurt, ready to be warm and pushed inside. No one else was home so I flopped on the bed and sent the guys a quick text.

Sophia: Ash and I are up at the yurt.

Doc replied with a thumbs up a few seconds later.

Ed: We'll be there soon.

Ash put my suitcase next to the door and perched hesitantly on the edge of the bed.

I sat up and took off my boots, tossing them next to the doorway.

"What do you think of the yurt?" I couldn't think of anything else to say that might break the awkward silence.

"It's nice." His shoulders hunched more.

"Ash, it wasn't your fault." I sighed and put my arms around him, hugging him from behind.

He really tensed at that, but I held on, giving him a chance to relax. His hair smelled like the shampoo the guys were using, mixed with a hint of woodsmoke. I rested my cheek against his shoulder and waited while his shoulders slowly unknotted.

"Want me to let go?" I asked once he had somewhat relaxed.

"No." His hand found my arm and he held me against him, so I pressed against his back and just rested there until all of the tension eased out of him.

About the time his shoulders eased, we both heard the diesel engine. Ash tensed again and I reluctantly let go.

A few minutes later, Ed and Allan came in the yurt, brushing snow off their shoulders. I caught a quick look outside the flap. Darkness had fallen and the snow had really started to come down.

Allan came over and clapped Ash on the shoulder before leaning in and giving me a quick kiss.

Ed hopped up on the bed next to me and pulled me against him. I leaned in for a kiss and he devoured me. I moaned appreciatively.

It had been a long week only seeing my guys at school. I hadn't even been able to touch Doc. Perhaps I could fix that today. Of course, with Ash here, and no separate rooms, it was more complicated.

Doc and Nikolai came in, letting in a blast of cold, snowy air.

"Guess we're not going anywhere for a while," I said.

Ed hopped up and joined Allan to start dinner. Doc took his place, not touching me, though he sat close.

Nikolai shook his head. "No, it will be a deep snow."

I put my arm around Doc, playfully tugging at his ponytail holder.

"I bought more," he said with a small grin.

Calling on my magic for the first time since we had freed Ash, I disintegrated the one he used and ran my fingers though his silky hair. His smile broadened.

Then I poked him in the shoulder. "Guess who's not actually my teacher anymore."

He actually blushed a little, though his eyes sparkled with mischief. "I'm not actually a teacher at all anymore. At least until fall."

He didn't look upset so I matched his smile with one of my own and shifted around so I could kiss him. Doc hesitated as he pressed his lips to mine. I buried my hands in his hair and pulled him against me. Doc's hands kneaded my back and I groaned as he found a few knotted muscles. I settled into Doc's lap while he gently massaged my back and I leaned into him, content to be held.

"So, what to do about parents?" Nikolai asked.

"Depends on how long they're staying," Ed answered. I looked over at my guys and sucked in a breath. Somewhere they must have gotten the message that I liked shirtless cooking because both of my wolves were currently half dressed. Their jeans hugged their hips and the claw scars across Allan's shoulder blades were just begging for me to run my fingers over them. I knew Ed had a similar set of scars across the back of his thigh.

Doc's arms tightened around me when I licked my lips. Ed glanced over his shoulder and winked at me.

I growled softly, knowing he would hear. Allan chuckled. I stared at their asses and ground my teeth.

Doc caressed my neck before tilting my chin up and kissing me right over the pulse on my throat. My breath hitched. The only one of my boyfriends not torturing me was Nikolai and I didn't expect him to hold out long.

Thunder crackled around us and I jumped, not expecting that in the middle of a snowstorm. It did serve to distract me from my arousal, at least a tiny bit.

"Thundersnow!" Ed exclaimed. "I love it when it thunders during a snowstorm."

I took the opportunity to study Ash. He didn't look annoyed, as I had expected, or even like he was trying to ignore our antics. Instead he studied me closely. I glanced at Nikolai. The mage was looking at Ash, just as intently. That might be why he hadn't decided to join in on the fun. Nikolai sensed my attention and glanced over at me.

His eyes flicked to Ash then back to me before he shrugged and hopped up on the bed behind us.

Doc nibbled at my neck.

"Hungry?"

"A little," he admitted.

I tipped my chin back, inviting him.

He hesitated.

"You shouldn't let yourself get too hungry."

Doc sighed. "Later, after you all eat."

I snuggled into his chest again, wondering why he was feeling shy all of a sudden. Ash still studied us, but I couldn't read the expression on his face.

Doc went back to rubbing my back gently while we waited for Ed and Allan to finish dinner. I tried not to drool as I watched their coordinated movements as they went through their nightly dance of preparing us dinner. Someday I really should help them, but it was so nice to just watch.

I reluctantly climbed off of Doc's lap when Ed and Allan finished dinner and we all gathered around the table. Ash ended up on one side of me and Ed sank down on the other. I pushed my knee against his and he put his hand on top of my thigh for a moment, leaving a burning warm spot and making me squirm a little on my cushion.

Thinking about how I could maybe get one or two of my guys alone, or all of them, without kicking Ash out, kept me occupied through dinner.

Once we had finished, I offered my arm to Doc. He shook his head. "You need to keep your strength up," he said. "As soon as this storm breaks, you three have to build us a cabin."

I wrapped my arms around him, inhaling his leather scent as he hugged me tightly. "You sure?"

"I'll be okay."

"Don't starve yourself," I whispered. I knew he was feeling a little uncomfortable with his vampire side after indulging it so deeply when rescuing Ash, but he still needed blood.

"You can have some of mine if you want." Ash stared at the table while he spoke, and I could tell it had taken a fair bit for him to offer.

I glanced up at Doc at the same time Ash did, just in time for us to both see him twist his lips. He cleared the expression from his face quickly enough, but Ash had seen.

Before we could explain what demon blood did to Doc, Ash nodded and headed out the door.

I sighed. "I'll go get him."

"Sofia, be careful of the storm. I don't want to have to rescue someone else from a blizzard."

"I will be." I knew he referred to our adventures at my parents' house during Thanksgiving. I took a minute to throw on my coat and boots and then plunged into the snowstorm after Ash.

Fortunately, he wasn't far. He was leaning against his snow-covered Camaro, arms crossed, shoulders hunched. It was probably a good thing it was snowing, or he might have left.

"Ash, demon blood makes Doc sick."

He turned, head tilted.

"It's actually so bad for him, that the first two times he drank demon blood, it almost killed him. I saved him the first time. The greater demon saved him the second."

Ash touched his neck. "He drank my blood to help the mage free me."

"The greater demon did something to Doc. He can drink demon blood now, but it still isn't good for him. It just won't kill him. She knew he would help Nikolai free you, even if it would nearly kill him to do it."

"Oh." He sighed.

I came up next to him and put my arms around him. "Ash, we want you with us for as long as you want to stay."

He hesitantly hugged me back, finally pulling me close, threading his fingers through my hair as I leaned into his chest, his other hand firm against the small of my back.

Snow swirled around us, but he was warm enough that I didn't get cold while he held me. He tilted his head down so he could lean his cheek against my head. We stood there until my feet got cold. I shifted, and he released me.

"Toes are freezing," I explained.

He squeezed my shoulder. "You should head back."

"You should come with me."

"Thought you might want some time alone with your pack."

Ash was perceptive, but even if the cold didn't bother the demon there was no way I would leave him out in a snowstorm.

"I can wait, Ash. Come join us."

When he hesitated, I grabbed his hand and dragged him back in the direction of the yurt. He didn't resist and soon we were back in the warmth of the yurt, snow melting off of us.

The guys were dealing out cards. Someone had found a deck recently and they had rediscovered the joys of card games. No one said anything, just dealt a hand for Ash and me and made space for him to sit next to me at the table. It put him between me and Doc and once the cards were dealt, Doc put his arm around Ash and gave him a quick side hug, before going back to the game.

Ash might have been fighting back tears, but I sensed that he didn't want any extra attention at the moment, so we just played the card game and stayed close to him while still trying to let him have some space.

Chapter 14

Sofia

"Let's run!" Ed exclaimed.

The storm had abated, and we were ready to be out of the yurt for a little while. It was comfortable, but with six of us in there we were a little crowded. Darkness had fallen early both from the storm and the time of year.

Allan jumped up from the cushion, obviously in agreement.

Ed turned his puppy eyes on me and arched an eyebrow.

He was right, it was time to run. I looked at Doc who smirked and nodded.

"Nikolai, Ash, would you like to join us?" Doc stood and headed over to Allan. He would have to take blood from one of the werewolves to transfer the ability to shift to us.

Nikolai tilted his head. "Run?"

"As a wolf."

Nikolai's eyes widened. He looked at me and I nodded. "I do not know spell to shapeshift."

"Transference," Doc reminded him.

"Ahh."

"I can force the change if you can't do it yourself," Doc explained.

"I will join the pack," Nikolai replied hesitantly, agreeing to the experience.

We all turned to Ash.

"Can you shapeshift?" Doc locked his gaze on Ash.

His eyes darted between Doc, Allan, and me.

"No," he finally replied.

"Do you want to try?" Doc offered in a gentle voice.

Ash hunched his shoulders, gaze going to the ground, but he nodded.

Doc held out his hand to Allan. The werewolf stepped to Doc and slipped his hand into the vampire's. Doc pulled him close and tilted Allan's head back, lowering his fangs to the werewolf's neck. He still hesitated, but finally he took a breath and bit down.

Allan's eyes rolled back in his head. He groaned as Doc took his blood, hands clutching the vampire's back. After a moment, Doc released Allan, though he held the werewolf until he steadied.

Allan's eyes shone and the look he gave Doc would have made me jealous if he'd looked at anyone outside the pack like that.

Doc's gaze was equally heated.

I echoed Allan's groan, completely turned on.

The guys all stared at me, and for a moment I thought the run might be delayed, but we all got a hold of ourselves and refocused on the run.

Doc approached Ash first. "You don't have to."

Ash took a breath and nodded. "I want to."

Doc removed one of the magical reservoir bracelets he wore and sank his fangs into his wrist. Blood welled on his arm and he offered it to Ash. The demon took his arm and hesitantly pulled it to his mouth. Doc shut his eyes when Ash licked the blood, breath quickening.

Though he had to have noticed Doc's reaction, Ash didn't act like he had.

Doc looked at the demon. "You might want to strip."

Ash tugged off his T-shirt. I couldn't help staring at his muscular torso. If I had thought I was turned on before, I about cried when his hands dropped to the button on his jeans.

The guys zeroed in on me and I realized I whimpered out loud.

Ash's eyebrows rose and I blushed hard, ducking my head. Where had that come from? I must be getting greedy, wanting all the men.

Doc licked his lips and turned his attention back to Ash. "Do you think you can change on your own?"

The slither of fabric made me clamp my lips shut against another moan as he finished slipping out of his clothing.

I darted a glance, staring at Nikolai and Allan instead of Ash. Of course, they were both staring appreciatively at the presumably naked demon.

"I don't think I can. Using magic without orders is still difficult."

Ash was having a hard time using his magic anytime he had to really think about what he was doing. More than three hundred years of conditioning had left him a little dependent on others telling him what to do. We were helping him with this, but it would take a while to undo.

"Will you let me help you? I will have to control you."

I turned to look at the two of them. Doc mostly blocked my view of Ash, but I did catch the demon's nod. Fear widened his eyes, but he submitted to Doc's mind control when the vampire took Ash's face in his hands and looked deeply into his husky blue eyes.

It took a while, but finally Ash's skin rippled. He gasped and collapsed to the ground, Doc sinking down with him. He cried out and I watched, fascinated, as his muscles bulged and twisted, his bones stretched or shrank, and white fur sprouted from his skin. It happened quickly, and except for his initial protest, it didn't appear he was in pain.

Ed quickly pulled off his clothing and began his own change so he could be there for Ash.

Ash staggered to his feet, wobbling on four legs. His head swung around, ears forward, hackles up as he worked to understand his new perception.

"It doesn't take too long to get used to," Doc reassured the demon.

Ash huffed and took a few experimental steps before Ed came over and rubbed his cheek against the white wolf's. He followed closely while Ash staggered his way around the yurt until they were at the door.

"Ed will help him get his feet under control while we get the rest of you shifted," Allan explained.

Doc offered his arm to Nikolai next. The mage wrinkled his nose but didn't hesitate to drink the offered blood. Licking Doc's wrist suggestively and pulling matching groans from me and the vampire.

"You all are killing me," I protested.

Allan laughed. "It'll be worth it. We can have the other type of fun later."

It had been a bit of a dry spell with Ash around. We would start building the new cabin soon, and then we could have some privacy. Of course, the way the guys were looking at Ash, well, to be fair, the way everyone but Ed was looking at Ash, maybe we wouldn't need the privacy.

Nikolai shed his clothing and crouched to the ground. He shut his eyes, concentrating, and after a moment, managed to shift on his own.

He also managed four legs a bit more gracefully than Ash had. I wondered if he had some sort of experience doing this before, but I would have to ask later. The dark brown wolf came over and rubbed against my leg. I ran my hand through his thick, silky fur, laughing when he licked my hand.

"Okay, your turn." Doc came over to me. "Ready for this?"

"Hope so."

He bit his wrist and offered it to me. I took his blood, moaning as the power coursed through me. I could feel Allan's energy transfer to me through the blood I drank. Our pack bond let me feel how I needed to shape it and I nodded at Doc. "I've got it."

I slipped out of my clothing and wrapped the wilderness around me, it penetrated my very being and changed me into something far more adapted to its depths than my human form.

The four legs were harder to get used to, but it didn't take long before I managed to coordinate them and it was my turn to rub against Doc and Allan. They pet me and I shivered as each hair transmitted their touch through my skin. So intimate.

I could also smell Doc and Allan's arousal. Now I knew why it caught their attention any time I was turned on. The intoxicating scent pulled me to them.

Allan laughed. "Go outside while we change. Get used to your feet so we can run."

Huffing indignantly, I slunk out of the yurt. Ed, Nikolai, and Ash came over to me. We all sniffed and rubbed on each other, blending our scents. The feel of belonging heightened as we spread our scents on each other.

A minute or so later Doc, now a black wolf, and my darker blond wolf, Allan, joined us and I rubbed on them. Doc wolf grinned at me, licking his lips. His canines were longer than a normal wolf's. It took a little time, but once all of us had thoroughly bathed in everyone's scents, Allan and Ed moved off into the woods.

The rest of us followed, and we started out at a light jog so the three of us not used to four legs could get used to moving. If I didn't think about it, the movements came naturally, and soon I could focus on my surroundings.

The crisp breeze brought so many new smells to my nose that I had a hard time sorting them out. Some I recognized, others I didn't understand until information filtered to me through the pack bond from the real wolves in our group. It was like learning a whole new language, but at least I had a way to cheat as I borrowed my pack mates memories and knowledge.

That musk was a rabbit, an interesting smell, but I caught the idea that the boys were after a deer tonight. The cool dry smell was an outcropping of granite, the one Allan and I had first made love on. Acrid pine tickled my nose and the recent snowstorm left its heavy smell on the air.

Sounds had more meaning now. I heard my pack mates breaths, the sounds of their pads softly covering the snow, feet spreading wide so we didn't sink in far. The soft scratches of ground rodents. The hoot of an owl. The nearly silent flutter of feathers and the squeal of a rodent's life ending. Rustling through the pine needles as the light breeze wandered through the pines.

Though not as strong as the time I had borrowed Doc's vampire vision, I became aware of heat signatures. My pack mates stood out, but soon I could sense the difference between the snow and the trees, as my ability to use my new senses expanded.

My vision dwindled in importance as my nose and ears conveyed so much more information in this form.

Ed chuffed and we all slowed. He tilted his head and I listened, trying to sense what he did. Allan's ears and nose were pointed in the same direction that Ed looked so I focused in that direction.

Heat, nervous energy, musky scent. Deer.

Hunger and excitement warred with each other as my mind caught up to what my nose already knew. The hunt. Food.

Doc shouldered me when I would have taken off after the scent. Obviously, a rookie move, but I couldn't help the step I took before he interrupted me. He gestured with his muzzle toward Ed and Allan, and I understood through the bond that they would lead the hunt.

Ash was somehow part of our shared communication and I sensed agreement from him and the others.

Following Ed's instructions, we fanned out, trotting through the snow. Doc and Allan broke off and circled around. We would attempt to drive the deer to their ambush. I had no idea if these were actual wolf pack tactics, or if they were adapting human ones for the situation, but it didn't matter.

Ash and I flanked to the right and Nikolai went left with Ed.

We broke into a lope, weaving nearly silently through the pines as we bore down on our prey.

I didn't let myself think about what we were doing or I might have faltered, simply let the wolf running through my veins take over, guide me, encourage me to hunt. Hunting was life, and it was the right thing for us to do.

Ed sent instructions through our bond and we altered our course. Allan's fierce joy and Ed's more enthusiastic glee at hunting with a full pack filled me, lifted my paws, made my heart sing.

The deer scented us, but we had allowed that. The four of us closed in, driving the deer toward Doc and Allan. They would take advantage of Doc's vampire nature and Allan's skill to bring the deer down. With inexperienced wolves in the hunt, it was wise to put our best on the take down. Tonight we wanted certain success.

The bitter scent of fear quickened my feet, sped my heart. The deer knew we were coming. The prey sprang from their hiding space and raced away from us.

We ran for a time, driving the deer, relishing the wind rippling through our fur, the ground passing beneath our feet, the feel of pack as we worked in sync to feed the whole group.

Our energy changed as Doc and Allan actively joined the hunt, closing in, bringing us closer to our goal.

Ed ordered us to move and we altered our position moments before the deer turned, seeking freedom. Our shift cut off its escape and sealed its fate as the creature darted right into Doc and Allan's waiting jaws.

The creature squealed as Doc latched onto her throat. Heavy copper scent filled the air. Saliva dripped from my jaws. I flicked my tongue along my lips, mouth open to taste the smell.

Now I had an idea of what Doc experienced when he smelled blood.

Allan leapt, grabbing the deer's haunches and between the two of them, brought the prey down. Doc ended its life quickly, as humanely as he could, lapping the blood from the deer's throat.

Allan tore at the haunches.

I growled softly and the others gave way as I stalked forward. Though I hadn't intended to push Allan off the kill, he made it clear he offered me the first bite, other than the blood Doc had already consumed.

Could I do it?

I let the wolf decide. Hesitantly, I licked at the bloody haunch. Coppery, delicious.

My teeth closed on the warm meat and I pulled. A chunk came away and I chewed, swallowed. I didn't think, just took another hunk of flesh.

That seemed to be the signal. The others dove in. Allan and Ed, well used to feasting on fresh deer, fell in with relish. Ash and Nikolai were more hesitant, but soon joined me, gorging on the steaming meat. Doc licked the blood and we made use of this feast that nature had provided.

With five full grown wolves tearing at the meat, there wasn't much of the deer left by the time we had gorged ourselves. Even Doc acted content, though I wondered how deer blood compared to human. Maybe in this form it was just as good for him.

Once we finished, we licked our lips and cleaned our paws and the sudden urge to howl came over me. I'd never heard the guys howl before, outside of the one time they had rescued me from the Andersons, and I wondered why.

As if sensing where my thoughts were headed, Ed huffed a wolfy sigh and shook his head like a human would.

I tilted mine, wondering why we couldn't howl.

The knowledge came to me. *Too close to people.*

I flopped on the ground and grunted. That was lame.

The other brown wolf in our group snorted and blue motes of energy rose from him. Apparently, I could still sense, and probably even use my magic, like Nikolai was. He was making a barrier.

Satisfaction came across the pack bond as he tilted his muzzle to the sky and let loose with a wailing cry.

Ed and Allan perked their ears, almost quivering with excitement. They couldn't take it any longer and both added their yipping call to Nikolai's song.

Doc and then Ash joined the song and finally I added my higher pitched call to theirs.

Though there weren't exactly words, we were communicating. While we knew no one else should be able to hear us, we sang that this was our territory, our pack, and we would defend it.

The howl vibrated through us, binding us even more tightly, until I couldn't tell where one of us ended and the other started.

We called our togetherness to the heavens until we came to a rightful end of the song and fell silent.

Ed and Allan especially, were still nearly vibrating with excitement at being able to make noise. It felt right. It was what pack did.

Ed got up from where he sat and pounced Nikolai, mock wrestling with him, to thank him for letting us experience this.

Nikolai, though new to wolf form, was still a better fighter and had Ed pinned in short order.

Doc got in on it, tackling Nikolai off of Ed and they scuffled for a while, more evenly matched. Nikolai had more skill, but Doc was far stronger, even in wolf form. Ed finally settled the matter, darting in at the last minute and pinning Nikolai to the ground.

Allan woofed slightly in laughter and Ash came and sat next to me, shoulders touching, while we watched the others roughhouse.

Finally, tiredness dragged at us, and we sensed it was time to return to our den. This time Allan led the way, and we all trotted around the edge of the property, taking a lightly roundabout way back to the yurt, marking the edges of our territory with all of our scents before heading through the woods back to where we could sleep.

I was too tired to attempt to change back on my own, and I guessed that I would shift just like the guys did, in my sleep. I nosed my way into the yurt and launched myself onto the bed. Ed, Allan, Doc, and Nikolai did the same, but Ash went over to the cot where he had been sleeping.

Allan yipped at him sharply and Ed jumped off the bed and shoved Ash toward us.

For a minute the white wolf stared, as if uncertain, but another push from Ed got him to jump on the bed and join us in one large pile of puppies.

As Ed had said at least a few times, pack should sleep together, and Ash was part of our pack.

We all curled up in a tangle of limbs, resting on each other, comfortable and falling easily into sleep.

Chapter 15

Ed

Waking up in a pile of naked men would have been weird if it weren't his pack, Ed reflected the next morning, feeling more content than he had in a long time. Someone was jabbing him in the back with some morning wood, but he didn't really care. His head rested on Sofia's thigh, and her scent intoxicated him.

He tilted his head so he could look at more than her hip. Ash had curled up around Sofia, his platinum blond hair draped over her chest, covering one breast almost completely. Doc lay curled around Ash. Nikolai was curled up on the other side of Sofia and was the one pressed into Ed's back. Allan had squeezed in and was using her other hip as a pillow.

Judging by the breathing, he was the first one to wake up. He recalled that Doc tended to sleep longer after running with him and Allan and he guessed the other three would, too. It was not something their bodies were used to, and they would probably feel a little hung over today.

He hoped that they wanted to run again. He hoped taking the deer hadn't turned any of them off. Even Ash. Having Ash in the pack felt right, and he wanted the demon to stay, wanted him to run with them again soon. And Nikolai…thinking to cast the spell so they could howl? Ed hadn't been able to howl like that in years. He sighed contentedly, full of love for his pack.

He was drifting back to sleep when Nikolai bolted upright.

That woke everyone else, though Sofia was still buried.

"What's wrong?" Doc grumbled.

"Someone tripped wards," Nikolai said warily.

"Fuck." Doc scrambled out of bed.

Nikolai waved his hand and cast his cleaning spell over all of them. That was probably just as well since they probably all smelled a bit earthy. Ed didn't mind, but he was a werewolf.

Everyone dressed quickly while Doc and Nikolai slipped out of the yurt.

A quick glance at the comforter showed that they really needed to clean that, too. Probably before they had guests in the yurt. Wolf hair, some streaks of mud, and he smelled a hint of deer blood.

"Hey, Sofia." His heart stuttered when she turned her gray eyes on him. Lavender motes from the magic she held danced through them. Her lips curled into a pleased smile and he wanted to melt into a puddle at her feet.

"Yeah?"

"Could you clean the comforter. It's a bit, uh, wolfy."

Her eyes crinkled in amusement as her smile broadened and she nodded, waving her hands over the bed. For good measure, she included the rest of the yurt.

Sofia's easy expression reassured him. She didn't act upset or repulsed by the run the night before. If anything, she looked relaxed despite the unexpected visitor.

He heard a trio of footsteps trudging through the snow. Doc was nearly silent, and he might not have noticed the vampire if he hadn't been accompanied by the quiet, but still human Nikolai and someone else. The third person didn't even attempt to walk quietly.

"You live in a big tent?" The voice belonged to Doc's old *friend* Adriana.

What was she doing here? He had known the pack wouldn't be done with her, but he had hoped the real world wouldn't intrude on them until at least after the new year. Couldn't they have waited until afternoon? He growled under his breath.

Sofia put her hand on his arm and squeezed sympathetically.

"It is a yurt," Nikolai replied stiffly.

"You live in a yurt?" Adriana rephrased her question.

"Temporarily," Doc said as he threw back the flap that covered the entryway and gestured for Adriana to enter.

"Why?"

"Because we are redesigning Doc's cabin. We will rebuild shortly," Nikolai snapped.

Ash flinched, but only Ed noticed. The four of them were all standing there staring, almost like they'd gotten caught doing something wrong. It was pretty awkward, and he cast about for some way to make it better.

His stomach grumbled. Food. He could make food. The non-werewolves might not be hungry after the feast last night, but he and Allan were.

He rushed over to the small kitchen area and put the kettle on to boil while he started everything else. Allan, probably understanding what he was doing, dove in to help.

Ed listened while he went through the familiar routine of making breakfast.

After a quick greeting, Adriana jumped right into why she was visiting. Or at least part of why, by the glances she kept darting toward Doc. She really wanted to know something about him, too.

"Nikolai, your Russian counterparts have never heard of you. They say you're to return to Russia immediately."

Nikolai snorted. "Am not from Russia. Am from Detroit. Will not be going anywhere I don't wish to."

"Detroit?"

Ed didn't need a werewolf nose to smell her disbelief. He glanced at them while the pancakes cooked.

"Yes, Michigan. Big city, dirty. Lots of cars. Much happier here. Free country, yes? Don't need permission to live in Colorado." He crossed his arms.

"Can you, uh, prove that?"

"Of course." Nikolai waved a hand negligently.

She arched her eyebrows.

Nikolai's eyes narrowed and he dug out a wallet and handed Adriana his driver's license.

Ed knew Doc had some pretty good contacts in the making up new identities department. He hoped Nikolai's would withstand a heavy look. Adriana took a picture of his license and sent it to someone before handing it back to the Russian.

"Who trained you."

"Family, of course. They died in a fire."

"Convenient," Adriana muttered.

Nikolai's face reddened. "Nothing convenient about it," he snarled.

"My apologies." Adriana apparently realized she had hit on a delicate subject and backed off.

"And you trained Sofia?"

"The demon trained Sofia." Nikolai continued to glare at Adriana. "I simply filled in a few gaps."

She shook her head and glanced at her phone when it beeped. Her frown deepened before she sighed.

"Whoever made up your background did a very thorough job."

"Adriana, why are you here?" The menace in Doc's voice cooled the temperature in the yurt a few degrees.

She shivered. "I, uh, will of course inform the Russians that your background is properly accounted for even though no one has heard of you." She stammered for a moment before getting her composure back. She turned on Doc. "You are not a mage. You don't even have the same ID information that you did the last time I ran across you."

"Do you?" he asked, voice no less frosty. "Not all mages age normally. You certainly haven't. Does your ID have your actual birthday on it?"

She blinked.

"Maybe you should let it go," Nikolai suggested.

Ed got the next round of pancakes cooking, really glad he was just a werewolf and didn't really have anything to hide. At least from Adriana.

Ash took plates and set the table.

On reflection, he cursed himself for making food. If Adriana stayed, she'd be paying a lot more attention to Doc than normal. Would he be able to get away with not eating anything?

Sofia had perched on the edge of the bed and was glaring at Adriana, lavender flashing in her eyes. If Adriana wasn't careful Sofia was going to roast her. The burning scent of anger rolled off his mate.

"So, you tore your cabin down because you didn't like it, and are all living in a yurt? With one bed?" She was clearly trying to change the subject, but she chose a poor topic.

"The cabin was a casualty in the war with the Andersons," Doc bit out. "We're rebuilding it now that the Andersons are handled. We didn't want it to get burnt down twice in short order. Figured that would gather too much attention."

"I see." She turned her attention to Sofia and flinched at the glare she received. "Are you comfortable with the arrangements."

"If I wasn't, I wouldn't be here." Sofia scowled.

"Ash, have you made any further decisions on your path now that you are free of the Andersons?" She switched subjects again.

Ed knew they were all grateful for the help Adriana and her people had provided, but there was so much they should have done long before Sofia had ever gotten involved, that no one was feeling terribly charitable toward those invasive questions.

"I am staying here." He stared at the plate of pancakes he held, looking uncertain, but his voice was firm.

"Very well. Should you change your mind we will help you find new accommodations. Unrelated to that question, none of us have had a chance to talk to a demon. If you become willing to answer questions for us, please contact me. We have a lot of them, but we also understand you've been through quite an ordeal. We also could have use for you. All of you." She looked at everyone in the yurt for a moment. "You're a powerful group and there are many people out there like the Andersons who have gone unchecked for far too long because we simply don't have the ability to take them on. You do. Think about it. We'll be in touch." Adriana headed toward the door and Nikolai pulled the flap open for her.

We heard her car start, but no one moved until Nikolai nodded and took a deep breath. "She is outside the wards. Now you're cooking like I do." Nikolai gestured toward the pancakes.

Ed yelped and scooped them off the magical stovetop. "They're only a little singed," he replied defensively.

Nikolai laughed.

Sofia groaned and sank down at the low table, sitting on one of the cushions. Ash sat next to her and Doc sat on the demon's other side. Allan claimed Sofia's other side and Nikolai sat next to Allan. Ed squeezed in between the mage and Doc.

"Are you okay?" He hoped nothing was wrong. He scented the air, but she smelled all right.

"I just want that vacation I mentioned." She leaned her forehead on the table for a moment before sighing and grabbing a few of the pancakes.

Doc handed her a mug of tea he had somehow procured.

"What kind of vacation?" Ed shoved a pancake in his mouth, ignoring the burnt side.

"Just. A vacation. Here. Not having to go anywhere unless we want to. Not having to deal with anyone else. Just the pack."

Doc smiled. "Hopefully, we can manage at least a day of that."

She leaned against Ash and put her forehead on his shoulder. "Please?"

The demon awkwardly put an arm around her.

She stayed in that position when she spoke. "Okay, let's stop talking about all of that. Let's talk about last night."

When she didn't continue right away, Ed stopped breathing. She'd hated it. She was never going to run with them again. Fuck, he should never have pushed her to run with them.

"I don't even know what to say, or how to say it." She sat up again.

Damn it, damn it, damn it. Ed kicked himself.

"Fuck that was amazing," she finally breathed out. "I mean...the way the wind whispered through my fur. The scents, the sounds. Hell, the hunt...we have to do that again soon. Like, all the time."

His heart skipped about five beats and then he finally figured out how to breathe again.

"You liked it?" He winced at the way his voice squeaked.

"Duh. What part of 'fuck that was amazing' did you not hear?" She grinned at him.

He blushed. "I was worried."

She didn't give him a hard time about it, just accepted his emotion.

"I also enjoyed running as a wolf. I would enjoy doing again." Nikolai agreed.

Ash nodded. "I felt like I belonged for once."

The sadness in his voice sobered them, but only a little. Sofia and Doc both put their arms around the demon.

"You belong with us, Ash," Sofia insisted. "For as long as you want to be with us."

Ash twisted around until he was looking at her. He cupped her chin with his hand and brushed a strand of hair out of her face. She didn't pull away, meeting his cautious gaze with her own open one.

No one spoke, or really dared to breath. Ash needed to feel accepted, needed to know that they wanted him around, and no one wanted to do anything to push the demon away. He'd been mistreated for so long, Ed knew it would take a while for him to trust the rest of the pack, but hopefully they'd get a chance to prove to him that they really did want him there.

Sofia leaned forward, inviting Ash in.

He could sense through their pack bond that everyone felt peace with this move and knew Sofia felt that acceptance, too.

Ash wasn't part of the bond, and he hesitated. His hand dropped away from her chin and his shoulders slumped.

Sofia clenched her jaw briefly before leaning forward, tangling her fingers in Ash's long hair, and pulling his mouth to hers.

The demon stiffened, and she didn't push him beyond pressing her lips to his. After a moment, he returned his hands to her face, holding her as he kissed her deeply, as if he were kissing Sofia to her very soul, trying to decide if her acceptance was real, or just a trick. Ed smelled Ash's desperate hope and desire conflicting with fear.

His heart broke a little for the demon. Three hundred years, or more, he had said he fought his bonds. Ed couldn't even imagine. There was no way any of them would be able to undo several lifetimes of torture, but he wanted to try.

Without breaking off their kiss, Sofia moved until she was straddling Ash's lap. She left one hand in his hair, as if to keep him from running away, but she dropped the other one down to the demon's broad shoulder and caressed his arm.

Ash rumbled in his throat, and some of his fear scent dissipated, replaced more heavily by lust.

Ed glanced at the others. They looked as content as he felt while the demon lost himself in Sofia's embrace.

They finally came up for air. Ash stared at Sofia with wonder in his mottled blue and white eyes.

"You know," she said slyly. "I had always thought you were just after Doc."

Ash's jaw dropped and he cleared his throat, his eyes darting over to the vampire, a hint of panic overcoming the wonder.

"Uh…"

"It's okay. Ed's the only one not after him," Sofia whispered and pressed her lips to Ash's again. "He is pretty hot," she said against his lips.

Doc smirked, possibly finally owning up to that particular aspect of their pack dynamic.

"Mmhm," Ash agreed as he focused on the woman in his arms.

Ed quietly got up, working on clearing the table, though Sofia's hungry moan distracted him. Ash cupped her ass, holding her close. The rest of them had the table cleared by the time Sofia let Ash go. Though the demon certainly wasn't complaining. He looked happier than Ed ever remembered seeing him.

"Should we start the cabin?" Nikolai suggested. "It will snow again soon."

Ash tore his gaze away from Sofia and glanced around the yurt, looking slightly panicked again. Obviously, he had known everyone was there, but maybe he hadn't quite thought through the implications of kissing Sofia.

Doc, probably trying to reassure Ash that it was okay, put his arm around Ash's waist.

If he hadn't been watching the demon, he wouldn't have caught the hint of mischief that flashed thorough his eyes. Ash turned quickly and grabbed Doc, pressing his lips to the vampire's.

Doc's eyes went wide, but he didn't have any reason not to kiss Ash back and Ed found himself wondering just how good of a kisser the vampire was. He was certainly getting a lot of practice recently.

Nikolai huffed, rolling his eyes. Sofia laughed.

Ash released Doc, a smile tugging at his lips. "Yes, we probably should go build a cabin."

Sofia hopped off the bed where she had perched while watching Ash and Doc. "Great. I can't wait to get this done. Bigger showers, here we come!"

Chapter 16

Sofia

Kissing Ash was definitely the right thing to do. He had a spring in his step I'd never seen, and though I wouldn't exactly call him cheerful, he stood straighter and a small smile tugged at his lips. The move he'd pulled with Doc had showed he was relaxing a little.

If only I had been able to wake up more slowly and enjoy the tangle of limbs and possibilities it had presented.

We probably had been a bit short with Adriana considering she and her people had come through as they said they would and helped take out the Andersons, but her questions were getting frustrating and worrisome. Of course, she also presented an interesting possibility. Especially with Ash in our pack, we were powerful. Should we help others? Or should we stay hidden away in the mountains? Could we do both?

All I really wanted to do at the moment was enjoy my guys and work my way through college.

My phone chimed while I pushed my feet into my snow boots.

Mom: We'll be there in a week if the weather cooperates.

Sofia: Sounds great. Got a place to stay?

Mom: Yes.

She sent the name of one of the bed and breakfasts in town. I was impressed she had gotten reservations. Ski season was in full swing. I'd been a little worried that they would want to stay with us.

Nikolai handed me my jacket. His calloused hands caressed mine and he winked.

I wanted to fold myself into his arms, but we had a cabin to start and snow to beat. The storm bore down on us with a heavy pressure that had me a little worried now that I focused on it.

"We should be able to get this all done today," Ash said as we headed out into the crisp mountain air.

"Really?" I couldn't imagine building an entire cabin in one day.

"The shell, anyway. The little details will take longer." Ash glanced at the sky. "We'll likely be snowed in for a few days, so we'll have plenty of time to rest and put the finishing touches on everything."

"Wow. Okay." I hadn't expected it to go that fast.

"We're all powerful," Ash explained. "You and Nikolai work together well. It will make this all easier."

Nikolai didn't comment and I glanced over at him. A slight frown creased his brow as he studied the spot where the old cabin had stood.

"Nikolai?"

Blue magic danced in his dark eyes. "Ready?" He didn't answer my unspoken question, but I sensed confidence through our bond.

"You and Nikolai should join your magic and then let me in. I can guide us."

Nikolai called his magic and I groaned as it washed through me, tugging my magic to the surface and lighting me on fire. Working magic with him hadn't affected me this strongly in a while and I wondered if Nikolai had done it on purpose. His hands slid around my shoulders and he pulled me against him as we held our magic and waited for Ash.

The demon hesitated, staring at the ground, platinum hair obscuring his face as he hid from us.

Finally, I reached out my hand and took his. "It's okay, Ash. Join us."

"It's so different with the two of you. I've had to work magic for and with that family for so long and there was never any affection. To feel the love in your bond." He shivered. "It's frightening."

"How can we help?" I squeezed his hand.

"I'm just..." He didn't finish but I could guess. He was afraid of letting us in, of getting hurt again.

"Ash, I can't promise we'll never hurt you, but we won't do it on purpose. Just like you don't know you won't ever hurt us. Mistakes happen. I can promise that we do want you with us, and that we will do our best to avoid causing you pain."

He tilted his head so that he looked at me through the long fall of his hair. My Viking demon was breaking my heart with his fear, but I couldn't make this decision for him.

Ash took a deep breath and called his amber magic. He took a step closer and kept a hold of my hand, but tension sang through the uneasy set of his shoulders. His amber magic melded with our dark blue and lavender, creating a colorful lightshow that stood out against the white backdrop of snow that covered everything.

"Ready?"

"Yes," Nikolai answered for both of us.

Ash let go of my hand and moved so he could touch both of our shoulders. His warmth washed through us as we let him into our bond so he could direct our efforts.

"Oh," I gasped as the raging fire of his magic washed through me. I'd felt it before, when I'd taken his magic from Doc, and my body accepted it, pulling more from him and feeding it to Nikolai.

The Russian rumbled in pleasure. "Benefits to working in groups you trust," he murmured.

Ash didn't respond, but we could sense his cautious hope at our acceptance. After we all had a moment to get used to being melded together by our magic, Ash gently took control. I could see what Nikolai meant about trust, though. Ash could have controlled both of us completely, instead of just directing our magic.

Still, we had a cabin to build and the land was willing to aid us. Now I understood what Nikolai meant when he said he wasn't good at elemental magic. Where he could shape some of the land's magic to his will, the environment around us practically begged for Ash to take its magic and use it.

"It helps that the land likes us," Ash explained when I commented on it. "It wants us to stay."

Slowly, we gathered the elements we needed from the land around us. At some point we also pulled energy from Ed, Allan, and Doc and mixed it in with the power from the land. Our pack bond flared to life as we told the land everything we hoped for in our new home.

The power of this place responded enthusiastically. Trees nearing the end of their lives volunteered, stone, soil, and even the transient nature of the snow came at our call and solidified as Ash wove the energies into the design we had come up with over the last week.

I didn't know how long we worked, all of us joined with our land to build our new home, but Ash was right, we did get the shell done in one go. After it was formed, he slowly released us.

"Wow." Darkness had fallen but the moon was full and though our immediate area was bare of snow, it was bright enough that I could see what we had created.

Doc, Ed, and Allan came over to us. Ed put his arms around me and I leaned against his solid warmth.

Exhilaration at what we had done warred with the fatigue that pulled at my limbs. Ed kept me upright. Doc supported Nikolai, and Allan stood close to Ash in case the Demon needed help, but he seemed okay.

"That's amazing," Ed breathed out.

Managing to push some of the weariness away, I walked forward until I could touch what we'd created. Stone gave way to logs as I ran my hand up the wall. Slate covered the roof. I touched the storm shutters and lightly ran my hand over the smooth glass before peeking inside.

"Go on," Ash suggested.

I hurried to the door and worked the handle. Lever style so wolves could open the door easily.

Grinning, I rushed inside. Beautiful wooden floors creaked ever so slightly under my feet as if the house spoke to me as I moved from room to room. It was just as we had imagined it. The large fireplace, a bigger kitchen, individual rooms for everyone, and a large master bedroom. I ran my hands over everything as I explored and the energy of the house responded to my touch, tingling up my arm and down my spine, caressing me.

I stuck my head in the master bathroom. Large shower, large bathtub. I couldn't wait to give them all a try. Each room had a window seat with a fantastic view. Something else I had wanted, and the others had agreed with.

Laughing with joy at what we had created, I ran back outside and gestured for the guys to come inside.

"This one won't burn," Nikolai said as he explored. "Magic won't allow it. Land will fight back if this place is attacked."

"The land likes all of us here," Ash said again. "It resisted when I burned the old place down. It simply didn't have the power to fight me then."

I went over and hugged Ash. "In reality, you did us a favor. Look at what we've made."

His lips curled, but the smile didn't reach his eyes.

Allan came over and put his arms around Ash and me. "You really did. This is fantastic."

Ed joined in the group hug, then Doc and Nikolai, all of us pouring our love and appreciation into the frightened demon.

He spoke hesitantly after a few minutes. "You're welcome? I guess?"

I laughed. "It all works out. Guys, can we move the bed in here. I want to sleep in our new cabin tonight."

"You three rest," Doc ordered. "We'll take care of moving everything we have over. We can make a list of the other things we need to buy or make and build a plan while we're snowed in."

∞ ∞ ∞

Sure enough, the next storm hit hard. We could have used magic to get out if we really needed to, but there was no need to go anywhere for a few days. By the time I woke up the next morning, snuggled in with my pack, the house communicated to us that we were buried in snow.

"That's going to take some getting used to," I said, wrapping my arms more tightly around Ash and burying my face in his long hair.

Ash tensed under my arms. "What is?"

"The house isn't talking to you?"

"Ah, no." He sounded incredulous for a moment.

"Yeah, it just told me to stay in bed, everything is buried in snow." I grinned.

"Did it now," Doc rumbled, pressed up against my back.

"Well, I might have added the stay in bed part."

"Is really talking to you?" Nikolai propped himself up on his elbow and looked at me. He had fallen asleep on the other side of Ash.

"Yes."

"That's so cool," Ed added from the other side of Doc.

"I like the stay in bed part," Allan agreed.

"What, not a starving werewolf this morning?" I joked.

"We ate really late so we could sleep in," Ed admitted.

"Good." I snuggled back in with Ash and Doc rested his cheek against me. We all wore sleeping clothes and had a light sheet thrown over us. The house was the perfect temperature to keep me comfortable.

"This seriously is the best," I murmured. The house pulsed joy at my acceptance.

Ash took my wrist and caressed the smooth spot where my magical pack tattoo had prevented scaring from the binding cuffs. The skin there was very sensitive and I moaned, pressing into Ash's back.

"Starting shit?" Ed sounded intrigued by the idea.

"Counting pawprints," Ash replied.

"What?" I propped myself up so I could see my wrist where he had it cradled in his hand. "Oh. See, now you're really stuck with us, Ash." Sometime, probably when we were building the cabin, an amber paw print had joined the rest. Now I had six, Amber, Blue, Lavender, Gray, Sky blue, and black. One for each of my guys and me.

"I didn't do it on purpose." Fear threaded through Ash's voice and his muscles went rock hard where I leaned over him.

"It is Sofia's fault," Nikolai replied. "She claims people."

"Hey, you said it yourself when we claimed you. We couldn't have done it if everyone didn't agree."

"True." Nikolai twisted around to face Ash. "It's good." He took Ash's wrist and traced the smooth skin that disrupted his more extreme scars from the years of being bound. "See. One for each of us."

Ash sucked in a breath as Nikolai touched the sensitive skin.

I snuggled back against him, and Doc squeezed me tight. It had taken a bit of convincing to get Ash to snuggle into bed with us last night. He wanted to be there, he was just scared. If we had excluded him, I had no doubt that someone, probably me, would have started things with the guys already. As it was, I still wanted to start shit, I just wasn't sure how Ash felt about group activities and I didn't want to chase him out of the bedroom.

Ash's breath quickened as Nikolai continued to drag his fingers over the demon's arm. I hadn't been completely sure if Nikolai was just into vampires or if he actually liked men, too. As he brushed his fingers up Ash's arm, sliding over the demon's shoulder and then traced a line up his neck, I decided Nikolai liked vampires, women, and men, possibly in that order.

Ash tilted his neck as Nikolai traced his way along the demon's jaw before tangling his fingers in Ash's hair and pulling the demon to him.

I loosened my grip so I didn't restrict him, though I left my arm around the demon's waist. Doc, Ed, and Allan watched, all of us curious as to how this would go.

Nikolai pressed his lips to Ash's. The demon only hesitated a moment before returning the mage's kiss. Tension still corded his muscles, but he dug his fingers into Nikolai's hip.

The mage groaned and pressed into him, trapping my arm between their bare chests. I slid forward, sandwiching Ash firmly between us. Ash's skin burned hot under my lips as I kissed his shoulder, then worked my way to his neck, staying soft with my touches. While I enjoyed rough handling, I guessed Ash had probably experienced enough pain in his life that what he needed right now was tenderness.

I freed my hand from between the two men and traced my fingers down Ash's muscular side. He and Nikolai came up for air about the time I reached his hip. I slid my fingers under his sleeping pants and continued to trace his hip. Ash panted, a low groan escaping his lips as I moved my fingers up and trailed them gently along his stomach, caressing Nikolai at the same time as I worked my way up to his chest.

Nikolai moaned appreciatively.

Ash twisted around until he could kiss me. I didn't let him hesitate, just dove in, pressing my lips to his, while Nikolai went to work on Ash's neck and shoulders, brushing his long hair out of the way so he could get to skin.

I devoured Ash's lips while his hands slipped under my light shirt. Another pair of warm hands joined Ash's, tugging my shirt. One of my werewolves. I broke off my kiss with Ash long enough to glance over. Ed's sky-blue eyes shone over a happy grin before he pulled my shirt off.

Ash tried to pull away, maybe to let Ed have me, but I grabbed his shoulder, meeting his eyes. "Stay?"

He raised his eyebrows. "Are you sure?"

"Yes," Ed answered for us.

Ash studied us for a minute before his eyes trailed down my naked torso, caressing me with a look, making me feel tight and loose at the same time with the hunger in those husky blue eyes.

He still didn't touch me, and Nikolai finally took his hand and put it on my chest, just above my breast before burying his face in Ash's neck.

The demon's eyelids fluttered closed and his lips parted with pleasure. His hand trailed lower, cupping me, playing with one of my nipples until it was a hard peak in his fingers, warming my skin and making me melt inside.

Ed dragged his hand down my ribs until he could hook his fingers in my pants and tug at them.

I lifted my hips and he slid them off. His lips worked their way down my back, over my hip, burning through me.

Pressing my lips to Ash's, I pushed on his shoulder until he rolled onto his back. I slid my leg over his stomach until I straddled him. His firm erection pressed into me, the thin layer of his sleeping pants all that was between us.

Ash panted, eyes wide, burning into me with a combination of desire and fear. Placing my hands on his chest, I leaned forward until my mouth hovered above his. "I'm not going to hurt you," I breathed onto his lips.

He worked his hands up my hips, burning fire along my sides until he gripped me around the waist. I waited, letting him make the decisions. I had made sure he knew he was wanted, now everything else was up to him.

Finally, his lips twitched into a wicked smile and he brushed them against mine, before seizing hold of me and flipping us over until he was on top, pressed against my core, heavy weight pushing down on me. He leaned on one elbow, his other hand raking a trail of pleasure down my body as he moved it lower, until he cupped my hip.

I moaned into his lips as he devoured me, claiming all of my attention as he ground into me with his hips. Already soaked, I ached for more and I pushed back, hooking my leg over his firm ass.

"You sure?" He whispered, though his voice conveyed strength I hadn't heard in him before. More confidence. He knew I wanted him, and at least right now he believed it.

"Very," I replied with a grin and slid my fingers into the hem of his pants, tugging at them until he helped me take them off.

I was distantly aware that the others still surrounded us, but they had backed off, letting Ash and I have this moment together.

He pressed slowly into me and I arched up, tilting my hips as he filled me. Ash watched me as he pushed into me, and I tried to let him see how good he was making me feel at that moment.

He filled me completely, and I groaned in pleasure as he pulled out slowly.

"Ash, I'm glad you're with us," I gasped out.

The demon paused, shooting a quick glance around as if he had forgotten the others, but whatever he saw from the rest of the pack must have reassured him because he returned his attention to me, picking up some speed as he filled me again.

He moved one hand to my breasts and kissed along my jaw until he nibbled at my neck, just below my ear.

I grabbed his hips and pulled him into me with more force, not wanting him to be careful with me.

"Sofia." His breath tickled my neck. "I don't want to hurt you, either."

"You won't," I answered. "But if you're about to, I'll let you know."

He took me at my word, thrusting harder, until I was panting with need. Pressure built in my core, begging for release.

I dug my fingers into Ash's firm ass as Nikolai slipped his hand between us and brushed his fingers along my clit.

"Yes," I hissed.

Ash reclaimed my lips with his mouth while his thrusts and Nikolai's skillful fingers brought me to the verge and then sent me crashing over.

I cried out as pleasure ripped through me. Ash kept going, bringing me close again as he groaned and came inside me, shaking with his release. Nikolai sent me over the edge again just after Ash and the demon clutched me as he shook.

Ash collapsed onto my chest, face buried in my neck, and I thought he might have been crying.

I held him, arms and one leg wrapped around him.

Nikolai held the demon from the other side, then Doc, Allan, and even Ed found a way to squeeze into our group hug.

No one said anything, letting Ash recover on his own. After a few minutes, he slid out of me and the guys backed off a little, giving him some space.

He met my gaze with his, husky blue eyes shining with unshed tears. "Not sure you're going to be able to get rid of me now," he said quietly.

I smirked at him. "After that, I hope not."

Ash blushed, but the wariness lifted from his eyes. He leaned on an elbow next to me.

Ed ran a hand up my arm and I turned to face him, grinning. He arched an eyebrow and my smile widened as I leaned toward him.

He kissed me, wrapping his arm around my shoulders and pulling him close to him. We lost ourselves in each other, tongues exploring. He dragged his hands up my back and I hooked a leg over his hips. One of his hands wandered lower, while the other gripped my hair gently, but firm enough to give him control of me.

I groaned, loving him taking control of me. Another pair of strong, warm hands gripped my wrists. Allan.

The older werewolf pulled my hands above my head, then, as if he and Ed had talked about this, flipped me over so I was on my stomach. He pulled me forward until I could reach his erection with my mouth if I wanted to. He didn't demand anything.

While I was contemplating the position, Ed grabbed my hips and raised my butt up in the air.

I got my knees under me. Allan kept my hands pinned and Ed kept control of my hips. I wasn't completely trapped but getting out of their strong grips would have taken magic, or a simple request. Heat pooling in my core, I squirmed against their hold, letting them control me.

Ed rumbled in pleasure.

I scooted forward, taking Allan in my mouth. He groaned and released one of my hands so I could grip him and work him with my mouth and my hand.

We both gasped as Ed pushed swiftly into me from behind. It took a few tries, but we got a rhythm down, him shoving into me, me working on Allan. Before long, Allan's grip on my wrist tightened, and he tangled his fingers in my short hair. He didn't control my movements, but cupped my head as I brought him pleasure.

"Sofia," Allan warned me.

"Mmmm...." I moaned around him, my own core responding to Ed's hand on my clit and his erection thrusting into me. I gasped as heat and pleasure pooled through me and exploded.

"Oh, God," Allan cried out, thrusting into my mouth and getting his release at the same time I did, hands clenching, body trembling.

Ed joined us a moment later, his own gasp of pleasure sending tingles through my body as we all collapsed into a messy, panting puppy pile.

Drunk with pleasure, I lay there. Limp and not really willing to move. What a way to wake up. My heart swelled with love for my men.

After a while, Ed and Allan slowly pulled away from me. I grumbled in a protest that was quickly cut off as Nikolai's strong, calloused hands dragged me across the bed and into his arms.

"You did not like my last shower. Must see if you approve of the new one."

"I liked it!" I objected.

"Said it was not big enough." He picked me up. "Doc, you must supervise."

Several low chuckles met Nikolai's proclamation as he carried me into the new master bathroom. Doc joined us a moment later.

Nikolai set me down in the shower, which was quite a bit larger than the one in the old cabin and certainly larger than the small one Nikolai had magicked for us. Smooth limestone made up the walls of the shower, and lightly frosted glass doors closed it off from the rest of the bathroom. The house's magic tingled along my skin when Nikolai set me down and held me long enough for my shaky legs to support me. Once he stepped back the water poured out of the showerhead, just the perfect temperature.

"Wow, that's freaking amazing."

The magic pulsed with pleasure.

"So is that."

"Yes, I felt that, too. Quite amazing. So, how is shower?" Nikolai crossed his arms and stared at me.

"Um." I ducked under the water, letting some of it rinse out my mouth, and slick some of the sweat from my body. "Perfect."

"Good." Nikolai said, but didn't make any move to join me.

Doc wore an amused expression on his face.

I shrugged, found soap, and started to clean myself, though I kept an eye on Nikolai as I ran the soap suggestively over my breast.

His eyes widened, but he clenched his jaw, clearly intent on acting insulted about my assessment of his last shower.

Doc chuckled, slipped his hands around Nikolai's waist, and pulled his pants down.

The mage grumbled, and though it had been obvious before that he was turned on, now he was turned on and naked.

"There is a problem with the shower," I purred.

"What?" the mage muttered. Maybe he had been a little annoyed.

"I'm all alone."

"I can fix that problem." Doc slipped his arm around Nikolai's waist and half dragged, half carried him into the shower with me.

"See, room for three is a good thing, Nikolai," Doc caressed the mage's name with his voice and Nikolai's expression softened considerably.

"It wasn't that I didn't like your shower," I said as I put my hands on his chest. "It was that I couldn't fit more than me and Allan in there."

"Ahh. I understand now." Nikolai winked before kissing me on the forehead. "So, how would you like to break in shower?"

"Sex is always a good way to break things in," I murmured and nibbled at his jaw.

"Up for a little more?" Doc moved around behind me, hands on my hips.

"Yeah." I turned so I faced my vampire and twined my fingers in his wet hair, pulling his lips to mine. Nikolai pressed into me from behind and I stood sandwiched between them

Water warmed us, making us slick and my body slid against theirs as I shifted around, rubbing my stomach against Doc's firm erection, and my ass against Nikolai's. They groaned and Doc captured my mouth with his, while Nikolai bit at my neck.

"Sofia, would you like us both at once?" Nikolai asked as his hands wrapped around me to fondle my breasts where the pressed against Doc's chest.

215

"I...sure." My heart raced at the idea, and I was a little nervous. Doc's hands tightened on me. I was sure my nervousness called to the predator he was. He probably also liked the idea. He and Nikolai were close, and this would be a whole new level of intimacy.

"Don't have to," he murmured as he continued to nibble on me.

"I want to try, at least once. I've never done anything like that before."

He rumbled appreciatively as he played with my nipples and Doc's chest at the same time. "We will stop any time you want."

I nodded.

Doc reclaimed my lips while Nikolai called on his magic. I cried out as he pushed it through all of us. Doc shuddered against me. He was nearly as sensitive to the magical resonance Nikolai and I had as I was. Probably because he'd taken so much of our blood over the last few months.

Calling up my magic, I did the same, until blue and lavender motes swirled around us and we all trembled. Nikolai dropped his hand to my clit and rubbed. I arched up against both of them, gasping as his hands, now slick with water, magical lube?, caressed my sensitive nub.

"Fuck," I groaned as my legs shook. I would have collapsed if the men weren't holding me up. My core tightened and I rocked between them, on the verge, almost scared Nikolai was going to leave me there.

Doc lowered his head to my neck, nipping just enough to barely draw blood, and hit me with his vampire power.

I lost all control of my legs and sagged between the two of them as my body shook with my powerful climax.

"Couldn't resist," Nikolai whispered as he put his hands under my arms and lifted me back to my feet.

I leaned against Doc's chest, Nikolai supporting me from behind while I recovered.

It took a few minutes before I could stand again.

"Ready?" Nikolai caressed between my legs from behind, rubbing my clit, my opening, moving further back.

I ached for him to fill me and whimpered when he didn't sink his fingers into me. Nikolai ignored my objection and ran his fingers around my ass. Definitely magical lube. Of course, he knew how to magic that, too. I almost laughed, but Doc distracted me, nipping along my throat, the points of his fangs pressing into my skin as he pulled my attention to him.

Needing something to do with my hands, I squeezed his firm ass, groaning as Nikolai pushed a finger into me.

"Okay?"

"Yeah," I replied breathlessly.

He pushed another into me, thrusting a few times with his fingers, bringing me whole new sensations of pleasure as I dug my hands into Doc's butt cheeks.

After a while, he pulled his fingers away and he pushed the head of his erection against me. "Yes?"

I nodded. "Yeah."

Doc lifted me so I was the right height and I wrapped my legs around his waist. He held me as Nikolai slowly pushed into me. I cried out in a mix of pleasure and surprise at the new sensations as Nikolai slowly stretched me.

"Just relax," Doc said softly. "I've got you." His strong hands never wavered, holding me tight as I shuddered against him.

I had to wonder, again, just how much Doc and Nikolai were into each other, because it sounded like he knew what he was talking about. The thought made me grin, though I didn't need to know details unless they shared with me. My imagination was enough, and I did relax as Nikolai finally buried himself in me.

"Keep going," I prompted when he hesitated. "It's good, just different."

The mage held my hips and slowly worked his way back out before thrusting in a little harder. I groaned. Yeah, this was definitely good. I knew my men would take care of me and I trusted them. So far they hadn't disappointed.

"Ready for Doc?" Nikolai asked once I was nice and loose in his hands.

I whimpered and nodded, not quite able to articulate how ready I was to have both of them filling me. I had never imagined anything like this.

Nikolai took over holding me, while Doc guided himself to my opening and carefully slid in. He groaned, not quite able speak either as I wrapped my legs back around him and held on as tightly as I could manage.

The two quickly worked out a rhythm, thrusting and withdrawing, bringing me to new heights of pleasure as they filled me more than I had ever thought possible. Our skin slid together, warm and slick under the perfect temperature of the water that caressed us.

"Fuck yeah," I gasped. The guys both moaned in response.

Before long we were all groaning, trying to draw out our pleasure as long as we could, but so close to coming that even Doc was shaking, though I had no fear he would drop me.

Heat pooled in my core and burst, making my entire body shake as my orgasm hit me harder even than the one Nikolai and Doc had given me not long before. I couldn't even cry out, just gasped. It was a good thing Doc held me because I lost all control of my body as I came undone. I clenched around Doc and he and Nikolai came together, thrusting hard into me, both crying out.

The held me like that for a moment, buried in me, holding me tightly. Nikolai pulled out of me first, then Doc. He set me down and we all sank to the floor of the shower, holding each other as our bodies recovered.

"Yeah," I said after a while. "We can definitely do that again."

"Good," Nikolai replied.

Doc chuckled.

Nikolai climbed to his feet and offered me a hand. I accepted, though I stumbled into his arms when my legs still refused to cooperate fully.

Nikolai laughed then hauled Doc to his feet.

"See, bigger showers are good." I winked at him and blushed at the hungry look he gave me.

"Yes, this will require much experimentation. Never done that in a shower before."

"Really?" I arched an eyebrow at him then glanced over at Doc, who also had his eyebrows arched.

"Um, well, no showers in the old days, and I meant with three." It was the mage's turn to blush.

Doc simply looked pleased.

Yep, they were definitely that into each other. It made me happy.

Nikolai grabbed the soap and he and Doc spent a great deal of time making sure I was completely clean before Nikolai and I washed Doc, and then the vampire and I turned our attention on the mage.

It was a good thing our shower was magic, or we would have run out of hot water long before we finally stepped out of the shower.

Chapter 17

Sofia

"Whatever you three were up to in the shower, I want to try that next time." Allan winked at me.

Blushing, I took the tea Ed offered me and sank into one of the chairs. Decadent languor settled in and I relaxed and enjoyed the attention as Ash brought me a plate and Allan put some juice on the table.

Ed, Ash, and Allan had already eaten so Nikolai and I stuffed our faces while Doc cleaned up the kitchen.

"Looks like we have a reasonably self-cleaning kitchen, too," Doc said after a minute. "Just need to put things away."

"Sweet." Ed hopped up to help.

Someone's phone buzzed and Doc grumbled and headed into the living area.

The werewolves perked up when Doc answered.

By their narrowed eyes, the news wasn't amazing, and anxiety destroyed my good mood. What now?

Doc came back in, jaw clenched.

"Do I even want to know?" I sighed.

"We knew that Melinda Anderson wasn't captured. Well, apparently she broke Alex and one other mage out of wherever Adriana and her people were holding them."

"Well, that's amazing." I sagged in the chair and stared at the ceiling. "One morning. Just one morning where things can be awesome, and nothing goes wrong right after."

No one laughed, and I could sense general agreement from all of them.

"So, what do we do?"

They all looked to Doc who shrugged. "I guess be ready. It would be dumb to assume that they're not coming after us."

"My parents are coming." I groaned.

"Hopefully, they'll need time to regroup." The flat tone Doc used told me he believed that about as much as I did.

"I could tell my parents not to come, I guess."

"It will be okay, Sofia." Nikolai patted my shoulder. "When do they arrive?"

"This weekend." Crap, I still needed to go Christmas shopping, too. "Assuming the roads clear."

"It won't snow for at least another week," Ash said. "Maybe more."

"Good and bad," Nikolai mused.

"We should warn them that the Andersons aren't as handled as we had hoped, but that things will probably be okay," Doc said.

"I'll text them." Easing out of the chair, I grinned at the light soreness in my muscles from this morning.

Wandering through our new cabin, I again marveled at what we had accomplished.

I had left my phone in the room I had claimed as my own. The light flashed at me and I checked my texts. Victoria wanted to know when I was coming down to shop and Mom checking in saying they thought roads would be clear by the time they needed to leave.

I sent a quick text back to Victoria.

Sofia: Do you mind if Mom joins us?

Victoria replied right away.

Victoria: No! Sounds great.

Sofia: Cool. I'll check with her and get back to you.

Victoria: Sounds good. Sunday would be a good day for me. Or Monday.

I touched the screen and changed over to my mom's window. What to say?

Sofia: Hey, Mom. Want to go shopping with me and Victoria in Denver Sunday or Monday?

While I waited for her to reply, I curled up in the window seat and stared out my window. No cold leaked through the clear panes as I stared out at the snow covered pines that made up my view.

One of these days our little haven in the mountains truly would be secure. I had hoped we were already there, but we still had a little ways to go. Damn them, anyway.

My phone chimed.

Mom: That sounds wonderful, honey. If you don't mind me coming along.

Sofia: I don't mind. It will be fun.

Mom: Let's go Monday. Give us a day to settle in.

Sofia: Great. We rebuilt the cabin and in less good news, I guess we still have to deal with the Andersons. Should be safe on the property though.

Mom: We'll be careful, honey. Looking forward to seeing you.

Sofia: Love you.

Mom: Love you too.

I did a quick weather and road check on my phone. The roads were supposed to be snowy but drivable, and the next few days would be sunny and warm. By the time they arrived, the weather would be great. After informing Victoria of the plan, I put my phone down and went back to looking out the window.

Someone knocked quietly on my doorframe.

I patted the window seat in front of me and Ash came in and sat down.

He didn't speak, eyes roaming the view outside my window. His long platinum blond hair called to me. The silky strands flowed through my fingers when I touched them.

Ash breathed out quietly and I took that as a sign he liked the attention. We didn't speak, just hung out while I played with his hair.

"You really want me?"

Even with my demon enhanced hearing, he was difficult to hear.

"Yes, Ash. I do. We do." Leaning forward, I rested my forehead against his broad shoulders and tightened my arms around the demon. His silky hair tickled my face and heat from his body warmed me.

"Do you want us?"

"I do."

"Good."

His hand found mine and he held me against him.

We stayed like that until Ed found us. Ash straightened, though his hand remained over mine.

"We're picking out furniture. Do you two want to join us?" Ed bounced on his toes, eyes twinkling in excitement.

"Sure."

Ash squeezed my hand before releasing me. We stood and followed Ed into the living room.

∞ ∞ ∞

It took a few days to get some of the new furniture for the cabin. Though we didn't expect to really need them often, one of the first things we did was buy beds for each of the rooms. We also got couches and a huge kitchen table.

We still weren't sure how the visit with my parents would go, but we didn't necessarily think they needed to know we all shared.

"It'll be okay, Sofia." Doc put his arms around me where I sat hunched up on the couch.

I leaned into my vampire and snuggled against his chest. My skin tingled when he slipped his hand under my shirt and rubbed small circles on my back with his cool hands. Fortunately, most of the side effects of really vamping out while fighting the Andersons had worn off and he no longer had any sunlight sensitivity. We were all relieved about that. Grumpy daytime vampire had gotten a little old.

"Mmmm," I mumbled happily.

His hand stilled.

"They here?"

"Someone driving a diesel is. Probably your folks."

Nikolai joined us a moment later, drying his hair with a towel. My eyes roamed his lean muscles, jeans riding low and revealing just enough to make me drool.

"Put a shirt on," I said reluctantly. "Too distracting otherwise."

Nikolai paused drying his hair, winked, and headed toward his room.

Doc sighed. By the time I glanced up at him, I couldn't tell if it was for the loss of eye candy, or because my parents were almost here.

I tangled my fingers in his long hair and pulled him in for a quick kiss. He devoured my lips, leaving me breathless when he released me.

Groaning, I pulled out of his embrace and got up, heading for the door so I could go meet Mom and Dad.

Cold air pricked at my cheeks as I stepped into the brisk afternoon. Dad's gaze shifted between Ash's Camaro and the newly built cabin, a frown creasing his brow. Mom saw me before she got too focused on anything else and came over to me, wrapping me in a hug.

"How are you?" Mom studied me closely before glancing at the cabin. "Impressive."

I grinned. "Magic. Come on, see the inside."

Ed and Allan looked out from the kitchen, where they were working on dinner for everyone, when we walked in.

Ash had perched himself in one of the window seats in the living room and looked like he might want to melt into the wall. Nikolai poked at a fresh fire in our fireplace and Doc had stood to greet my parents.

Mom liked all my guys. Nikolai, especially, had charmed her. Dad was tolerating everyone. Of course, neither of them knew for sure I was dating all of them. They might suspect. We hadn't exactly been careful at Thanksgiving, with everyone so happy to see me in one piece and alone in my own head.

Nikolai hugged Mom while Doc shook Dad's hand. Everyone else traded greetings before Mom noticed Ash hiding on the window seat. To his credit, he hadn't actually used magic to vanish.

"You're just surrounded by attractive men, Sofia. Who's your other friend?"

My eyes widened and Ash ducked his head, though I saw a hint of a smile tug at his lips.

"Mom, Dad, this is our friend Ash. He's staying with us for a while."

Ed and Allan disappeared back into the kitchen. I didn't blame them. I couldn't remember if I had mentioned Ash to my parents or not, but there was a good chance I had.

Mom's face twisted up as if she were trying to remember. "Ash? That sounds familiar. Have you mentioned him?"

"Um. I can't remember. Here, let me show you around the cabin." I grabbed her hand and began the tour.

Dad trailed along behind us.

"So, we haven't finished getting stuff for the cabin, and obviously we don't have any decorations or anything."

"You did this all with magic?" Dad asked after we ended up in the kitchen where Ed and Allan were almost done cooking. We sat around our large kitchen table.

"Yeah. Ash, Nikolai, and I, and, uh, Doc, built it." I'd almost forgotten to include Doc. We hadn't even made any of our stories overly complicated, and it was still hard to keep track of everything.

"Wait, Ash," Mom said, her eyes darting to the demon. "Doesn't he..."

"No." I cut her off. Obviously, I had mentioned him before. "He was under their control. He's free now."

"Oh." Mom eyed the demon. "Well, they sound like terrible people."

Ash nodded his agreement but remained silent.

"So, what now? They're still out there?" Mom wrapped her hands around a mug of tea that Doc slid in front of her.

Dad was a coffee drinker, but we didn't have any in the house since I still hadn't gotten over getting drugged with a latte.

Ash lifted a shoulder, staring at the table as he answered. "Melinda is powerful." His lips twisted when he said her name. "But Sofia is more than a match for her now. So is Nikolai. She has experience, but Nikolai can match that, and the demon left Sofia with a lot of knowledge. If Alex is working with her, that will give her a boost, but..." Ash shrugged again. "They don't have me anymore. I was the main reason no one would dare take them on before. They're probably out for revenge. We'll just have to fight them off for good this time."

"Oh." Mom's eyes scanned all of us. "I never really expected to have to deal with this world," Mom replied. "It's so different than what we're used to. I'm grateful Sofia has such capable help."

Dad still didn't say anything, though his jaw was tight.

"Hope you're hungry." Allan broke the uncomfortable silence as he brought plates over.

Nikolai helped him set the table. I watched the mage, marveling at how readily he had settled into our life. Though I was sure it was vastly different than palace life with servants and all that went with it, he had taken to our ways. Of course, we had adapted to some of his also. We were all much more open about using our abilities, at least when safe to do so.

"So, Nikolai, how are you settling in to modern times?" Mom turned her attention to the mage just as he casually brushed his hand across Doc's shoulder. Doc absently put his hand on top of the mage's for a moment. It was an everyday action for them, but I wasn't sure Mom had ever seen it before. Her eyes widened and she glanced at me.

I was currently sitting between Ed and Allan. Maybe I should have taken the spot next to Doc. Maybe I should just tell them and hope Mom and Dad didn't freak out too much.

"It is good. Not even sure I miss home." His eyes danced with mischief as his gaze settled on me.

I grinned back.

"Well, I'm glad to hear that. Ash, what are you going to do now?"

The demon shrugged. "Get used to freedom, I guess. They're letting me stay here as long as I need to. I really don't know."

She looked back at me, head tilted slightly before she shrugged. "I suppose I'm glad my daughter is surrounded by powerful mages and, uh, werewolves, to keep her safe."

The oven dinged, saving us from the rest of that awkward conversation. Doc and Ash brought over the baked pasta and garlic bread.

"And good cooks, too," Mom said as she tasted the pasta. "Sofia can cook, you know."

"She does every once in a while, but we like to cook more than she does," Ed replied. "And we're better at it."

I laughed.

Another awkward silence fell and I filled it by eating.

"So, how's the hunting up here?" Dad finally broke the silence.

We all traded amused glances. The memory of hot, fresh meat wasn't nearly as disturbing as I had thought it might be, even while eating. The memory of the wind in my fur and the ground under my paws as I raced after the deer we had taken down recently tugged at me.

"It's good," Ed finally answered. "There are a lot of deer up here. Especially on Doc's land. Do you like hunting?"

Dad nodded. "I try to get away during hunting season. I've never hunted in Colorado before. Thought about giving it a try."

Ed and Allan traded another glance before they shrugged. "We could take you next season. I think Doc knows some good areas to get tags for."

They glanced at Doc who nodded. "I've led hunting parties before. One of the many things I've done with my life."

Dad looked surprised. "That would be good."

For a while Doc and my dad fell into a conversation about different areas to hunt and how to go about getting the correct tags.

Mom and I traded an amused glance. We enjoyed game meat, so we never minded when Dad actually made it out, but it was often hard for him to get away and he'd given his game tags to friends more often than he'd actually made it out for his own hunts. Maybe we could change that next year.

By the time that conversation wound down, it sounded like they had agreed to give it a try next fall.

I supposed if that finally got him to accept the others, I was all for it.

Between the werewolves, guests, and Nikolai, we polished off the food. I couldn't remember a time when we'd actually had leftovers.

Ed and Allan left the cleanup to Nikolai and Doc and the rest of us went out into the living room.

Ed and Allan traded uneasy glances before Allan finally spoke. "We need to go, uh, run. It was nice to see both of you," he said to my parents.

"Nice to see you, too, Ed and Allan. I'm sure we'll see you again before our visit is over."

"Yes, we're hoping you'll join us for Christmas dinner." Ed shoved his hands in his pockets, looking nervous.

We were? I was touched that the guys wanted to include my parents, but it also surprised me.

"We would love to," Mom answered. "Are your parents joining us?"

"Uh, they're dead. So, no. Hopefully not." Ed bounced on his toes.

Mom put her hand over her mouth. "I'm so sorry."

Ed shrugged. "It was a few years ago. Werewolves attacked our family camping trip. Allan and I survived. Parents didn't. We like being werewolves, so it's mostly not a big deal. We miss them, but it's almost like it was a different lifetime. So much has changed since then."

Mom, probably overcome by some sort of parent instinct, went over to Ed and gave him a hug. Then she hugged Allan, too.

"Go run. We'll see you later." She smiled as she watched them head down toward their bedrooms. They could leave out the backdoor unless they really wanted to see how my folks were handling me hanging out with werewolves.

"I had no idea," Mom said when they were out of normal human hearing range.

"They handled it pretty well," Doc said. He didn't go into details and Mom didn't ask.

Nikolai waved his hand at the fire after putting a fresh log on. Blue magic sank into the wood and flames sprang up.

"Anyone want to play cards?" We hadn't replaced any of the electronics yet, so we didn't have a TV or video games or anything yet. We had spent a lot of time learning various card games.

"Yes!" Nikolai particularly liked playing cards.

Mom and Dad did, too, so we settled in by the fire with a couple of decks of cards.

We had to play on the floor since we didn't have a table for the living room yet and I sat between Doc and Nikolai, my knees brushing against theirs.

Mom gave me another contemplative look especially when Nikolai treated me to one of his random casual touches that he liked so much.

I just focused on the game, trying not to squirm under her scrutiny. We might just have to have that conversation, but I wasn't ready to do that now. Maybe Monday. Victoria would help. I hoped. This really was complicated. Worth it, but complicated.

Chapter 18

Sofia

We took Dad's truck down to meet Victoria and left the guys at the mercy of my dad. Or maybe it was the other way around. I wasn't quite sure. Doc and Nikolai were going to take him shooting. As long as no one killed each other I supposed it wouldn't go too badly.

Mom and I talked about easy things on the way down the mountain. It was a long drive but nice to spend some time alone with her.

Victoria decided to meet us in Estes so we didn't have to drive all the way down to Denver and by the time we arrived, both Mom and I were ready for lunch.

"It is beautiful here." Mom looked around as we walked toward the café Victoria wanted to meet us at. "I can see why you like it here."

"Yeah. The mountains already feel like home. Even with everything crazy that has happened."

"I'm glad, honey. You've found yourself some nice boys."

Nearly tripping over a curb, I sucked in a breath and tried to calm my heart. She didn't seem to notice me trip, gaze fixed on the river while we meandered through the light crowd. Though a lot of smaller shops were closed on Monday, enough were open that I thought I could find something for everyone.

"Christmas shopping this year is complicated." I studied a glassblower's display as we walked past.

"Oh?"

"I don't know what to get everyone."

"How about things you can do as a group. Games? You like cards. I bet there are a lot of other games you could get, too. You'll have plenty of snowy days stuck in the cabin."

"That's a great idea. I could just get a whole bunch of games for all of us to play. You're a genius."

"I would also like to get something for the guys," Mom said. "Maybe your dad and I could get something for the cabin since you don't have much right now."

"A nice table to play games on in the living room?"

She grinned. "Great idea."

We found the café. Rich buttery pastry smells curled around us. I focused on the sugar and sweetness and the hint of bergamot and tried to ignore the heavier coffee smell, though, as time passed it bothered me less. Maybe once we'd finally defeated Alex I would celebrate with a latte. Or at least attempt to celebrate with one.

"Victoria!" I hugged my friend when I found her waiting inside.

"Sofia! Mrs. Collins! It's so good to see both of you." She hugged Mom after me.

We grabbed a table, ordered, and fell into a discussion about Christmas plans.

The food lived up to the smell, and I groaned as I stuffed the last bit into my mouth. "So good."

"Hey, how's the new cabin?" Victoria asked once the plates were cleared away and we sipped our tea.

"Great. Not much in it yet, but we're really happy with what we have already accomplished."

"I was thinking of a housewarming style gift for you all for the holiday. What do you need?"

"Um. Wow, that's a really good question." I ran through all the things I eventually wanted, but they weren't something to ask a friend for. "Maybe something for the kitchen?"

"I'll think about it," Victoria said. "You let me know if anything comes up while we're wandering around."

"Deal."

We paid and left, intent on taking advantage of the warm afternoon sunlight while we shopped.

All of us had bags by the time we made it back to the parking lot where we had left the truck. Victoria's car wasn't far away, and we put our purchases in the vehicles so we could grab an early dinner before everyone headed home.

I slipped a small box I'd managed to buy without Victoria noticing into her hand. "Merry Christmas."

She blushed and handed me something, too. "Open it when you open the rest of your gifts."

"You, too."

We stashed those boxes in our vehicles and headed back to the pizza joint we'd seen. Victoria claimed that it was almost as good as our normal spot.

The skin crawled on my arms and I looked around, wondering what had caught my attention.

Was that? A familiar head of blond curls bobbed in the crowd, but then it was gone.

"Sofia?" Victoria scanned the crowd.

"I thought I saw someone I recognized. Sorry. It's not important."

She studied me while we went inside but didn't pressure me to tell her what was wrong.

"It was probably nothing." I insisted when we sat, though I did put my back to the wall and carefully cast a concealment around us. The magic would hide us from casual notice.

Victoria noticed, but Mom didn't.

Instead she plunged into the topic I had been dreading for a while now. At least she had waited to ask until Victoria was around.

"You're dating Doc, right?"

"Yeah."

"He seems awfully comfortable with the way you act around the rest of them."

"Act how?"

"You all touch. All the time."

I lowered my voice. "It's, um, well, at least partially a werewolf thing. Touch is very important to Ed and Allan."

"But what about Nikolai, who, by the way, is interested in your boyfriend if you hadn't noticed." Her tone stayed mild.

"Um." I cast a desperate glance at Victoria, who shrugged. Lot of help she was.

"Yeah, uh, Nikolai likes Doc. It's fine. He's fine with me and, um, all the guys. Touching, I guess. He's used to living with werewolves."

"They're all so nice. I just hate to see any problems come up because of misunderstandings."

I wasn't exactly saved by the arrival of our pizza, but it gave me a few minutes to think. I really just needed to tell her. What else could I do? Victoria gave me a subtle thumbs up.

"Yeah, about that. I guess, I'm just dating all of them. One big happy pack."

To her credit, Mom didn't choke on her pizza. She managed to swallow and take a big drink without too much trouble.

"I see."

"They're really all pretty adorable," Victoria said.

"And they're all okay with it?"

"Yeah."

"Does all of them include Ash?"

My cheeks heated and I stared at my hands. "Um. Yeah."

"Oh, got the demon, too! You go girl." Victoria gave me another thumbs up.

"Demon?"

If Mom hadn't know before, she knew now so there was no point in denying it. I really couldn't remember if I had mentioned what Ash was before.

"Yeah, demon."

She shook her head. "How did you manage to get so lucky?"

She didn't sound mad, so I risked a glance. "Lucky?"

"It's hard enough to find one compatible person, let alone five. Especially ones willing to share."

"I don't know. I'm glad I did though, or I'd be dead. Alex found me before Ed and Allan did."

Mom's eyes widened and she nodded. Perhaps that was why she didn't seem to be having as hard of a time with this as I had expected. She really did like them all, and they had saved my life. That counted for a lot.

"Let's not tell your father." She took a sip of her drink, as if that settled things.

I shared a wide-eyed glance with Victoria before I nodded acceptance. "Yeah, that's probably best. He finally seems to have gotten over some of his dislike of Doc."

"He just wants the best for you."

"I'd say Sofia hit gold there," Victoria replied. "They all love her."

"I still think Nikolai is after your boyfriend." Mom sounded like she couldn't decide if the idea should bother her or not. She really liked the mage.

Clearing my throat, I shrugged. "Yeah, they're into each other. It's fine. There *is* only one of me."

Mom's eyebrows rose. "I guess I didn't really see Doc as the type."

"Honestly, I think he's just into Nikolai. They kind of clicked." Mom really didn't need to know that everyone but Ed was into Doc to some degree or another and that he was willing to reciprocate. That he could pretty much light up a person's entire body without even touching them didn't hurt. Vampire powers were intense. I knew a lot of it was just Doc, though.

If we were going to help this group of Adriana's, Doc might have to get more comfortable using his powers. There had to be a balance between hardly using them and going so far that he would have issues with sunlight on a regular basis.

We also had to figure out how to deal with the issue of it just not being safe to know that Doc was even partially a vampire. Of course, there was also a pretty good chance they already knew. I couldn't imagine Alex keeping his mouth shut about that.

"You're thinking hard about something." Victoria interrupted my musings. "Smoke is coming out of your ears."

"Sorry." I put the problems out of my mind. Those were issues for another day.

"So, are you all having sex?"

I snorted my drink through my nose.

Mom's tone conveyed mild curiosity, but I wasn't sure I wanted to have that conversation with her ever.

"I…" I choked.

"Just be careful, honey. I want to be a grandmother, just not yet." She smiled at me.

"IUD" I managed to gasp out. "Remember?"

She gave me a serene look.

"Also, Nikolai taught me a bunch of useful spells. I'm good."

"I can't imagine you're bored."

"The possibilities are endless with them," I managed to get out.

Victoria laughed.

"So, Nikolai knows all the mage spells. Doc doesn't seem like he knows as much as Nikolai, though I'd swear he's older."

"Nikolai grew up in the past. Doc grew up having to hide."

"Good point. I'm still getting the idea there's a lot about him you're not telling me."

"Pack secrets, I guess."

"I suppose I can accept that as long as you know everything."

I nodded.

"Maybe you should get some toys."

There went my drink through my nose again.

Victoria cackled.

"Mom…" I finally managed to gasp out when I stopped choking. "There's five of them. What could I possibly need toys for?"

She smiled. "I'll give you some ideas on the drive back up the mountain. It will keep us occupied."

"Okay." I wasn't sure I wanted to have that conversation either, but apparently, she was more adventurous than I had thought. Not completely comfortable with that insight into my mother's life, but glad for her, I struggled between curiosity and not wanting to know.

Her eyes twinkled with amusement. "I really am happy for you. I just want to make sure you get the most out of your somewhat unusual situation."

"Thanks," I blurted, though I was also relieved. If it ever came up with my dad, at least my mom would be on my side.

"It's getting late. As much as I hate to break up our afternoon, we all have long drives and darkness comes early."

"It was great to see you, Mrs. Collins." We stood and Victoria insisted on paying.

Though I kept my eyes open for any signs of Alex, I didn't see any and by the time we made it to the truck I had convinced myself I had imagined seeing his blond curls. I couldn't be too careful, so I cast spells on both of the vehicles checking for tracking spells or anything more nefarious. Not finding anything only made me feel a little better but the vehicles started normally and we headed out, Victoria heading back to Denver, and me and Mom back to Sunnyglade.

Chapter 19

Sofia

"We wanted to help you decorate," Mom said as she came into the cabin a few days later. "If you don't mind?"

"Decorate?" Nikolai looked up from the tablet. He still had a lot to catch up on. Until we had heard the diesel coming up the driveway, I had been cuddling with him in the recliner he and Doc had turned up with the other day. I had shared with the guys that Mom now knew for sure I was dating all of them, but that we all agreed it was best if Dad didn't know.

Now I was sprawled on the couch, using Doc's thigh as a pillow, both of us reading.

"Yes, holiday lights for the house, some decorations for a tree, that sort of thing."

Ash, Ed, and Allan came in from outside in time to overhear.

Dad followed her inside with a few shopping bags full of stuff.

"That's great."

Ed and Allan shared a glance before looking at my mom. They both looked stunned. "We haven't decorated in, well, years. We usually get a tree, but, well, we felt bad cutting one down this year after they did so much by helping us rebuild."

Dad frowned. "What?"

"Uh, the land, uh, helped." Ed scuffed his feet.

Dad looked at me and I shrugged. "It likes us here."

"I see."

"If you want a tree," Ash said quietly, "I can help with that."

"Sure!" I beamed at him.

Ash nodded and went over to the open space in front of the big windows that overlooked the valley. My skin tingled as he called his magic. It wasn't the same intensity as with Doc and Nikolai, but it still affected me.

He folded his amber colored magic until it hovered in a tight square in front of him, then slowly expanded and grew, shifting through the space in front of him and changing shape until it resembled a tall pine composed of amber magic.

Ash blew across his palm and more amber magic joined the tree shape. Slowly it coalesced into a solid amber pine tree. Another hit of magic and the colors altered until the needles were vibrant green and the bark a rich brown. Pine scent, always somewhat present, filled the room.

Jumping off the couch, I took a deep breath and ran over to the tree, brushing my hands across the prickly needles.

He'd gone so far as to craft it into a Christmas tree holder and wound a red skirt bordered with running wolves around the bottom. One for each of us, though they were all white.

"It's perfect, Ash."

He ducked his head, cheeks red, lips curled in a bit of a smile. Deciding I needed to hug Ash more than I needed to hide from Dad, I wrapped my arms around the demon.

Hesitantly, he hugged me back.

"Time to decorate!" I declared. Dad handed over one of the laden shopping bags.

"This means we need Christmas cookies." Ed bounced on his toes.

"I'll bake, you decorate," Ash ordered.

"Deal." Ed took the bag from me and I got another from Dad.

Nikolai joined us while Doc watched and pretty soon the living room looked like a bunch of kids had just opened their gifts. Packaging was everywhere as we pulled out strings of house lights, packs of ornaments., and a few other odds and ends to lend a Christmassy touch to the cabin.

Dad, Nikolai, and Doc headed outside with the house lights while Ed, Allan, and I went to work on the tree. Mom went to the kitchen to help Ash bake.

It took a couple of hours but between the fresh pine from Ash's tree, the sugary sweetness of the baked goods, and our efforts at decorating, the place looked extremely festive.

Ed and Allan sat in front of the fire, contented smiles on their faces as they looked at the tree and ate cookies. I sat on one end of the long couch and nibbled on a sugar cookie. Ash and Mom had started up a card game and Doc, Nikolai, and Dad had just come inside from hanging the lights. For once I couldn't wait for it to get dark so we could fully appreciate their efforts.

Doc and Nikolai sat on the couch by me and Dad joined Mom.

The winds picked up outside and Ash and I traded glances. Normally we sensed weather shifts a few days in advance. It was something to do with how tightly demons were tied into the energies and elements of the world. That was part of why Ash was so good at using the land to build things. I still had a lot of that from when the demon had possessed me.

"That's strange. A storm is kicking up."

"It's winter, honey," Mom said.

"Right, but Ash and I usually sense it coming. This one is unexpected. It wasn't even on the weather." I had actually checked since I wasn't quite used to the ability.

"Interesting." Doc got up and went to the window. "We got done just in time."

Uneasy, but not sure why, I went over and joined him.

Doc, sensing my distress, put his arm around me. "We're safe in here."

"Yeah, I know. It's just strange. I've been able to predict the weather for weeks now and it feels weird to not have sensed this coming."

"Ash, did you sense anything?"

"No. It is unusual, but not completely unheard of."

"Don't sense magic," Nikolai said, uneasily. "Is probably natural." He didn't sound convinced.

Doc pulled a hair tie out of his pocket and pulled his long hair back into a tail. "I'm going to check and make sure everything is tied down, if the wind is going to kick up like that."

"I'll help." Allan joined Doc. Neither of them remembered to grab a jacket since they really didn't need one.

Moments after the door shut, Ash bolted to his feet and clutched at his head.

Nikolai swore, leapt to his feet, and blasted Ash in the chest with the same spell we had taken the demon out with before we'd released him. He crumpled to the ground.

"Nikolai!" I was interrupted as pain seared through my chest. I clutched at myself and staggered, falling to my knees. Moments later I heard Allan yelp.

The Russian mage was already casting another spell, this one a shield as he rushed out the door, Ed on his heels.

I struggled to my feet, ignoring my parents except to make sure they were still all right. Mom knelt by Ash.

Ed and Nikolai dragged an unconscious Doc back inside while Allan hobbled in after and slammed the front door.

"What the hell! Doc!" I shrieked and hit my knees again beside the very unconscious vampire. "Nikolai!"

Nikolai rolled Doc onto his back and brushed some stray hair out of his face. I stared at the wooden bolt protruding from the vampire's chest in shock.

We had wards. Why weren't they triggered? How were we under attack?

"Ready?" Ed asked his brother.

I glanced at them. Ed had his hands wrapped around another wooden bolt that was imbedded in Allan's thigh.

Allan nodded and Ed pulled.

Allan howled in pain, collapsing backward, skin rippling as he almost shifted. "Fuck," he gasped.

I grabbed the bolt in Doc's chest, but Nikolai stopped me. "That is not a good idea. He will wake up violently. Last time I did this, nearly died."

"Wake up?" Dad was standing behind me. "That's through his heart. There's no way he survived that."

Nikolai and I locked gazes, not answering my dad.

The house shuddered.

"Lock the doors, no one gets in," I shouted.

The house responded, sealing even more tightly. I didn't even think the magical attacks would get through, at least not any time soon.

"He can wait until we defeat the Andersons," Nikolai said.

I switched to Russian, in a sort of last-ditch effort to keep my parents in the dark a little while longer about Doc's vampire nature. "He's half human. This can't be good for him. Hell, feel the bond, he's fading." I fought off panic, knowing it wouldn't help me save my lover.

Nikolai swore colorfully and at length. "Will take me out of the fight." He swallowed nervously. He didn't make me decide, just hooked his arms under Doc's. "Ed, grab his legs."

They carried Doc into the bedroom, Allan limping after them. I followed, shutting the door in Dad's face.

"Sofia!"

I ignored him.

"Dan, help me with Ash," Mom called.

"Okay, will pull this out. He will probably attack me. If not, needs blood right away. Try to keep him from killing me." Nikolai gritted his teeth and gestured for the others to get back. He cast the healing spell on himself that helped with vampire bites and muttered something, maybe some sort of prayer.

The house shrieked in pain as a particularly nasty spell attacked it. Sparing a bit of attention, I pushed some of my energy into restoring the house. It pulsed with gratitude.

I turned my attention back to the guys just in time to hear Doc's feral growl as he tackled Nikolai off the bed. They both hit the floor hard and Nikolai gasped a strangled cry of pain.

We let Doc feed until Nikolai started to look a little panicked. He clawed weakly at the vampire's back. None of us would be the same without the mage, and Doc would never forgive himself if he killed Nikolai. I had to stop him. I just hoped I could.

"Doc," I grabbed his shoulder.

He growled, probably not completely conscious through the bloodlust. I used a little of my own magic, shoved it through Doc and zapped him.

I probably should have let him have one of the werewolves next, but I hadn't thought that far ahead. Doc released Nikolai and turned on me. He was so damn fast, I was trapped in arms before I even comprehended that I was no longer leaning over him. I barely managed to shove my wrist in his face before his fangs sank into me. There was nothing pleasurable about this bite and I bit my lip so I wouldn't yell in pain. I did not need my parents hearing that.

Doc drank some of my blood, but I'd shoved the wrist with the pack tattoo in his face and I used that extra bit of connection to shove my magic at him again, calling him back to himself.

He released me almost as fast as he had restrained me and fell back, blinking as if trying to figure out what was going on. His eyes fell on Nikolai. "Shit, Nikolai." He scrambled over to the unconscious mage.

I joined him and cast another healing spell.

"Are you okay?" I put my hand on Doc's shoulder.

"Physically."

Nikolai gasped, his eyes fluttering open. He looked around at us before giving us a loopy grin. "Didn't die," he said happily.

Doc's shoulders sagged and he sighed. "You're insane."

"Yes," the mage agreed. "Also, I will not be casting magic for a while. Drained."

We all groaned at his horrible joke. Even Doc.

"I need to reinforce the house," I said. "They're hitting pretty hard, even as sturdy as the house is."

Doc growled.

"Will be okay. Help me up."

I hauled Nikolai to his feet and Doc stood. Allan leaned heavily on Ed but they both made it to their feet, as well.

"You've, um, got a bit of blood on your face." I gestured.

Doc rubbed at his face with his sleeve. "Better?"

"Um, kind of."

"Is good enough," Nikolai shrugged. "Not going to be able to hide my neck anyway. Parents will have to deal."

"Yeah, I'm pretty sure the not instant death from the stake through the heart was a big clue, anyway." I was more worried about dealing with my parents than the Anderson's. How fucked up was that?

Doc put his arm around Nikolai's waist and supported him, and Ed supported Allan as we stalked back out into the living room.

"How are you not dead?" Dad's eyes widened and he blanched as he took in Nikolai's bloody neck and Doc's angry expression.

I hadn't noticed in the darker bedroom, but the shadows danced around Doc's feet unnaturally, and his movements were completely unhuman. His eyes had gone wholly black and I suspected a lot of blood would be spilt before he would truly get himself under control again.

"What happened to Ash?" Doc ignored the question from Dad.

"Blasted him. Ash was worried about the Andersons possibly being able to control him, even now. They had him for three hundred years. Seemed like a good idea to knock him out. It was his idea." Nikolai sank down onto the couch, groaning. "Let's not do that again any time soon."

"How about never." Allan grumbled.

"It's time to end this," Ed snarled.

"Agreed. Okay, here's what we're going to do. We need to know how many of them there are, and their positions. Ed, you shift and sneak out. I'll cast Nikolai's invisibility spell on you. I'm going to go out front and nuke them. Allan, Nikolai, stay with my parents in case they need defending. Doc, what do you want to do?"

"I'm going to rip their throats out." The deadly calm in his voice covered me with goosebumps. "I should have done it years ago." He stalked over to the door and tilted his head, listening. "Well, that's different," he muttered.

"What now?" I hugged myself.

The house screamed as they hit it again, and we all flinched. I poured more energy into the house's shields.

"They found themselves a vampire." Doc smiled.

I might have wet my pants at the expression on his face if I knew he would never hurt me.

"Clearly not the only ones," Dad muttered. It wasn't loud but we could all hear really well.

Doc cast about until he saw the bolt Ed had pulled out of Allan. He grabbed that and tucked it in his belt.

Ed, now a wolf, stalked back into the room. He rubbed against me and I trailed my hand along his back.

Mom and Dad both stared. Ed ignored them, bumping against Doc.

"Out the back?"

They both nodded.

"I'm going out the front. I'll keep them occupied and I'm seriously going to fuck them up."

My parents didn't even object to my violent intent. They must really have understood the danger we were in.

"Not by yourself." Nikolai grumbled as he pulled himself to his feet.

"You're not in any condition to help," I objected.

"Blood." He held out his hand in Doc's direction.

Doc slipped off the magic reservoir and bit his wrist, holding it out for Nikolai.

My parents were getting all of our pack secrets in one giant dose. If we survived this, we were going to have a very interesting conversation later.

The mage wrinkled his lips but drank until Doc's wrist healed.

"Will be fine in a minute. Need weapons."

Doc vanished from the room and returned a minute later with a sword I'd never seen before and his spelled long knife. He handed the sword to Nikolai, who's hand slid over the handle like he caressed a lover.

Come to think on it, I'd never seen him use a sword before, though I knew he was quite accomplished with one. He acted familiar with this weapon, however, and I wondered if that was something I had missed while being possessed.

Dad acted like he was going to join us when we headed for the door.

"Dan." Doc tossed him a set of keys. "There are a few guns in the safe. Closet in the main bedroom. Take position at that window." He pointed at the big picture window. "The window will allow you to put the muzzle of the gun through it. Magic, of course. You're welcome to shoot anything that isn't us."

I cast Nikolai's invisibility spell over Ed, but Doc waved me off when I offered to do it for him, too. "Won't need it."

Dad stared as Doc and the invisible Ed headed for the back door. The house adjusted as it let the two slip out and then sealed back up.

"I guess I can see why you told us he was a mage," Dad said, voice dark, as he headed for the gun safe.

I glanced over at Mom. A smile played across her lips despite the situation. "Dan, grab one for me, too."

"Of course, honey."

"Be careful, Sofia," she said as Nikolai and I headed for the door.

Allan growled in frustration, but he stayed with my parents.

I threw up the strongest shield I knew and opened the door. Nikolai followed me out, sword at the ready.

A new wave of magical destruction battered my shields, but they held. I expanded my awareness into the pack bond so I could get a sense of our opponents from Doc and Ed.

I caught a vague sense of something inhuman. That must be the vampire. Doc was intent on hunting it. Probably wise, the vampire was likely the most dangerous opponent. Another human with the smell of magic about him covered the back door, though he hadn't seen Doc and Ed slip out. Ed stalked that one.

Three human mages were out front. I recognized Melinda, Alex, and Sam.

"Fucking traitor," I muttered.

Nikolai had tuned in to our bond also, so he knew who I talked about. "Could be prisoner."

The magical barrage died down and Alex stepped out of the trees, followed by Melinda and Sam.

Sam did appear to be a prisoner. Her arms were tied behind herself. Melinda shoved Sam to the ground in front of her.

"It's dangerous to be your friend," Alex mocked. He aimed a shocking bolt of green magic at Sam.

She screamed when it hit her and collapsed to the ground.

That got Doc's attention, but we all assured him that focusing on the vampire was the most important.

"That's quite the bite you've got there, Nikolai. We weren't sure if that would kill Cassidy or not. Too bad." Alex smirked.

Shouting in rage, I dropped my shield long enough to lob a fireball at Alex.

Melinda had watched for that and shot deadly lightning back at me, but the house shields protected me.

Alex looked a little singed, but had mostly blocked my attack, though the smug expression had vanished from his face.

The demon had left me with the knowledge I needed to defeat the Andersons. It was up to me to wield the magic. This was going to take a while.

Reckoning

Chapter 20

Doc

The shadows called to him, and for once Doc didn't try to fight it. He gave into his vampire side more completely than he ever had before. He was pissed, he was still hungry, and he knew he would need every edge possible against a full vampire. He had hunted and killed them before, but in the past he had always had the element of surprise on his side. This time the vampire knew he was coming and it might be more difficult.

Doc slipped into the shadows, wrapped them around himself, and faded completely from view.

The one he stalked circled the house. He sent a quick warning to Nikolai through the pack bond before slipping from shadow to shadow as he followed.

The mage guarding the back of the house screamed, though the sound cut off abruptly. The coppery tang of magic laced human blood carried on the gusting wind, tugging at Doc's attention. Ed had taken care of the mage. The vampire he stalked paused and then nearly vanished from Doc's awareness.

Fuck.

A whisper of stillness in the gusty wind was his only warning. Claws ripped through his flannel shirt, popping a few buttons and lightly scoring his chest. He snarled and threw himself backward, ignoring the fiery sting. A swipe of his hunting knife met only air.

255

Doc flowed through the shadows until he had put some distance between him and the other vampire. The presence was about as solid as a wisp of fog, but he managed to keep his attention locked onto it. If he could keep the vampire focused on him, it wouldn't go after Sofia or Nikolai.

"You're good, for a half breed." A masculine voice floated on the breeze, not quite coming from any one direction, but Doc thought he still had a fix on the vampire's location.

"Is this where you try to get me to switch sides?" The shadows coated him as he dashed to a new position.

Moments later, the wind eddied around his previous location and he saw a flash of silver before the vampire vanished into the swirling wind.

Snow flurries joined the gusting wind, further obscuring his vision. He slipped fully into his ability to see in the dark. The vampire had let his body temperature cool to the ambient temperature, but he could get clues to the other's location by the air currents.

"No," the other responded finally. "I'm going to kill you. Then I'm going to drain your friends. It will be quite the power boost. Then I might kill those asshole mages. I haven't decided yet."

Doc guessed the mages had coerced him into helping, but that didn't mean the vampire wouldn't kill everyone else first.

The other's voice shifted with the winds and Doc couldn't get a fix on his location by sound.

Snow came down in earnest, big flakes reducing visibility to nothing.

Crouching, listening, watching, Doc waited for a clue.

The winds shifted. Acting on impulse, Doc lunged forward. His knife met resistance. The rank, cooper tinged reek of old vampire blood coated the air.

An iron grip clamped down on his wrist and shoved Doc forward, throwing him off balance.

He jerked away, managing to free himself, but losing the knife in the process.

Hissing, the vampire solidified out of a swirl of snow and stalked forward. Doc saw the knife, blade stuck in the dirt. He used all of his vampire speed to rush forward and grab it.

The other vampire came forward at the same time, and Doc got the knife up in time to sink it into the other's stomach, but it missed his heart and the full vampire didn't give a fuck if he had a knife stuck in him, even a spelled one like Doc's. It hurt but wouldn't be enough to take him down.

Doc tried to get away, but the other vampire trapped him close, wrenching his neck around and digging his fangs into Doc's neck.

His brain short circuited as pleasure so intense it hurt ripped through him.

Pain he could have fought right away, this undid him long enough that the vampire had a solid control over him before he managed to come back to himself.

The vampire drained his strength away as he tried to free the knife from the vampire's ribs, but his arm was trapped, and he couldn't get free. Grasping for Nikolai's magic from the blood he had taken from the mage earlier was like trying to catch the wind that swirled around them. It was there, but he'd already lost too much strength to manage it.

His legs gave out and blackness circled his vision, though he still fought.

Something slammed into them and the vampire lost his grip, tearing at Doc's neck as he was ripped away.

Not taking time to try and figure out what had happened, he leapt forward, falling on the vampire. This time he didn't miss the heart.

Doc got his first good look at his opponent. His blood covered the vampire's chin. Pale skin, dark hair, European features. It wasn't anyone he knew. He gathered his strength, jerked the knife out of the vampire's chest and slammed the blade down on his neck. He crumpled to dust as Doc's knife separated his head from his shoulders.

"Fuck," Doc gasped as he collapsed to the ground.

A blond wolf straddled Doc's chest and licked at his neck.

He didn't have the energy to push Ed away, and really, Ed could have his blood if he wanted it. The werewolf knew what he was doing.

Ed whined.

"I'm okay, Ed." He rolled over and struggled to his feet. They needed to rescue Sam and kill the others. "Thanks for the save."

Ed perked his ears and Doc dug his fingers into the werewolf's ruff for a moment.

Hunger flared through him, but he wasn't in as bad a shape as he had originally thought now that he wasn't under the other vampire's control. His strength returned quickly, and he wrapped the shadows around him again.

"Let's go."

Chapter 21

Ed

He slunk through the swirling snow at Doc's side. The vampire had wrapped the shadows around both of them since Sofia's invisibility spell had apparently worn off when the vampire had clawed the shit out of him. Doc's blood had helped his werewolf healing take care of most of it and he ignored the minor discomfort as they worked their way through the forest.

Snow obscured his vision, but his other senses compensated, and he knew this forest better than he knew anything. The energies of the land guided him until they were crouched not far from where the mages battled.

Sam lay forgotten in the snow, hands bound and apparently unable to perform any magic.

Sofia battered at Melinda's shields, while Alex cast offensive magic. Nikolai blocked the spells with his sword somehow, standing in front of Sofia so she could concentrate on battering away at the others.

Sofia blazed with her lavender magic. Ed had to tear his eyes away so he could focus on helping Doc. He wanted to watch his mate destroy the enemy. They were weakening. Sam's presence limited Sofia's options, and they needed to rescue her so his mate could finish this.

"I'm going to go after Melinda," Doc said. "See if you can drag Sam out of the way."

Ed nodded. He could grab the ropes that bound her and drag her away.

He followed as Doc rushed out of the shadows. Neither of the mages had time to react as his knife slid across Melinda's throat. Blood sprayed, and she spun, catching Doc with the edge of a spell and sending him flying into the trees. He disappeared into the shadows. Ed could still sense his pack mate through their bond, but Doc was probably out of the fight while he recovered.

Alex shouted as Melinda sank to her knees.

Sofia hit Alex hard with a blast that flung him backward. He lay still.

Ed used the distraction to dart forward and grab Sam's wrists, teeth locking down on the ropes that bound her. He dragged her away in the distraction.

Sam didn't struggle, eyes wide but seeming to recognize that Ed was helping her.

Once she was as safe as he could get her, he backed away, not trusting the mage as he hid himself in the underbrush and watched.

She looked around wildly, making it to her knees.

"Ed? Allan?" She stuttered, teeth clacking together as she shivered in the cold air.

Sam wore jeans soaked from the snow and a thin sweater, not at all dressed for the outdoors. Still, Ed couldn't bring himself to get closer. He could have helped her stay warm, but was she the enemy?

She staggered to her feet and fell again.

Ed's attention shifted back to the mages at Sofia's shout of dismay. Somehow Melinda was back on her feet and Nikolai was sprawled on the ground, unconscious. Blood coated the front of her jacket, but her neck was whole.

"She's got some sort of leach spell going," Sam said. "Not sure who it's attached to, but whoever it was, just died. I think she's got one more. We're going to have to kill her again before we can really bring her down."

Ed huffed. Of course, she couldn't be easy to kill.

"I can help," Sam said when Ed crawled out of the underbrush.

He ignored her and sent a thought to Sofia hoping she would understand he needed a big distraction.

Moments later, Sofia unleashed a tornado of magic and snow and sent it straight for Melinda.

That got her attention. Ed dashed toward the enemy, leapt, and clamped his jaws around her neck, snapping it.

Pain seared through him, and bones snapped as he crashed into the trees. He would recover, but it was going to be a few minutes before he could fight again. Laying there, he watched Melinda stagger to her feet and deflect Sofia's attack.

Thunder cracked through the snow and Melinda jerked. Not thunder, gunfire.

She staggered and the gun boomed again. This time Melinda went down and stayed there.

The front door on the house opened and Sofia's dad came out followed by Ash. Dan held a rifle and Ash's hands glowed with magic.

Together the three of them cautiously approached Melinda.

"I think she's actually dead," Ash said.

Dan clenched his jaw. "Good. What are we going to do with the bodies?"

Ash's hands flared amber before the motes settled on her body. It rapidly desiccated into dust.

Sofia gagged.

"It only works if the person's already dead, if that helps any," Ash said quietly.

"Yeah, kind of."

They turned their attention to Alex.

Before Sofia could even ask what they were going to do with Alex, the demon found Doc's knife, scooped it up and slammed it down into Alex's chest.

Sofia's eyes widened and her dad twitched the muzzle of his rifle toward Ash before he took a deep breath and pointed it at the ground again.

Sofia turned away while Ash destroyed his tormentor's body. Ed couldn't blame him. Not really.

"That's it then," Sofia said, voice flat. She hugged herself.

Her dad put his arm around her. "Where's everyone else?"

That jerked Sofia out of her daze.

Ed woofed and tried to get to his feet. His body didn't want to cooperate, though he could tell his bones were knitting.

Ash tucked Doc's knife into his belt and zeroed in on the unconscious vampire. Sofia and her dad came over to where Ed lay.

"Hey, you okay." She knelt next to him.

He whined.

"Here. I don't have much energy left." She cast a weak heal spell on him. Her magic tingled through him, helping a little.

Dan handed the rifle to Sofia and knelt next to Ed. "Don't bite me, okay?"

Ed nodded and Dan carefully picked him up. He yelped but managed not to struggle. Dan grunted but managed to lift Ed. "Well, you don't lose any weight when you change. Let's get you inside."

Sofia went over to Nikolai and rolled the mage over on his back. Ed could hear his heart beating steadily.

"Nikolai." She shook him and he groaned.

"Am okay," he muttered and managed to sit up on his own.

Sofia grabbed his sword and took it and the rifle inside while Nikolai staggered after her, clutching his head.

Dan put Ed down by the fire and Ash came in a minute later, Doc's arm over his shoulder as he helped the vampire inside. Doc collapsed into Nikolai's recliner, groaning. Nikolai sank to the ground next to Doc and leaned against his legs, resting his head on Doc's knee.

Allan came over to Ed.

"You okay?"

He nodded. Allan sat down next to him ran his hand through Ed's ruff.

Ash went back out into the storm. He hoped the demon was going after Sam.

Sofia put the weapons on the kitchen table and came back into the living room.

Ed watched as her eyes went to her parents. Dan stared at Doc, eyes wide. Sofia sighed tiredly, went over to the recliner, and half collapsed into Doc's lap.

Dan twitched, but didn't say anything.

He watched until Doc wrapped his arms around their mate, leaned his cheek against her head, and held her close. Nikolai lifted a hand and let it rest on Sofia's thigh.

Satisfied that everyone would be okay, he let the exhaustion take him.

Chapter 22

Sofia

I didn't move when Ash came back inside with Sam, feeling numb. We'd gotten our asses kicked, but we had still won. Everyone would recover, and the enemy was really handled this time. I shied away from thinking about Ash plunging the knife into Alex's chest. I didn't blame the demon, I just didn't want to think about it.

Sam shivered violently and Ash brought her over to the fireplace.

"Mom, could you get the comforter off of my bed for Sam?" I kept my eyes on the other mage but hoped Ash could handle her if she tried anything. None of the rest of us had any energy left.

The demon worked at the bindings on her wrists, carefully cutting with Doc's knife.

Mom came back and wrapped the blanket around Sam once Ash had her free. She didn't say anything, just huddled near the fire wrapped in my lavender comforter.

"You know how I wanted a day where we had a really nice time and nothing bad happened?"

"Yes," Nikolai answered.

"I'm still waiting."

Doc laughed, though it sounded strained.

Just then someone's phone buzzed.

Doc sighed. "It's mine. I'm not answering it. There is no one who could possibly want to talk to me badly enough right now."

"Adriana?" Nikolai said.

Doc muttered something impolite mostly under his breath. "I think that's what voicemail is for."

After Doc's phone fell silent, mine started up.

"It's definitely Adriana, or Victoria. They're the only two people I know who have both our numbers and aren't in this room." I didn't move.

"Who's Adriana?" Mom asked.

"Magic council person," I answered.

"Oh."

"They've been marginally helpful."

"She just wants in Doc's pants," Nikolai muttered, jealousy coloring his voice.

Doc sighed.

"Everyone wants in Doc's pants," I said, momentarily forgetting my parents didn't need to know that. "He's hot."

Dad made a strangled sound and Mom put her hand on his shoulder. Sam laughed.

Ash unfolded from the ground and left, probably to retrieve my phone. If it was Victoria something might be wrong. If it was Adriana, she could wait.

The demon came back a minute later and handed me the phone.

"Sofia, don't tell her about any of this," Doc cautioned. "We have no idea how they're interpreting any of their so-called rules."

"We can disappear into Siberia," Nikolai said.

"I don't like the cold as much as you do," Doc grumbled.

"Doesn't bother you, don't know why you don't like it," the Russian countered.

"I do get cold, just not as easily as you do."

"Do not get cold easily." Nikolai huffed.

I laughed tiredly while I stared at the number on my phone and debated calling back.

"So, vampires are affected by weather?" Dad asked. It was probably the best way he could have broached the subject.

"I don't think so," Doc answered. "At least not easily."

"But..."

"I'm not..."

"Yes, you are," Dad barked.

"I was going to say, I'm not a full vampire. You've seen me in the sunlight. That's real, too." Doc didn't look at Dad while he spoke, just continued to stare off into space as he quickly repeated the story of how his mother had been attacked right before he was born.

I remembered Sam didn't know any of this and glanced at her. She had paled considerably, and it was clear she hadn't guessed that possibility at all. She glanced toward the door, but a shiver wracked her body and she huddled closer to the fire instead of bolting.

"Guys, shut up for a minute. I'm going to call Adriana back."

Everyone fell silent.

Adriana picked up quickly. "Sofia. We were just checking on all of you."

"We're fine, why?"

"We still haven't managed to track down Alex or Melinda Anderson. Have you seen them at all?"

"No."

"Okay. Have you considered our offer any further?"

"To help you guys? We're thinking about it, but I'd also like to get through school, too."

"Of course. Please keep us updated on your plans. We really want to talk to Ash, and we need to talk to Roy."

He tensed. "What about," he spoke up enough that the phone would catch his words.

Adriana sucked in a breath, clearly not expecting Doc to respond right away. "Uh, just some of the things Alex said while we had him."

"I'm sure Alex is a completely trustworthy source of information," his voice dripped with sarcasm.

"Well, yes, we have taken that into consideration."

"Why don't you focus on finding Melinda and Alex and actually containing them this time. Maybe then we can talk. It's the middle of a blizzard here, and no one is going anywhere for a while, regardless. We'd like to get through the rest of the holidays without another disaster or confrontation."

"Sure, Roy. It's probably not that urgent, anyway. Sofia, thanks for calling me back. We'll leave you alone for a while."

"Thanks, Adriana. If we do come across Alex, we'll let you know."

"Be careful, Sofia. I'm sure they're not happy with any of you."

"Well, we're not happy with them, either. I'm certain they realize that." I clenched my hand on the phone.

"Happy Holidays." She hung up.

"Okay, I'm texting Victoria and then everyone is turning their phones off!" I almost threw the thing, but I didn't want to have to buy another one, so I sent Victoria a quick text letting her know we were all right and that I was turning my phone off for a while.

Ash took the phone from me and left the room for a moment.

"Okay, quiet, peace? Raging blizzard? Can we just have dinner and not deal with the real world for a while?" I snuggled into Doc who tightened his arms around me.

"Sure, honey," Dad said after a moment.

"Sam, are you okay?" Doc finally asked her.

"Starting to warm up."

I groaned. "Maybe we should cleanup."

Doc sighed. "Yeah."

Nikolai grumbled in protest when I moved off of Doc's lap but accepted my hand when I pulled him to his feet.

"You two first."

Doc nodded, tiredly got to his feet, and headed for the master bathroom. After a quick glance at my parents that I think only Mom noticed, Nikolai headed off for one of the other bathrooms. She smirked as she watched the mage head down the hallway. Mom really had accepted my pack dynamic pretty easily.

Allan climbed to his feet and followed Doc into the master bedroom. I took his spot next to Ed on the floor and gently ran my hand along his shoulder, thick fur warming my hands. He didn't move, though his side rose and fell evenly.

Sam stared at me, eyes wide.

I ignored her.

"You knew all that?"

I turned my attention to the other mage. "Yes. And if you tell anyone, I'll personally end you."

She blanched.

Fortunately, my parents still didn't protest my violent intentions.

"Do you want me to get you home before the blizzard gets to bad?" Ash offered.

"Yeah, maybe that would be best," Sam said. "I think I'm warm now."

"You taking the Camaro?"

Ash winked at me. "Traction spell."

I giggled before sobering. "Sam, I'm sorry you got caught up in all this."

She shrugged. "None of this was your fault, Sofia. The people who caused it are, uh, missing. Right?"

I nodded.

"Hopefully we'll never see them again."

"Yeah."

I glanced at Ash and he nodded. I wasn't sure what he would do, but whatever it was, he would reinforce to Sam that she could never speak of any of this.

They went out into the storm, leaving me alone with the sleeping werewolf and my parents.

"So, I think I'm safe now." I forced a smile.

Dad rubbed his hands together and hunched his shoulders before nodding.

"You okay?"

"Never killed anyone before, but yes, I'm fine."

That was probably as close to admitting he wasn't fine as Dad would come. Mom put her arm around him. "One of those shots was mine, Dan. And she was going to kill our little girl. We did what we had to."

Dad nodded before his gaze strayed to the bedroom. "You're dating a vampire."

"Um, yeah. Half vampire anyway."

"That can do magic?" He crossed his arms.

"Well, uh, he has these reservoir bracelets that store magic. That's how."

"You could have told me." He furrowed his brow.

"Honey," Mom said. "You would have flipped out."

He opened his mouth, probably to protest, before clicking his teeth shut. "Maybe."

"I can't figure out why George lied to me, though."

"Doc threatened him. There's a reason everyone is afraid of vampires," I admitted. George, Dad's werewolf friend, hadn't been able to figure out exactly what Doc was for a while. When he had figured it out it was because Doc had threatened him into silence.

"You're safe here?" Worry made him sound almost sad.

"Yeah."

"You're sure?"

"Honey, they're all in love with her. None of them would hurt her. Our daughter couldn't be safer, and if you hadn't noticed, she's pretty badass herself. It'll be okay."

"All?" He turned his attention to Mom, who simply grinned.

He dropped the subject. "Let's get dinner started. I may not know a ton about the supernatural community, but I do know werewolves eat a lot and I'm sure they're both going to be very hungry."

Mom and Dad headed to the kitchen. I pulled the comforter over Ed, thinking he would probably change back soon, and went to my room. I wanted a change of clothing and a shower, and if Nikolai happened to still be in the shower when I got there, well, that would just be too bad, wouldn't it?

∞ ∞ ∞

Ash made it home before the roads got impassable without serious magic and Doc gave up his spare room to my parents since it really was better for them to stay instead of risking the drive back down.

They ended up staying up at the cabin for a couple of days while the storm raged and then we waited for roads to clear. During that time, they both relaxed considerably around my pack, and my guys got more comfortable around them.

By the time they got ready to leave, I half expected some other disaster. Nothing happened though, as they headed back down to their bed and breakfast to collect their things and head home. With promises to call or text

271

when they arrived home, they hugged me and everyone else goodbye and headed home.

"Well, that went better than I expected," Doc said after they were gone. He held me in his arms as we all watched the pickup head down the driveway.

It was still a few days until Christmas, but none of us were going anywhere for a while, except maybe the grocery store. My parents had decided to leave a touch early because of another incoming storm, so we had celebrated with them early.

"What now?" Ed asked.

"What do you mean?" I replied.

"Well, the Andersons are really defeated. What will happen next?" Ed glanced around at all of them.

"Um, well, I mean, school?" I shrugged. "Lots of sex?"

Allan laughed and Ed blushed but nodded enthusiastically.

"This is a good plan," Nikolai agreed.

"Adriana did mention wanting our help to face other threats like the Andersons..." I wasn't sure how I felt about that.

Doc nodded. "It's a possibility, for the future."

"Yeah, maybe after we're done with school. By then, we'll be so strong together that no one will be able to stop us." I grinned, but the expression fell from my face when I noticed Ash scuffing his foot on the floor, avoiding the conversation.

"What's wrong, Ash?"

"You're sure you want me?" He hunched his shoulders.

I stepped up the demon and slid my arms around his waist. "Ash, I love you. I don't think I've told you that. You're part of my pack, and we all want you. Can you sense that through our bond?"

He met my gaze with his husky blue eyes and slowly nodded. "I can. I just...I needed to hear it. I love you,

Sofia. All of you." He raised his eyes to include the rest of the pack. "Thank you."

"We love you, Ash." Nikolai said for the guys. "We want you with us."

Ash took a deep breath and I brushed a tear off of his cheek before kissing him gently.

"What do you want to do now?" Allan asked.

"Tonight, I want to run."

Ed bounced on his toes in excitement and the others murmured agreement.

"Right now, I want to make up for the time my parents were here." I grinned mischievously. "And then we can see if we've broken the curse."

"Curse?" Nikolai looked around warily.

"Yeah. Whenever we have an amazing time, something bad happens right after."

"Oh." He headed for the door. "Let's hope."

Doc picked me up. I giggled, not protesting.

"Everyone, turn your phones off," Doc ordered.

Nikolai opened the door for him, and we went inside. Doc set me down so I could take off my boots and turn my phone off. I left it on the low coffee table my parents had gotten for us, and everyone else did the same with theirs. This time, if we got interrupted, they were going to have to knock on our door.

With that thought in mind, I sent a quick request to the house to discourage visitors. It pulsed with agreement.

Before I could head toward the master bedroom, Ed scooped me up, sky-blue eyes shining.

"I can walk."

"And we can carry you." Ed kissed me on the forehead.

The others followed us into the bedroom. Ed set me on the bed, and I scooted toward the middle so everyone could pile on.

Nikolai grabbed me first, devouring my lips with his. Warm hands heated trails up my back as Ash pushed my shirt up and I broke away long enough for him to tug my top off. Allan claimed my lips while Nikolai went to work on my pants.

It didn't take long before we were all happily wrapped up in each other's arms.

While I couldn't know if the next few months would bring us the peace I craved, I did know that we weren't about to take any of the time we had together for granted. We had firmly woven ourselves into each other's lives and nothing would come between our pack bond.

Ever.

The End.

Author's Note

Thank you so much for reading my reverse harem tale! More is coming soon! Reviews are so very important, especially to new authors and are greatly appreciated! Even a line or two will do!

About the Author

Dakota has two passions in life: writing and cinnamon tea. Tea so strong she ought to be able to see her future when she drinks it, and the writing? Well, she hopes it makes you see stars when you read it. She creates reverse harem romance novels filled with things that go bump in the night. That handsome werewolf walking down the street? The suave vampire you're just dying to get a taste of? You'll find them enraptured by charming, smart ladies ready to make those bad boys work for their affection. When not writing, Dakota can be found on the back of a horse out on the trail or tending the animals on her farm.

Other Works

Mountain Magic Trilogy (complete)

Becoming
Demon's Touch
Reckoning
The Men of Mountain Magic Novellas

Ocean Enchantment Trilogy

Siren's Catch
Siren's Song
Siren's Storm (forthcoming)

Pizza Shop Exorcist (complete)

The Price of Possession
The Price of Exorcism
The Price of Magic
The Price of Souls
The Price of Rebellion

Horsemen Against the Apocalypse Duet

Seeking War
Apocalypse Interrupted (forthcoming)

Dreambound Trilogy (Complete)

Nightmare's Dance
Nightmare's Fall
Nightmare's Flight

Pizza Shop Monster Hunter
Monster's Price (stands alone)

Companions of the Convergence
Only Human in Strangeville (stands alone)

www.ingramcontent.com/pod-product-compliance
Lightning Source LLC
Chambersburg PA
CBHW070316260626
47160CB00003B/860